HER GUARDED HERO

A BLACK DAWN NOVEL BOOK 5

CAITLYN O'LEARY

Dedicated to those who are serving and who have served.

1

THE RIFLE SHOT WAS FOLLOWED BY A WOMAN'S SHOUT. NOT A scream, a shout. He heard rapid horse beats. They were coming towards him. Dalton Sullivan ducked behind one of the Ponderosa pines, his gun in his hand.

The horse and rider came into view. Another rifle shot. This time there was a scream. It didn't sound human. The horse reared up. Scratch that, the beast was literally standing up on his hind legs as if he was a person, but somehow the rider stayed on.

"Siren calm down." He heard a woman's calm voice.

So, it was a woman on the horse, but she couldn't stay on for long, no matter how soothing her tone. Dalton took in the blood on the palomino's flank. The woman must not have been hit by a bullet, because she wouldn't still be holding onto the horse. Dalton watched as her golden hair streamed and whirled around her, glinting in the sunlight.

Amazingly, the horse came back down and shot its legs backwards and bucked again, but somehow the woman stayed planted. Once more the horse bucked and twisted, and the rider moved fluidly with the animal, like they were one perfect being.

It was when another shot rang out that she bent sideways and lost her balance. Grimly, he watched as she literally flew the twenty feet toward him. She tucked and rolled like a pro, but still the forest floor was pretty damn hard here in Lake Tahoe.

Dammit! Why wasn't she wearing a helmet?

She swung out her arms, trying to reach for any kind of underbrush that might stop her from rolling down the hill, but there wasn't a lot. Dalton ran and jumped over her slim body, bracing himself in front of one of the tall pine trees so that he could cushion her stop. She groaned when she rolled into his waiting arms.

She looked up at him, dazed. He saw blood dripping down her face from what looked like a laceration on her scalp. Her hair was in the way, he couldn't see if it was deep, but it was bleeding like a son-of-a-bitch, he hated head wounds.

"Siren?" she asked softly. He ignored her. He needed to check her out and see how badly she was injured.

She grabbed at his sweater and levered herself up, her gaze was fierce. "Did you see my horse?"

Dalton admired her grit, but that didn't mean he wasn't worried about her. He gently pulled her hands away.

"You need to lie back. I need to check you out," he said gently.

"Did you see Siren? I think she was shot."

Last Dalton had seen, the horse had run off down the steep hill towards the pristine blue water of Lake Tahoe. "Seeing how well she was running, I'd say she was fine. It's you I'm worried about. Do you promise not to move if I go get my backpack?"

As soon as he stood up, she rolled over on her knees and started to get up.

"Dammit Woman, I said stay still."

"I'm fine," she gasped. Then she groaned and rolled back over. "Okay, I'm not fine. I'll just rest here for a moment."

Dalton dashed over to his pack and was back in under a minute. Her blonde hair was quickly turning to orange from all the blood. He had field medic training, all the SEAL's on the Black Dawn team did. He knelt beside her and foraged through his backpack and grabbed at a clean pair of white socks. He gently placed one against her forehead.

She immediately grabbed it out of his hand and pressed it against her scalp.

"I'm fine," she assured him.

Sure, she was.

Now that she was holding the compress, Dalton started to check the rest of her out. He was pretty sure nothing was broken after the way she had gotten onto her knees, but he wanted to be sure. "Tell me if anything hurts."

"I'm good," she said as his hands competently checked her out. When he touched her right hip, she sucked in a deep breath.

"How bad is it?" he asked her.

"Nothing's broken. But I'm going to have a hell of a bruise."

She seemed coherent, which was great. He grabbed his first aid kit out of pack and opened a cleansing wipe packet. He needed to see what he was dealing with. He wiped the gash on her forehead clean and she winced.

"You're going to need stitches."

"There goes my modeling career," she quipped.

He paused, then said, "I'm sure a plastic sur-"

Her laughter cut him off. "I'm teasing. Trust me, one more scrape or scar isn't going to bother me. Kind of adds a little bit of character."

Dalton eyed her with a little more interest as he started to tear open the butterfly bandage packaging, so he could apply them.

"I'm glad you came prepared. Were you a Boy Scout?"

"Eagle Scout," he answered as he applied three of the bandages to the cut. "There, that should do it." It was the damn bruise he was worried about. There was a lot of swelling.

Dalton really wanted to go after the shooter, but there wasn't a chance in hell he was leaving a wounded woman in the middle of the forest.

"What's your name?"

"Aurora Chance? What's yours?" Good, she was lucid.

"What day is it?" he asked.

"You haven't answered my question yet," she protested.

"Dalton Sullivan. Now what day is it?"

"Monday. I need to go get my horse, can you help me?"

Good God, she was serious. She looked like a ghost, her two large brown eyes and purpling bruise were the only spots of color on her face. "No, we're not going after your horse."

Aurora clutched at the arm of his sweater. "She's hurt. I know one of those bullets hit her."

"You're damn lucky one of them didn't hit you," he bit out.

"That's a lot of gear for hiking," she said as she pointed to his backpack.

"Do you have any idea who was shooting at you?"

Her hand clenched tighter, biting through to his forearm. "It must have been one of the damned poachers. They've been running rampant around here for months."

"There is no way that one of your 'damned poachers' would have taken three shots at a horse and rider. Maybe one stray shot I'll grant you. Not three. Someone was deliberately shooting at you."

Those brown eyes got wider, but he didn't see any fear, instead he saw anger. "Somebody shot at my horse? At Siren?"

"And you, let's not forget you."

"But it's Siren whose wounded. Seriously, we need to round her up." Aurora pushed up from the ground on unsteady legs and looked around. Dalton stood with her so that he could catch her if she fell, and it looked like she might.

"You're in no shape to go after your horse, and right now I want to get us a little more cover. These two little trees don't make me feel safe enough."

She turned around on wobbly legs, "Okay, where to?"

"You're coming with me," Dalton bent and picked her up, then bent again and snagged up his backpack.

"I can walk," she protested.

"Sure, you can, Sunshine. He strode over to seven trees that grew close together. He gently lowered her behind four of the narrow tree trunks. "Stay put. I'm going to check things out."

"Siren?" she asked hopefully.

"I'm going to look for the shooters. We're not safe, until we make sure they're long gone."

5

He watched as she bit her lip. She finally nodded her head in acceptance.

"Besides being an Eagle Scout, who are you?" she asked when she saw the gun that he pulled out of one of the compartments of his backpack.

"I'm one of the good guys. Will you promise me to stay put?"

She worried her bottom lip again.

Goddammit, she was going to go after the horse. He just knew she was.

"Listen Aurora, Siren is in as much danger as you are from the shooter. You keep your ass planted." He made it a command. He was good at commands.

"But-"

"We'll argue when I come back, okay? I need to go now. Promise me you'll stay, okay?"

She nodded, then winced.

"Don't move your head, just rest against this tree. Can you do that?"

"I don't think I'll have a choice," she admitted ruefully. He pulled out a clean t-shirt from his pack and put it behind her head. "Hopefully that's soft enough for you." She hummed her appreciation as she leaned back.

"I'll be back as fast as I can," he promised.

"S'okay."

He took few moments to pull out some other things from his pack.

"Here's Gatorade, Trail Mix and a couple of protein bars. I want you to finish the Gatorade while I'm gone." He gently pulled her away from the tree and helped her into a rain jacket that he had in his backpack. He zipped it up to her chin, then he rolled up the sleeves.

"That should keep out the chill."

Then he took off on a silent run.

FROM HALF-MAST EYES, Aurora watched as her savior morphed into a predator and then disappeared. She shuddered. Was it pain? Shock? Or was she replaying the feel of his hands on her body? She was twenty-six years old, and in her entire life, she had never had such a strong reaction to a man. She took a deep breath, and instead of smelling the fresh mountain air and pine trees, she took in the lingering masculine scent of Dalton Sullivan. She had to stop herself from sighing in pleasure.

Obviously, she'd hit her head too hard.

"It's the circumstances. Get over yourself."

She trembled again. Even though she was thinking of his dark Irish good looks, she knew that her shivering was due to cold. His rain jacket was keeping out the wind, but she needed more heat.

With gloved fingers she plucked at the fastenings on the back of his backpack that where she saw the rolled-up blanket. It didn't work. She yanked off the gloves using her teeth, even then it took her three times as long as it should have to undo it because her fingers were so cold. Aurora shoved herself up against the tree trunk so that she was sitting up.

"Halleluiah." She shook out the silver survival blanket and tucked it around her lower legs, combining that with Dalton's jacket, she basked in warmth. That answered that question, it had been the cold, not any kind of weird reaction to the man.

Still, as she nestled into the blanket, and let her body relax against the tree, she kept thinking about her close call, and Dalton's protectiveness. He hadn't been put off by her independence. Not once had he backed down. She smiled as she thought about it. He was just like all the other bull-headed men in her family, not that wimp she'd dated.

But Dalton Sullivan sure as hell didn't feel like family. Nope, as a matter of fact, he seemed larger than life.

"He's a tourist."

Shit, now she was talking to herself, and she was supposed to stay quiet and hidden. Get it together girl. Just because you thought all your hormones had taken an Alaskan cruise five years ago, and now they decided to come back and unpack their bags in the middle of a shoot-out, doesn't mean that you should go all psycho-girl.

Now, rest your head back and relax. Be the logical and practical Aurora we all know and love.

What had he been doing with a gun in the woods? And a wicked looking gun at that. He sure as hell wasn't a hunter. She was pretty sure that was a Sig Sauer, based on what she'd seen in her granddad's gun magazines. He'd said he was one of the good guys, and he sure knew first aid. She really couldn't imagine Eagle Scout boy, with his first aid kit and clean socks being some kind of criminal, but who goes around camping in the woods with a military pistol?

She was a millimeter away from slapping her forehead before stopping herself. God, she was so stupid.

"He's a soldier! You're dealing with a soldier!"

Crap, she was talking loud again.

Get it together girlfriend. Are you hearing me? No hormones. No hitting your injured head. No yelling out

8

loud when there are shooters in the woods. You're better than this.

Sure, she was.

Come on, what would Grandma Mae do?

God, she missed her grandmother, but the thought of her made her smile. Little Miss Liberal Hippie.

Time to meditate. That's what her grandmother would tell her to do.

She leaned back against the clean shirt. Did she smell Dalton?

Stop it, that's Febreze!

She took another deep breath. Ponderosa Pine trees. Mountain air.

Another deep breath.

In.

Out.

In.

Out.

Better. She snuggled deeper against the t-shirt and smoothed the survival blanket over her legs. Now Aurora closed her eyes and thought of the magic of the forest that surrounded her. She let herself float upwards, she flew miles toward her family's ranch. Valhalla. She pictured the beauty of the ranch with the horses running in the tall grass and remembered how her granddad used to ride with such strength atop his stallion.

She whispered her mantra.

"Beauty. Strength. Magic."

THERE HAD BEEN two sets of hoofprints near the four brass

shell casings. Dalton crouched down to get a better look. They were boat tail hollow points. Shit, they could have come from any jackass hunter. But he'd be damned, before he would believe that Aurora and her horse hadn't been targeted. Sure, the first shot could have been a mistake, if you wanted to believe in the tooth fairy, but there wasn't a chance in hell the second and third ones had been.

He got up from his crouch, eying the casings one last time. He was careful not to touch the brass, or step on the imprints left by the horses. He stood up and really looked around the site. This was a crime scene, and even with a forensics team, Dalton didn't think the sheriff's department would have much to work with, but that couldn't be his problem. Right now, Aurora was his first priority. He pulled out his cell phone but didn't get a signal. Dammit, it was about damn time to invest in a satellite phone. He missed those when he wasn't working on a mission. Disgusted he pocketed his phone, realizing he needed to get closer to the road, and started to head back to Aurora.

It took half the time to get back to her, and when he did, he didn't like what he saw. She was out like a light. He squatted in front of her and touched her shoulder, she didn't move.

"Aurora?" he whispered. She didn't move.

"Aurora?" he spoke louder.

"Hmmm?" Her eyelids fluttered open. She looked up at him, her expression dazed. "You're back. Did you find Siren?"

Dalton smiled. "I haven't searched for her yet. I was looking for the people who shot at you."

"Are you a super soldier, like Rambo?"

Dalton laughed. "No. Why did you ask that?"

"You just disappeared into the forest like smoke. I figured you were a super soldier or an Avenger. The soldier seemed more likely."

Her voice was beginning to fade and her eyes drifted closed again.

"Sunshine, stick with me."

"Hmmm?" She opened her eyes again and shook her head then sat up straighter. She grabbed at the t-shirt as it slipped down her back. "Sorry about that. I'm here. I won't go to sleep on you, again."

Dalton brushed the hair back from her face and looked at the butterfly bandages. There was some leakage, but not too much, but there was a hell of a bump forming on her forehead.

"Aurora, can you look me in the eye?"

"Checking for a concussion?" she asked with a smile.

"You got it in one." He nodded.

"I think I'm good. This doesn't feel like one."

Shit, if she'd had one before, she was more susceptible to having another one. "When was the last time you had a concussion?"

"Four and a half years ago."

Dalton relaxed. Good, it wasn't in the last year. Also, her eyes weren't dilated. Both things were good news. Aurora pushed her back against the tree, bracing her feet against the ground.

"What are you doing?"

"What does it look like I'm doing?" she asked with a slight grin. "I'm getting up, Ironman." She pushed off the silver blanket but kept the coat on. The sleeves fell past her hands and hung down almost to her knees. She must have unrolled them at some point to get more warmth over her hands. Dalton kept one hand under her elbow, the other around her back. He pulled out his cell phone again. Still no signal.

"Can you check to see if your mobile is getting service?" he asked.

"No can do, it was in my saddlebag." She gripped his bicep and grimaced.

"How are you feeling? Are you dizzy?"

She looked around. "Nope, not dizzy, and the good news is, there's only one of you. Last time when I flagged down a cop beside the side of the road after my car rolled, there were three of him."

Dalton sucked in a deep breath, bloody images flashed through his mind. "You were in a car accident?"

"I lucked out. The other driver fell asleep at the wheel and drifted into my lane. I swerved and went down an embankment. It could have been a lot worse."

"Were they drunk?" he asked numbly.

"No, they'd been behind the wheel too long. Poor judgement on his part." Aurora took a deep breath.

Dalton tried to decide if she was nauseated or she was remembering her close call.

"Come on, we need to go find Siren," she prompted him.

"What we need to do is get you someplace safe and warm, then talk to the police. After that, I'll go find your horse."

Her shoulders sagged. "I don't know what I was thinking. You going and trying to find Siren is ridiculous," she sighed. "What was I even thinking? Hopefully she'll be cold and hungry and head for the barn, or she's long gone, and I'll have to gather up some ranchers to help search for her."

"What happens if neither of those things work?" Dalton asked.

"Oh, as soon as I get home, I'll put in a missing horse report with the sheriff. Brody will put the word out to the other law enforcement in and around Tahoe. Granddad will work the phones. He's owned Valhalla for forty-five years, he knows everyone."

"Valhalla?" Dalton asked. He watched every step she took being sure to guide her along the flattest part of the forest floor.

"That's the name of our horse ranch."

"Is it safe to assume there is a little bit of Norway flowing through your veins?"

"Oh yeah, you could definitely say that. My great grandfather had fishing boats that went up and down the coast from Oregon on up to Alaska. Granddad was supposed to take over, but he was a rebel, he came to Lake Tahoe and fell in love with the land." Her tone was wistful.

"Why do I think there's more to that story?"

He wanted to keep her talking, her voice was still a little slurred and she wasn't walking well. The best thing to do was keep her mind focused and talking.

"Huh?" she asked.

"You were going to tell me about Valhalla," he reminded her. "You said there was a story behind your granddad ending up here."

She looked up from beneath her lashes. "You'd be right, there was a love story."

Shit. Really? Did he really have to hear about a love story after being embroiled in three others so recently?

"Okay, lay it on me."

"You don't sound very excited to hear about it."

13

"You could say I'm kind of burned out on love at the moment."

"Oh," she whispered softly. "She must have hurt you a lot."

Suddenly he was thinking of Lacey, and he didn't mean to. He hated thinking of his dead wife. He slammed that door shut in his mind.

"No, I meant that three of my teammates recently fell in love. I was really beginning to think that there was something in the MRE's."

"Huh?"

"The Meals Ready to Eat, that they give us on missions. Dex, Hunter and Zed all got engaged or married in the last year. It's been crazy. I was around for each one of their downfalls."

Aurora giggled. "I guess that sums up your perspective."

"What do you mean?"

"You just called falling in love a downfall."

Dalton paused and replayed his words in his mind. "I didn't mean it like that. For them it was the right thing," he sighed. "For me, it wouldn't be. That's all."

Damn, he hadn't meant for the words to come out so harsh.

Aurora peered over at him, but she didn't look offended or hurt.

"To each his own I guess. For my grandparents, it was definitely the right thing, kind of like for your friends."

Dalton considered how much further they had to walk. It was at least another two miles to the road. He could do without hearing about another great love story, but if it would keep Aurora's attention and keep her walking in a straight line, then he was for it.

"Okay, let's hear it," he said.

"Granddad had money that he'd earned long-lining. His father wanted to put him in charge of his fleet when he retired, but Granddad said to turn it over to his brothers Arvid and Einar instead."

"What's your grandfather's name?"

"Gunnar."

"I can get behind that," Dalton smiled.

"I bet you can," Aurora said cheekily. "A Sig Sauer is quite the weapon."

Dalton almost missed a step as he did a double take. "You recognized the gun I had?"

"Sure. So, Granddad went hiking around Lake Tahoe and fell in love with this meadow," Aurora said, continuing her story.

"Let's get back to how you recognized the gun I was holding," Dalton slowed down their pace until they were stopped, and he was staring down at her.

"Why is it a big deal that I know?" He could practically see the wheels turning in her head. He shouldn't have made such a big deal of it.

Aurora gave him a considering glance then smiled slowly. "You're not Ironman, you're a Navy SEAL."

"All that from the gun I carry?"

"That and the way you disappeared like smoke. Am I right?" Her eyes were sparkling.

Yep, no sign of a concussion.

"You're right," he admitted. "Petty Officer First Class, Dalton Sullivan, at your service. Tell me how you recognized the gun."

"Granddad's gun magazine. I think it goes along with his name. He's a big-time hunter, he still meets up with his brothers up in Alaska to go hunting every year. The poaching that has been going on around here is driving him insane. I know that he has been going out looking for signs of the poachers."

"Aurora, those weren't poachers. They had you in their line of sight."

She winced. "I really don't want to believe that someone would actually take a shot at me on purpose. I don't Dalton. Do I have to?"

He rubbed his hands along her arms and stared at her.

"Dammit," she finally said, her lip trembling. "Dammit, dammit, dammit."

One of her hands tentatively came up and rested on his chest. "I don't know why anyone would want to take a shot at me. I just don't." She looked so lost and bewildered. Then she began shaking her head in protest, her blonde hair went flying and he watched as she winced. Dalton stopped her before she pressed her fingers against her forehead to contain her pain.

"Calm down, Sunshine."

"How do you expect me to be calm if someone was using me as target practice?" Aurora gripped his hand like it was a lifeline. He noted she wasn't wearing her gloves anymore. She let go of him quickly. "Nope. I choose to believe you're wrong."

"What?"

"I get to choose my reality. You live in a world where bad things happen all the time, right? You're constantly having to protect and serve. There are bad guys that you're constantly fighting, so you always think the worst. Isn't that true?"

Dalton looked at her. She was serious. Before they had

gotten off course, hadn't she been going to tell him a love story? A fairytale?

"Dalton, answer me. I'm right, aren't I? You live in a world that is far away from mine."

"I suppose I do."

"They were poachers." Her grip gentled caressing his. How could something so dainty handle such a wild horse?

"Okay Aurora, it's within the far-reaching realm of possibility, in some universe that you live in that they were poachers."

Her smile ticked up at the corner. "Thank you for that, I'm glad you see it my way. Now let's get a move on and I'll tell you about my Granddad and Grandma so you're all caught up by the time we get to the ranch."

Sunshine was a good nickname for the woman. He'd really thought to get her to the road, get a phone signal and call the sheriff, afterall this was the day he normally spent alone, but maybe it was time for a change.

2

"Grandma had three brothers, and she could out ride them all. She was amazing on a horse. Back in the eighteen-hundreds the story was that two Comanche brothers came to live with the Washoe people, and that was where my Grandmother's family got their horsemanship skills."

Aurora watched as Dalton took a closer look at her features. Everybody always did when she mentioned her grandmother was Native American.

"It's the cheekbones and the eyes," she grinned.

"What?" he asked.

"Weren't you wondering how a blonde girl was part Native American?"

He looked down at her thoughtfully. "No, I was imagining you a hundred and fifty years ago, riding bareback, in buckskins on the plains in Oklahoma. It was spectacular the way you were able to stay on Siren. You would have been an amazing huntress back in the day."

Aurora felt her cheeks begin to heat. Sure, people had

said that she was good at what she did before, but nobody had ever painted such a stirring picture. She cleared her throat. "Well anyway," she said as she picked up her pace. "When he was twenty-two, Granddad bought the meadow and the big chunk of land surrounding it and thought he would farm it. He didn't have the slightest idea what he was doing," her chuckle turned into a pant.

"You doing okay?" Dalton asked as he put his hand under her elbow again.

"Sure," she grinned up at him. Her head was beginning to throb, but it was only a couple of more miles to the road. Of course, it was all uphill, or so it seemed. She looked up. Maybe at the top of that rise Dalton could get a signal on his phone.

"Let's take a break."

"I'm fine." Aurora gave him the same smile she gave new clients when they brought their horses to be boarded. When Dalton looked skeptical, she upped her smile's wattage to one she used to reassure those people who brought in abused horses and were worried that she might not be up to handling such delicate and in some cases dangerous animals.

Dalton sighed. "Aurora, you just took a major fall. I would give the same consideration to most of my team members."

She laughed, the word "bullshit," coming out with a snort.

Dalton raised an eyebrow. "Okay, maybe not. Especially Hunter Diaz. I'd expect him to still be able to carry my ass up the hill after being bucked off a horse." Dalton grabbed her hand and brought them both to a stop next to one of the tall trees. "Sit down next to me. I want to hear more about your grandfather and grandmother."

"I call bullshit again," Aurora smiled as she sat down next to him.

"Do you have cattle on your ranch?" he asked.

"Nope, just horses. Why do you want to know?"

"You seem to be obsessed with male cow feces," Dalton answered. "I would have thought it would have been equine feces."

Aurora chuckled. "I guess I don't like thinking about horseshit since I spend so much time mucking out stalls." She gratefully took the chocolate chip granola bar and Gatorade that he offered her.

It was weird having him watch her eat. He wasn't overt about it, but he was definitely making sure she was getting in her calories and drinking fluids. It was the same way he insisted she rest. She wasn't sure how to take it.

"Quit overthinking things and tell me more of your story. How did your grandparents get together?"

"To hear Grandma tell it, Granddad had more money than sense. He was asking all around for advice on what crops he should grow, not thinking to look around and realize that nobody was growing crops. Seriously, he was thinking the Lake Tahoe area was the same as the Central California breadbasket." Aurora shook her head, remembering how Grandma Mae used to tell the story when they were making blackberry jam and apple butter.

"What are you thinking?" Dalton asked. "Your eyes are lighting up with memories."

"I was thinking about Grandma and me in a hot kitchen putting up jars of preserves. We laughed for days doing that chore. She gave away half of what we made to people around the county. They'd come on over and everyone would tell stories and spread some of the sweet berry goodness on biscuits. She knew half the people in Placer and El Dorado counties." She put her bar wrapper into the empty juice bottle and handed it to Dalton. "You ready to go?"

"Hold up. Just sit back and finish the story."

"We're burning daylight."

"Horseshit. We've got plenty of time. Now lean against the tree and tell me more about this great love story. I'm fascinated by a woman's perspective."

Aurora gave him a long stare, but both his tone and expression were very kind, but she couldn't help but think he was making fun. Oh, to hell with it, just ask!

"Dalton, how come I get the idea that you're mocking me?"

Dalton jerked. "I wouldn't make fun of you. I was serious."

Dalton's jaw tightened, then he blew out a stream of air.

"Why is it so important to you?"

"For my friends, I want something that lasts, something that makes them happy. I guess I want the dream, even if I don't believe in it for me. I hear their women say they love them, and I..."

Aurora didn't prompt him to say anything more. "Okay. You want a woman's perspective. You want me to tell you that your friends won't get hurt, is that it?"

He looked off in the distance and nodded. She was exactly right.

"First, I think it's great that your friends have found love. For their sake, I sure hope it's like the men and women in

22

my family." Aurora purposefully kept her voice light and breezy. She thought back to her grandmother's stories. "Granddad was twenty-two, and only had experience fishing. He'd spent almost his entire life on the ocean, so even though he wanted to work the land, he couldn't give up the water. That's why he decided to buy near Lake Tahoe."

"I can't say I blame him. It's gorgeous here," Dalton said.

"Yeah, but it sure isn't farmland. So, here's Gunnar Olsen with all this land trying to figure out what to do with it. The contracting company he hires to build his home is owned by one of my great-uncles. That was how he met my grandmother, Mae Dressler."

"I can't imagine back then she was working on building the house," he said dryly.

"Don't be so sure, it was nineteen sixty-two. Not much of anything stopped her, she was considering all her options. She was twenty. She'd taken off a couple of years after graduating from high school to take care of her mother who was ill. Now that she'd recovered, everybody was pushing for her to go to college, she had the grades and test scores for it. According to her, she wanted to make a difference, and she wanted to protest the war, so she thought going to Berkley was the thing to do."

"But she didn't go?"

"She loved Dressler Ranch, where she grew up. She was as horse crazy then, as I am now. She said she was being pulled in two different directions, and she didn't know what she was going to do."

Dalton looked over at her, she could see that she'd caught his interest. "I take it she decided to stay in Tahoe."

"Not to begin with. She rode over to the construction site one day. She brought some cookies that she and her mom and baked for the men. That was when she met Granddad. She'd been hearing stories about him from two of her three brothers."

"Nothing good, I bet."

"Not to begin with, that's for damn sure. They thought he was a lunatic for not having a plan. The Washoe people are cautious. They're planners. Meanwhile, Granddad and his family were gamblers."

Dalton raised his eyebrow. "Explain."

"Every fishing season they'd go out on a wing and a prayer, hoping that they'd come back with a boat full of fish. Now, his family knew all the good places to fish, but still there were some seasons that they'd come back empty. It was a gamble. That's why Granddad felt comfortable thinking he could be a farmer. It was the same idea. He wasn't afraid to risk anything, work his ass off, and pray that the crop comes in."

"Yeah, but he didn't do his due diligence."

Aurora didn't hear censure in his voice which was nice. "Granddad was impetuous. I think that was one of the reasons that Grandma Mae wasn't impressed with him to begin with."

"Are you telling me it wasn't love at first sight?"

"God no, at least not for her. Now lust? That's a whole different matter."

"Are you saying your grandfather lusted after your grandmother?"

"Nope, I'm saying it was lust at first sight for my grandmother."

"And your grandfather?" Dalton asked.

"He always says that he thought she was the prettiest woman he'd ever seen. He doesn't mention lust. But when

Grandma and I were alone, she sure does. She used to call him her Viking. But her brothers' opinions mattered a lot to her, so she wasn't really impressed with Granddad's decision-making skills. However, she was thinking he might make a good summer fling before she went off to college. She'd just need to keep it on the downlow."

Dalton let out a laugh. "How was she planning on pulling that off?"

"It wasn't going to be easy. Her brothers were really protective. She suggested that Granddad might want to start raising horses, and if he did, he would need to learn how to ride horses."

Dalton moved their clasped hands, so they rested on his thigh and gave her a devilish smile. "Your grandfather must have loved that idea."

"Oh, he was fine with spending time with her. But according to Grandma Mae, she couldn't get him to go all the way, no matter what kind of moves she put on him."

Dalton shouted out a laugh. "I take it she was innocent."

Aurora tilted her head sideways to look at him. "You mean a virgin?"

"Uhm, yeah." Aurora smothered a smile as she saw a slight flush creep up Dalton's cheeks.

"She was, and she wasn't happy about it. She'd set her sights on Granddad to take care of that little problem and he was having none of it. Now, he never gets into those kinds of details when he tells his side of the story. He talks about how he fell in love with her, and how he had to convince her to stay in Tahoe and marry him."

"But I take it your Grandmother got into the nitty gritty with you."

Aurora plucked up a pinecone and tossed it up in the air,

easily catching it as it came back down and tossed it again. "It was when she was having the 'sex talk' with me when I was sixteen. She was telling me that she had waited to have sex until she'd met the right guy and she was almost twenty-one. But she'd really had to work for it."

Dalton grabbed the pinecone out of the air. "She didn't really say that."

"Oh yes she did."

"What happened next?"

"When Granddad rejected her at first, she went away for a year at Berkley."

"I bet she had lots of opportunities there to get things taken care of," Dalton said delicately.

"I asked her about that. She said, 'I could never get that damned Viking out of my head,'."

They both laughed.

This time Aurora didn't let him stop her when she got up off the ground. She offered Dalton her hand. "Need help getting up, Ironman?" she asked.

"You're a smartass, you know that don't you?" He pointed out as he easily eased up, grabbing his backpack.

He gave her an assessing look.

"I'm fine," she assured him. "Let's get up that hill so you can call someone."

AURORA WAS TALLER than most women, she had to be five nine. She took long strides up the hill with little effort now that she'd rested. Still, Dalton wanted her to take it easier. Even if she didn't have a concussion, she had to be a mass of bruises after that fall.

26

"Slow down, Sunshine. You haven't finished your story."

Sparkling brown eyes cut over to look at him. "You just wanted me to talk so I rested longer."

Smart too. Dalton grinned.

"Maybe. But now I'm hooked. Your grandmother wanted to lose her V-Card and had her sights set on your grandfather, but he was too much of a gentleman. You can't tell me that her brothers weren't watching the situation."

"Oh, they were all right." Her straight blonde hair sifted around her shoulders, catching the light as she nodded her head. "I'd go out to the Dressler Ranch when I was a girl, and all three of my great uncles would have that stoic hard-ass thing going on when they dealt with Granddad, but they were big ole softies when it came to Grandma, me and Mom."

"So how did your grandmother get around them?"

"She gave Granddad riding lessons."

Dalton rubbed the bridge of his nose.

"What, you don't have anything smart ass to say?"

"I'm not touching that comment," he agreed.

"Granddad had been busy while she'd been off to college. He'd started planting apple trees, and getting a barn built. Uncle Charles Dressler had convinced him that horse ranching was the way to go, but Granddad really wanted to grow things, that's the reason we have a ten-acre orchard. I think my favorite time of year is when the trees blossom and the ground is blanketed with blooms."

Aurora's face lit up as she talked about the flowering trees. A picture of her as a golden-haired child scooping up white and pink petals flashed through his mind. His step faltered, pain blasted through his chest when he pictured tiny little hands, black curls and big blue eyes fringed by dark lashes looking up at him with so much trust.

"Dalton?"

"Dalton?"

He shook his head and gave Aurora a wan smile. "Apple trees, huh?"

"Are you okay?"

"Sure." He gave himself a mental shake. He tried to force himself not to think of Reagan, he couldn't. Dalton jolted when Aurora's warm fingers touched his hand then she laced her fingers with his. He didn't look at her, instead he just soaked in the comfort that the soft contact provided.

Dalton appreciated how Aurora allowed him to continue walking in silence. Her presence, along with the beauty of the land finally soothed him to the point that he was able to resume their conversation.

"Did your grandmother ever go back to Berkley, or did they finally become a couple?"

"Oh, they both wanted the same thing. She might have thought she wanted a fling, but really, she wanted the whole nine yards. She came from a big loving family, and she admits now that deep down that was what she really wanted, despite being in the midst of the sexual revolution."

It should only take ten more minutes to get to the top of the hill, and he realized he wanted to hear how Gunnar convinced Mae to marry him.

"So, there were over-protective brothers, a hormonal young woman, and a man who was intent on marriage, what happened next?"

"All Granddad ever says is that Grandma Mae led him merry chase for six months before he was able to convince her to be his wife. But Grandma spilled the beans when I was sixteen." Aurora smiled and let out a wistful sigh.

He gave her hand a squeeze.

"She showed him the land, then he took her out onto the lake. Even though she'd spent her life living near Lake Tahoe, she'd never spent time on the water. She said that seeing that side of her man made her fall deeply in love. All thoughts of a summer dalliance went out the window."

Dalton chuckled. "She actually said *dalliance*?"

Aurora flashed dimples at him. "Yep, she used that exact word. Granddad had food and champagne on the sailboat."

"Good man."

"They sailed on the water for hours. Grandma said she took a nap, and she had a dream of the future with her Viking. Her mother, my great-grandmother, had told her that when that happened it meant that their souls were destined to be forever linked."

"Then they had sex and got married?"

"My God, you really aren't a romantic at all, are you."

Dalton was relieved to hear amusement in Aurora's voice, because as soon as the words were out of his mouth he realized how bitter they sounded.

"I am for other people."

"Well then you will be happy to hear that this couple fell in love." She swung their arms and laughed up at him. "Plus, according to Grandma Mae, the sex was incredible."

Dalton shouted with laughter. "Your grandmother didn't really tell you that."

"Oh yes she did. That was her way of telling me to wait to find the right guy."

"And did you?"

Shit, did he really ask that question?

"I'm twenty-four, I kind of got tired of waiting for my Viking, so I ended up kissing a frog." She swung their arms out. Then she peered at him sideways. "So, did your heart get broken once, or have you always known that the 'L' word wasn't for you?"

When he didn't answer, she swung their arms again, and she asked another question. "You can always say, "it's none of my business.""

"How about we say, it's complicated."

They walked a little further. "In that case, you should stick with dalliances," she nodded sagely.

He barked out a laugh. "I like you Aurora Chance."

The sad part was she was right. That's what his life had turned into, yearly dalliances, with nothing but the same lurking in the future. It seemed grim.

She tugged at his hand. He realized he was holding it too tightly and released it. He braced them both on the incline and pulled out his phone. He had a slight signal. He dialed nine-one-one. It didn't go through.

"Nothing?"

"Nada," he agreed. "You still good?"

"Yep." She didn't look so good, but she'd plastered a big smile on her face. The girl had game. He put his hand on her lower back and continued to guide her up the incline.

"This is better than a Stairmaster," she said breathing hard.

"You go to the gym?"

"No, but my friend Crystal does. She's always complaining about the Stairmaster. I imagine this is what it's like. I stick to work around the ranch. What about you?" she panted out the question.

"During down time there is a lot of physical training. Then we'll go on training exercises and maneuvers."

"Yeah, you look like you could wrestle a stallion to the ground."

"You should see some of the other guys on my team. I'm a small fry."

Aurora's laughter rang out through the forest. "Pull my other leg."

"Seriously. My friend, Hunter Diaz, makes me look like I ate nothing but gruel growing up," he grinned down at her.

"I'd like to meet him."

"He's engaged."

Where the hell had that come from? Why did he feel the need to tell her that Hunter was off limits? Ah hell, was he interested in Aurora?

"Let me check my phone again."

"Sounds good to me." She stopped and bent forward, putting her hands on her knees.

This time he got a signal and got through. As soon as they answered he explained their situation. He checked his GPS and said how close they were to the road.

"The sheriff should be here in thirty minutes," he told Aurora when he hung up.

"Let's keep walking," she said.

"No, I want you to rest."

"I'm fine. I want to be up there, so that you can then go down with one of the deputies and show them what you found. That way they can start after the poachers. I am so sick of those bastards," she said vehemently.

He chuckled.

"Poachers I say. Poachers."

He raised an eyebrow.

"You're not going to let me live in my own little world anymore?"

"Not with the sheriff on his way. You need to start thinking about who would want to fire shots at you."

He watched as her face scrunched up. Then her fingers flew to her forehead to tenderly touch her bruise. "But that's the thing Dalton. I don't have any enemies. I don't mean to toot my own horn or anything, but people really like me around here. I pay my taxes. I donate to charity. I even make jams and jellies and give them out like my grandmother did. People like me."

God, she looked so forlorn.

Facing her, he brushed back her hair, so he could look at the bandages on her forehead. They were holding, but the swelling around the bruise was even worse. "How bad is your headache?" he asked.

"We were talking about how nice I am."

"I believe you. I've found you to be extremely nice. Now tell me how bad your headache is."

"It's killing me when you make me think that someone is taking shots at me. Maybe it was just someone who wanted to scare me or something. I mean they didn't actually hit me."

"They hit your horse. You could have died." He still pictured her flying through the air. She could have hit her head on a rock. "Is your headache killing you?" he asked.

"Not really, it's fine. It's manageable."

"I think you're really in pain," he disagreed.

"I'm fine to walk the rest of the way up the hill." Her brown eyes flashed up at him. God she was stubborn.

"Aurora, you don't have anything to prove to me. I would tell most of my teammates to sit their asses down and wait."

"There is quite the dichotomy to your personality, isn't there?"

"You're not the first one to mention that." Dalton watched as she determinedly strode up the hill, then kicked himself as he noticed the flex of her ass. Yep, here he was supposed to be worried about her wellbeing and instead he was admiring how her jeans molded to her butt.

3

"YOU SCARED ME GIRL," SHE WHISPERED SOFTLY.

Aurora stroked the mare's neck and fought back tears for the third time.

Siren's breath wafted out and blew strands of Aurora's hair into her eyes. She wiped both hair and tears away, then sighed. Siren knickered softly in response.

Slowly, she smoothed her hand along Siren's coat, until she came to her flank, where Doc Barnes had given her sutures. Aurora winced at the discolored and swollen flesh. The vet had assured them that Siren would be back to a hundred percent in a couple of weeks. Aurora knew deep in her heart that there was no way anybody could have purposefully shot at Siren. Nobody could be that cruel.

Yeah sure. She could see Dalton's face in her head. He wasn't letting her get away from living in a fantasy. But seriously, who would want to shoot at her?

"Aurora!"

She grinned. Even at seventy-six, her grandfather could

still make himself heard from almost a quarter of a mile away.

She gave Siren one last look, then closed the mare's stall. Even though Gunnar Olsen was bellowing, she wasn't going to rush away from her charges, not when some of them were still shaken from Siren's sudden appearance earlier this evening. She stopped at various stalls, giving pats, rubs and treats where needed as she walked towards the barn door.

"Aurora, you have a visitor!" Gunnar bellowed again.

She reached in her back pocket to pull out her phone to find out what time it was, and then remembered that she'd lost hers, when it had fallen out of Siren's saddlebag. Still, it had to be around nine o'clock. Who would be dropping by now?

When she realized it could be one of the deputies, she picked up speed.

She stopped short when she saw an old beat-up, rusted, baby-blue pick-up truck in the driveway.

What the hell?

Then she spotted the tall, lean man talking to her grandfather. Even though she'd only spent three hours with him, Aurora was sure that she would be able to recognize Dalton Sullivan out of any crowd, and it wasn't just his height or his raven black hair. There was something underneath his calm assurance, he was like one her stallions at rest. There was a great deal of deadly power waiting to be unleashed. Dalton's low-key demeanor would never fool her, she would always see the man that he really was.

Aurora stopped short. What was she thinking? This was a fluke that she was seeing Dalton again, why was she considering that she would see him in the future?

36

"There you are! It's about time you left your babies! Get on over here, Darlin'." Gunnar Olsen waved his arm broadly. Aurora grinned. Even in the dusk she could see his white shirt and suspenders. The big Norwegian fisherman had started wearing suspenders when he turned seventy, he said it was the thing to do, even though there still wasn't a bit of gray in his blonde hair.

"Hustle up. You're not even wearing a jacket."

Aurora rolled her eyes. It didn't matter if she was twelve, twenty-six or eighty, this man would always be worried about her. As she got closer she could see Dalton's eyes watching her carefully.

"Shouldn't you be resting?" he asked as she joined the two men on the porch.

Was he for real? She looked at him closely and saw both concern and frustration on his face. "I took a nap earlier, before Siren came home," she said soothingly.

"Why aren't you wearing a jacket?" This time his question came out a little rough. What was his deal? He'd been at the hospital with her when the doctor had checked her out and said that she only had a mild concussion.

"It was beautiful when I left the house, and the barn was warm," she explained.

It didn't seem to appease him. He shrugged out of his coat and put it around her shoulders.

She noted her granddad's twitch of a smile.

"Let's all go inside. Dalton and I have been discussing his concerns, but I haven't told him what Brody told me while you were in the barn."

"Brody stopped by?" She hadn't heard the sheriff's patrol car.

Gunnar opened the door to the house, and Dalton put

his hand on her back and guided her in. She swore she could feel his heat even through his thick coat.

Down girl.

"Coffee?" Gunnar asked as he walked them through to the kitchen.

"I'd love some," Dalton pulled out a chair for her. She could get used to this.

"None for you," her grandfather said over his shoulder. "You get warm milk or hot chocolate, but I think warm milk would be better for you, the chocolate might keep you awake."

Aurora barely contained her snort of exasperation. "Seriously, I'm not your baby girl anymore. However, with that said, I want hot chocolate."

"And?" Gunnar looked at her expectantly.

"With those itty-bitty marshmallows please."

They both started to laugh.

Dalton's hand trembled as he took the mug from her grandfather, hot coffee spilled on his wrist, but he didn't react.

Aurora pushed his coat off her shoulders, got up and grabbed a dishtowel.

"Give me your hand."

"What?"

His hand was still up in the air. She gently pushed it down onto the table and eased the mug away from his grasp. She pushed the sleeve of his Henley shirt up and looked at his reddened skin. Aurora dabbed the liquid off his wrist and looked into his face. He wasn't there, and wherever he was, it wasn't good. It was almost as if the term itty bitty marshmallows had set him off, but she wasn't going to pry.

"Dalton?"

As lightly as a butterfly, she touched his cheek and smiled gently. "I promise that Granddad's coffee isn't that bad. It's strong, but if you douse it with some sugar and creamer it's almost drinkable."

There he was, she saw him come back to her. He gave her an awkward grin. "I'm in the Navy, I live on strong coffee." He grabbed the mug and took a long pull. Aurora watched him, ensuring that he would be okay before she sat back down.

"Here you go, Darlin'." Her grandfather passed her a mug of hot chocolate as he sat down at the table with his own cup of sludge. They sat in a comfortable silence, enjoying their drinks.

"I told you what I thought," Dalton said looking at Gunnar. "What did the Sheriff have to say?"

"He said that the same caliber and brand of casings have been found where three Bighorn Sheep and one Rocky Mountain Elk have been poached. Goddamn shame if you ask me. The Elk were endangered not so long ago," Gunnar said sadly. "But because of that, after he looked over the place where you found the casings, he's positive it was poachers."

Aurora slid her glance sideways to see Dalton's reaction. He gave nothing away. She looked back at her grandfather. It was as if they were involved in a staring contest.

"What already?" she demanded of the two of them.

"I trust his instincts." Gunnar said, nodding toward Dalton. "Nothing against Brody, but he deals with some tourist problems, a major crime once a year and forest ranger issues, but this man here?" Her grandfather's voice trailed off.

Dalton was looking into his coffee as if it held the secrets of the world.

"Yeah, I trust him too," Aurora sighed. "I'm actually surprised that Brody went along with the poacher's angle when there were three shots."

"She learns," he teased.

"Give it up, Navy Boy. I have a brain." She paused and blew on her cocoa. "Actually, so does Brody, he really said poachers?"

"He said he wouldn't rule anything else out," Gunnar said. "But he was of the school of thought that the obvious answer was usually the right answer."

"That's just plain lazy," Dalton said disgustedly. "I went over the spot where that shot was made, and it was purposefully made at you. It was set up. How often do you work your horses on that path?"

"At least three times a week," Gunnar answered. "It's what makes us unique, we train the horses outside of just the paddock and pasture. They're trained for the trail."

"What I don't understand is why somebody would target me. We don't have any enemies. The last time we got on somebody's bad side is when the Cordell twins were caught throwing rotten apples against our barn and we had to call their parents." She speared a glance at Dalton. "And before you make a deal out of it, it was six years ago, and the boys were thirteen. They're in college now. Believe me, they're not holding a grudge."

"Look, I'm not going to even try to figure out the who and why because I don't have enough information to make any kind of good assumptions," Dalton said with quiet assurance. "But I can say with confidence that your sheriff has his head up his ass."

At Dalton's words, Aurora saw her grandfather get a frightened and stubborn expression on his face. "You're going to need to leave."

"What?" she exclaimed.

"If someone is out to get you, and the sheriff isn't taking it seriously, then you need to leave the ranch. Maybe you can go down to LA for a while and stay with your cousin Lindy. Or better yet, maybe you can finally think about taking that job down at one of those ranches down South, like the one at Torrey Pines, they love you there. Hell, the one in Temecula has been after you for years. Just take a temporary assignment, test it out."

She stood up and slammed her fists on her hips. "Have you gone bonkers?" she demanded. "When has an Olsen, or a Dressler backed down? Or a Chance for that matter. Dad was never the type to shy away from a problem, heck he married Mom. How dare you suggest I tuck my tail between my legs and run." The blood pounded in her head and ears, she was so mad, which only made her head hurt so much worse.

Dalton's fingers smoothed over the back of her hand until she loosened her fist and he clasped their hands together. Then he tugged her back down into her seat.

"It's going to be fine," he said softly.

"No, it's not. Not if Granddad is thinking I need to be sent away, which is bullshit, I'm not going."

Gunnar looked at her through squinted eyes. "I'll pull in some reinforcements. Hal and Erwin aren't enough. Dammit, I'm so disappointed in Brody." He slammed his fist down on the table. She watched as three of her marshmallows dripped down the side of her mug.

41

Dalton cleared his throat. "I think I might have an idea. At least for a little bit."

Gunnar's head swung to spear the younger man with a laser gaze.

"What? Do you know a way we can get Brody off his ass to do something? Dammit, he's our friend, Aurora. He's known you since you were in diapers."

She covered her grandfather's fist. "He'll come around."

"Let's hope it's not before another attempt is made on your life," he huffed. He looked back over at Dalton. "What's your idea, Son?"

"I'm vacationing here for a week. How about I bunk with your two hands? That will allow me to keep an eye on things. Maybe take a look around and find out something."

She thought her grandfather might kiss Petty Officer First Class Sullivan.

"We have cabins a half mile away from the barn, it gives the men privacy," Gunnar explained, but then he hesitated. "I'd feel a lot better if you would stay closer to my granddaughter. We have two extra rooms here in the house. We can set you up in one of those. There's a good size TV in one of them."

"Weren't you here to hike and explore the area?" Aurora asked. She didn't need a babysitter, no matter how handsome he was.

"I was. But I like the looks of your ranch, and it's been a while since I've been riding, so I'd enjoy this even more."

Sure, he would. The man was just being a good sport.

"Look Dalton, we couldn't impose on you like this," Aurora protested.

"It's not an imposition," Gunnar said. "You heard the man. He wants to get back in the saddle."

"Your grandfather is right." Dalton said with a smile. "One of my former teammates has a big spread in Texas. That's where I learned to ride. I would really love to be able to show up the next time as a better horseman."

"Well Aurora can definitely help you with that. She's an expert, she not only trains and works with abused animals, she's a pro at giving riding lessons."

Dalton's lit up with amusement, while Aurora turned damn near purple.

Luckily her grandfather had no idea how she and Dalton had taken his words. Then Gunnar spoke up again. "Now wait a minute, you do realize that when you give him his riding lessons, you're going to do it while you're on the ground, now don't you Missy?"

"I'm going to be fine," she assured her grandfather. All I need is a long soak in the tub, and by morning I'll be right as rain."

"I don't think so. I saw how you were walking when you thought I wasn't looking. You were hunched over like Erwin is after a stint at the rodeo. You're taking it easy for at least forty-eight hours."

Aurora shook her head. "I can't do that, there's too much to do."

"Dalton will take care of it," Gunnar said as he pointed his index finger at the Navy SEAL.

"You can't just tell the man he's now a ranch hand." Aurora felt like tearing her hair out.

"Sure, he can. I'm used to taking orders. Just tell me what to do. I figure mucking out stalls is part of my duties," Dalton grinned.

"You've done enough already. Hell, you practically carried me up the side of a mountain, for Pete's sake." These two men were driving her up a wall. She gave them a weary grin and noticed that Dalton was staring. Dammit, she knew he was looking at her dimple.

"Young Man, I can't thank you enough for all that you did for my Aurora. It was a miracle that you were there for her this morning."

Dalton smiled at her grandfather. "I was glad I was there. Now let me go get checked out of the lodge, and I'll come back here. How does that sound?"

"There's really no need," Aurora said again. Both men turned to her with the exact pitying look. She was so outvoted.

"Don't listen to Aurora, you're staying. There's cable, and I cook a mean meal. You'll love it here."

She looked over at Dalton. "I really hate the idea of you ruining your time off just to babysit me," she sighed.

He turned in his chair, so he was looking straight at her. "You're right, I was looking forward to my time hiking around the lake."

"I knew it!"

"But," he continued. "I think spending time on a horse around this ranch will be just as soothing. What's more, I would lose my Eagle Scout badge if I didn't stick around and keep an eye on you," he grinned.

"I'm serious," she said.

His blue eyes darkened. "Okay, if you want serious, here's serious. There's not a chance in fucking hell that I'm not going to be on your ass until we find out who in the hell has targeted you. I am going to take them down."

"What you said doesn't make any sense." It was like he was speaking a foreign language.

"Honey, it's the boy scout creed." Her grandfather patted

44

her hand. He turned to Dalton. "Let me get you a key to the house."

DALTON TOOK the key from Gunnar. He had to admit, he really liked the man. They thought alike. Then he looked over at Aurora. Now they weren't always on the same page, but he had to admit, he really liked her too...a lot. He pushed up from his chair. "I better get over to Pinecrest Lodge. What time should I come back in the morning?"

"Are you really sure you want to do this?"

"He's sure," Gunnar answered.

"What he said," Dalton grinned.

"This next week is going to be hell, isn't it?" she sighed and grinned. He got another glimpse of her dimple.

"Not if you just do as your told," Gunnar said.

"Yeah sure, that'll be happening."

"It wouldn't be any fun if you did," Dalton said.

Her head jerked up at his words and she blushed, then she grabbed her cup of cold cocoa and took a long swig.

"We start early," Gunnar said.

"I've been known to work an early morning shift from time to time," Dalton deadpanned.

Gunnar's chuckle was deep and loud. "Aurora told me you're a SEAL. I'm betting you've worked an early shift, a late shift, and double shifts, and three days in a row."

The old man's laughter reminded Dalton of his friends. He was good people. "I'm still stunned that your granddaughter was able to figure out I was a SEAL, simply by the gun I carried. She pulled that out of her hat in a heartbeat. Hell, there a lot of vets from different branches that wouldn't have put that together as fast as she did."

Add that kind of lethal intelligence with how she filled out a sweater and she rang all his bells.

"Aurora's special," Gunnar agreed.

"Aurora's also right here, Gentlemen," she stood up shaking her head. "Are you really going to talk about me like I'm invisible?" At least she wasn't blushing.

"Hey Darlin', we were being complimentary," Gunnar defended himself.

Aurora rounded the table and handed Dalton his jacket. He took it, then tipped her chin back with his knuckles so he could better see her forehead. He grimaced as he saw that the swelling was worse than it had been that morning.

"Are you icing your head?"

"Are you a doctor?" she asked.

"I've trained as a medic. So, have you?"

"Have I what? Trained as a medic? Or iced my head?" Again, with the dimple. This time he was also getting brown eyes sparkling up at him.

"Either. But I'll be satisfied if you just answer yes to the ice."

"Yes, Mr. Medic, I've been icing my forehead." She walked over to the refrigerator and pulled out a frozen bag of peas from the freezer. "Voila."

Dalton looked over at Gunnar who nodded. "She's napped once, and laid down an additional two times, each time with ice packs."

"You two aren't going to be talking *about* me again, now are you?"

Aurora was getting feisty again. Damn, she had just started to settle down.

"Aurora, you gave me a hell of a scare today, and I'm betting Dalton here was a little worried too. Let us fuss a little."

"I already agreed to Dalton coming and acting as my keeper. Isn't that enough?"

"No," Dalton and Gunnar said simultaneously.

"Men are an odd breed." She turned and picked up his and her mugs and put them into the dishwasher. "So anytime after five a.m. will work."

"I'm in charge of breakfast," Gunnar said. "Cinnamon apple French toast if you make it here at five." The old fisherman finished his coffee. "Apple smoked bacon too."

"I think you've convinced me to be on time."

Aurora eyed him thoughtfully. "I'm betting you were never planning on showing up later than five, were you?"

He didn't bother to answer. "Thanks again for the coffee. I'll see you both in the morning."

As he walked out to his truck, considered what he had signed up for. It was really a threefer. One, he felt bad that an injured woman and her aging grandparent should have to handle a ranch and orchard on their own, so he was happy to step in. Two, when she had told him about the Valhalla ranch and then when he had pulled up the driveway at twilight he was hit with an odd feeling of comfort. Three, he was definitely going to find out who was behind those shots.

He took his time driving back to the lodge, carefully watching the dark road because he knew damn well that deer were prone to dart out. When he felt the vibration of his phone, he pulled it out of the inside pocket of his jacket and tossed it onto the passenger seat, not bothering to look at the display to see who it was. He had a good idea who was calling. It was the same man who had been calling the last three days.

Dexter Evans was getting to be more and more like a mother hen every month he spent as a father to Austin, and Dalton was suffering because of it. He should call Austin and offer to start a support group. Maybe invite Hunter in. Nah, Hunter was too into Aliana, he was rolling with Dex's meddling.

Then there was the way that Dex was getting in Wyatt's face about how he had ended things with his last conquest. Dex was on a mission to baby-sit the Western Hemisphere, and now Dalton was in his sites, and he didn't like it. He could hear the low hum of vibration over in the seat. Now who was calling? At least his teammate never called more than once a day, so this time it had to be someone different.

When he pulled into the parking lot of the lodge, he stopped the car and snagged the phone off the seat. He looked at the display and white-hot rage exploded through his body.

"Motherfucker!"

He slammed his elbow into the driver's side window, the loud crack was music to his ears.

"You bitch. You absolute bitch!" He stared longer at the number on the phone. Five years ago, he'd deleted the old woman's number off his phone, and anyone else connected to Lacey. It hadn't done him a damn bit of good. He'd thrown that old phone into the Pacific Ocean and gotten a new one. One that he gave to a select number of people. Very few people connected to the time before. Yet here he was looking at the number of his dead wife's mother on the five-year anniversary of his daughter's birthday. The death that Lacey had caused. What the fuck was Norma calling him for?

Flop sweat coated the back of his neck as he stared at the phone like it was emanating the stench of two-day-old road kill. The whole purpose of him coming to Tahoe, a place that had the deep, dark blue water of the lake and the rich green of the pines that it in no way reminded him of that San Diego road where his drunken wife had taken their precious child and hurtled them into the side of a rock. Now his former mother-in-law was calling?

He drew back his arm to slam it into the cracked window again but stopped himself.

"Get your shit together." He told himself.

The phone in his hand vibrated. Bile surged before his vision cleared enough to see that it was Zed Zaragoza calling. He let it go to voicemail. Zed didn't leave one. Seconds later a text came through.

QUIT SCREENING YOUR CALLS AND PICK-UP.

DALTON GRUNTED. It was the closest he could get to a laugh. The phone vibrated again, and he picked it up.

"What do you want?"

"Is Tahoe cold? It's beautiful here in Virginia." Zed sounded jovial. It was kind of scary.

"What do you want?" Dalton said again.

"You're not going to let me even try to kiss you before I go in for the kill?" Zed asked.

"I'm tired. It's cold. I don't have time for bullshit. What do you want?"

49

He heard the big man sigh. "You've been pinging my radar for the last forty-eight. Then five minutes ago I knew something big had happened and I had to call. It wasn't something that said I needed to call Dex and call in reinforcements, but I knew I needed to check in."

Shit. Shit. Shit.

Did he really need this tonight? First there'd been Norma who should be buried in the past, and now Zed. The big SEAL from Virginia had always been pretty empathetic for women and his friend Hunter, but now he was behaving totally out of character and calling him out of the blue. Dalton didn't need this shit.

"I'm not going to spill my guts," Dalton spit out bitterly.

"Remember one thing Sullivan, I'm the belligerent bastard out of the two of us, don't try to usurp my role." Zed's tone was mellow.

"Seriously, what makes you think you needed to call?"

Zed didn't answer. Then Dalton remembered a conversation he'd never really taken seriously. Hunter had said that Zed had some kind of sixth sense about things. Still, why would it relate to Dalton?

"You still there, or did you hang up on me?" Zed asked mildly. "I'll just call again."

"Don't you have a pregnant fiancé? Last I heard she was having morning, afternoon and evening sickness, shouldn't you be with her?"

"She's figured out that she can eat peaches, fettucine alfredo and Kool-Aid for dinner, it's her new favorite and she can keep it down, so she's sleeping. Anyway, it's midnight here. So, spill your guts."

Every instinct inside him rebelled, then cool air wafted in from the broken window of his truck, and Dalton realized he needed to vent about Norma. He didn't want to go into everything, but Norma, yeah, he needed to spew out that poison.

"My former mother-in-law called."

There was a pause. "Former is a different word than ex," Zed finally commented.

"My wife is dead. Didn't Hunter ever tell you?"

"Nope. Hunter keeps things close to his vest unless it's pertinent to a situation."

Sighing, Dalton had to agree. "Yeah, he only mentioned your voodoo after you showed up out of nowhere when he was in L.A."

Zed barked out a laugh. "How come I'm thinking that's not what he called it."

"Probably because you know Hunter. Still I don't know why you're signaling onto me."

"Man, you're blaring across the continent, I couldn't help but pick up on it. So, tell me why this former mother-in-law is calling today. I take it has something to do with your wife's death, right?"

Dalton gritted his teeth so hard he thought his jaw might break. "No, my daughter. Today would have been her eighth birthday if she'd lived. Her name is Regan Elizabeth."

"That's a beautiful name," Zed said quietly.

Vivid images of her silky black curls and navy-blue eyes floated behind Dalton's closed eyelids. He could hear her laughter, it would ring out like chimes. Regan's joy was contagious, he could still feel the fierce hugs that she gave him with her little arms. Every time, Dalton would breathe in the strawberry scent of her baby shampoo and savor the power of her love.

"She was a beautiful little girl. She was only three years old when her mother killed her."

He could feel Zed's shock through the phone.

"God, I'm so sorry. No wonder you don't want to talk to your former mother-in-law. Why Tahoe?"

"The last four years I've been climbing mountains. I wanted to do all the seven seconds, starting with K2, but there were permit issues, so I did Ojos del Salado first, then Mount Kenya, followed by Mount Townsend. Last year I climbed Mount Logan in Canada."

"And this year?"

Dalton took a moment to formulate his answer. "Mount Logan changed my perspective a little bit. I didn't feel quite the need to punish myself with the climb after witnessing the peace and beauty of Logan. I wanted to recapture the serenity." Dalton swallowed, he almost couldn't get the words out. Finally, "Hunter said you and Marcia are having a baby girl."

"Yeah." There was a wealth of satisfaction in Zed's voice.

"I'm glad for you. Girls are a gift," he said quietly. A gift and a curse, he thought to himself, but he would never say that out loud. The air coming into the cab of his truck was frigid, he could see his breath, it looked like a heavy fog of death.

"Are you listening to me?" Zed asked.

A stream of white mist came out of his mouth as Dalton asked, "What?"

"You're not tracking. Stay with me, Sullivan."

Dalton forced himself to pay attention. He needed to stay in the present. The past was the past. How could he tell Zed that some risks were beyond him? That it was better to face the certainty of nothing, than the tiny chance of soul-shearing agony?

"Dalton?" Zed asked quietly.

He blinked, his daughter's smile fading from his mind. "I'm here. What did you say?"

"Do you need me to have Dex or my guy Kane arrange it, so your former mother-in-law can't get through to your number again? Better yet, do you want me to arrange it so that her credit is tanked, and there's an arrest warrant out for her?"

More mist gusted out as Dalton chuckled. "Dex would never go for it. It's just not in his nature."

"Hell, I know that. Kane would do it. The arrest warrant would only be for unpaid parking tickets though. Unfortunately, he'd be kind of a pussy when it came to a little old lady."

Dalton grinned. Maybe it wasn't such a bad thing that Zed had called.

"You're not answering. So, I'll take that as a yes."

"No. No arrests," Dalton sighed. "I'm going to call Dex. He knows about Norma. I'm going to have him do a little digging and see if there is something going on I need to be aware of. There shouldn't be. I want those people wiped out of my life, but if there is something that is going to bite me in the ass, I want to know about it."

"Good idea."

"Fettuccini, Kool-Aid and peaches, huh?" Dalton's lip curled as he thought about the flavor combination.

Zed laughed. "I can hardly watch her eat it. It's grape Kool-Aid. There were three days in there where she wanted asparagus too."

All thought of Norma fled as Dalton pictured the plate

in front of Marcia and Zed sitting across from her. He burst out laughing. It felt great.

As both of their laughter faded, a comfortable silence took over. Finally, Zed spoke up. "I'm going to call you tomorrow, you better pick up your phone," he growled.

"I might not be able to. I have an appointment with some horseshit."

"Explain."

"It's a long story, and I'm tired. I'll tell you tomorrow. I'm going to bed."

"Fine, I'll call Dex for you," Zed said. "You go get your beauty sleep. But tomorrow I want to hear why you're making nice with the horsies."

He blew out a long breath. Who knew Zaragoza was so funny?

He looked over at the broken window. Nope, he wasn't going to go there. That shit was in the past. Dex or Kane would make sure she wouldn't call, and Norma would be history and he'd fix the window. Onwards and upwards. He'd play with horses and concentrate on Aurora.

4

———

OH, FOR GOD'S SAKE, WHAT WAS SHE THINKING? WHEN HAD she ever worried this much about what to wear? It was always jeans and a sweater, or jeans and a T-shirt, depending on the time of year. End of story. Aurora plowed through her drawer, reaching under all her sweaters and not finding anything that felt soft.

Dammit!

Where was the feel-good sweater? And not the damn pink one. Granddad would give her a ration of shit for it if she wore a pink sweater the first morning Dalton arrived. But blast it all, she knew there was a heather gray sweater that was really soft that would be great. She slammed her drawer shut and yanked open the next one.

Score!

She pulled on the sweater and did a cursory look in the mirror and groaned. Why had she even bothered to try? With the bruise on her head she was looking like the Phantom of the Opera without the mask. She sat down on the bed and put on her thick steel-toed boot socks that she preferred wearing with her cowboy boots, then pulled on her boots.

Leaping up she took a step toward the door and the room took a spin around her.

"Woozy-Daisy."

She gulped in three fast mouthfuls of air and felt a little better. She needed to get outside and get some real-live fresh air. That was all she needed. That and some coffee. Aurora left her room and followed the smell of apple-smoked bacon.

"Bout time you got up. You feeling okay?" Gunnar handed her a mug. She lifted it and almost choked when she tasted chocolate. Not that she didn't like it, but was he for real?

"Granddad, where's my coffee?"

"Not good for head injuries. I called Doc Barnes, he said so."

Aurora put the mug of hot chocolate down on the kitchen counter, grabbed herself a clean mug from the cupboard and poured herself a cup of coffee. "Dr. Barnes is the vet," she said patiently.

"He still had to go to medical school."

"He went to veterinary school, Granddad. Veterinary school. I highly doubt that the bulls were sneaking cups of coffee after they got injured in the bullring," she said wryly. She closed her eyes and took a long sip of the heavenly brew.

"You still didn't answer my question, how are you feeling?"

"I'm feeling so-so. I'm going to take it slow today." She nudged him with her hip and pulled the eggs and milk out of the fridge.

"Good, then I won't hear anymore guff about you actually up on a horse today, right?" he asked as he eyed her carefully. "Maybe just make some more calls about Aladdin and Siren and see if you can pinpoint their origins."

She scowled at grandfather. "I'm not going to spend my day shackled to a desk. Anyway, Crystal's been doing a lot of the legwork."

Aurora was happy when there was a knock on the door. Saved by the knock, she grinned to herself. Gunnar went to let Dalton in while she whisked together the eggs, milk, vanilla and cinnamon.

"Sit down with Dalton, I'll finish up," Gunnar said. He put her mug down on the table, and plopped down one in front Dalton as well, filling both before going back to the counter to finish the French toast. Aurora sank down in the chair, pleased when she noted Dalton's blue eyes perusing the fit of her sweater, but then he frowned.

"You're looking kind of pale."

"I'm fine," she protested.

"No, she's not," Gunnar inserted. "She already admitted she plans to take it slow, that means she must be feeling like crap. What's more she's drinking coffee when she shouldn't have caffeine." She turned and glowered at her grandfather.

"I can take care of things today," Dalton said quietly. "Gunnar's right, you should be resting."

"Great just what I need, two mother hens."

His eyes started to sparkle. She liked it.

"Whatchya thinking?" she asked.

"It's only fair I get to be someone's watcher. I just called mine this morning." He grinned broadly before bending forward to take another sip of his coffee.

"You have someone mothering you? Who is she?"

Oh shit, had she really asked that?

HE LOOKED up and raised an eyebrow, Dalton liked that she'd asked the question. Really liked it.

"There's no she," he answered slowly. "Just teammates. The nosey one is Dex. I woke him up out of a sound sleep and it served him right. He's been hounding my ass since I got here."

Gunnar put plates in front of him. "Sounds like how my brothers are. Hell, even since Arvid and Einar moved back to Norway they still call and kibitz."

"Older or younger?" he asked.

"I'm the baby and they don't let me forget it. My people last a long time." As soon as the words were out of his mouth a look of profound sadness passed over his face and he turned back to the stove. Dalton looked over at Aurora, she gave a small shake of her head. Dalton realized that the older man must be thinking of his dead wife. He couldn't imagine feeling that kind of love for a woman. A child yes. A woman? No.

"So, tell me more about your nursemaid," Aurora asked changing the subject.

"Dex is in charge of communications for our team." Dalton didn't explain that the man was also an experienced hacker and gathered all the intelligence for the Black Dawn SEAL team. "I think because he does so much communicating, he tends to act as a liaison between all of us and is constantly in touch. Whenever one of us goes off the grid, it drives him crazy.

"So, you went off the grid?" He watched as Aurora

swirled her bacon in syrup and licked it off the meat before taking a bite. He looked into her eyes and realized it was a totally unconscious action, but that didn't stop him from getting worked up.

It took him a moment to remember her question. "We all go off the grid from time to time when we have leave, it's the nature of the beast."

Aurora chuckled, and he took a bite of his apple French toast. "Gunnar, this is fantastic," he raved. Gunnar sat down with his own plate and smiled.

"I'm not the ranch hand I once was, but I'll make sure you have three squares while Aurora runs rough shod over you and our other two part-time ranch hands."

"Don't you cook for them?" Dalton asked.

"I'll send out lunch to the stables. They prefer to handle breakfast and dinner in their cabins." Gunnar answered.

"So, Dalton, did you tell your friend Dex that you would be working on a ranch?" Aurora asked.

"I did. He thought that was a great idea. Valhalla has one of the best reputations in the state of Nevada for training horses. I didn't realize I was in the presence of a real live horse whisperer." He was never surprised at the amount of information that Dex could get his hands on, but he was amazed at what the man had found out about Aurora.

Blushing, she bent and swirled another piece of bacon and delicately licked it. He had to stifle a groan.

"I'm just lucky that the horses tend to respond well to me."

"That's a load of crap. She's been like this since she was a little girl, she charms them. The foals used to follow her around," Gunnar grinned. Dalton liked the pride he heard in the man's voice.

"I look forward to seeing that today." Dalton saluted her with his coffee mug.

"It's really not as big as deal as those people made it out to be. I think sometimes people just believe what they want to believe because it makes them feel good." She dipped her head and concentrated on her food.

"Ah, good ole self-delusion."

"Are you a cynic?" Gunnar asked Dalton.

"You got to remember the Navy SEAL motto, The Only Easy Day Was Yesterday. I'm a realist."

"While I like that kind of attitude when it comes to protecting my granddaughter, I sure hope you have a better outlook when it comes to your personal life."

It was as if the room around him froze for just a moment as he was caught in his memories, but then it sped crazily back to life. Dalton nodded. "Yes Sir, personally, I know that my worst days are behind me."

At that moment, the room stopped its crazy ride, and thudded to a stop, and there was Aurora's smile. "I'm glad you have nothing but good things to look forward to, you deserve that," she said.

"I THINK YOU LIED MR. SULLIVAN," Aurora said archly. "You're a lot more comfortable around horses then you led me to believe."

She watched as he expertly saddled the brown gelding.

"Yeah, well, one of my former teammates has a ranch in Texas. I've spent some time there. Jack has horses and cattle. Any of us who came with him to visit his folks were expected to ride herd."

"I've never done that, what was it like?" She wanted to get him talking, she liked his voice. It was smooth, dark and melted over her like warm honey. What's more, he'd been so quiet when they'd left the house, it had taken her almost a half hour to get him to smile. It wasn't until she'd started in on Erwin's antics as a rodeo clown that he'd broken a grin. Now Dalton seemed to be behaving more like the man she'd met yesterday.

She watched his large hands competently cinch up the saddle and then gently stroke Teddy's neck. "Jack's parents are salt-of-the-earth people, they make you feel right at home, the same way Gunnar does. I'd ridden a horse a couple of times when I was in boy scouts, but this was something different. Jack is the only one of my teammates who wouldn't give me shit, he patiently taught me everything I needed to know so I could help with the round-up."

Dalton led Teddy out of the stall and presented him to her.

"I'd say Jack taught you well," she smiled. "I'll go get Aladdin and then we can go for a slow tour around the ranch."

"Which one is Aladdin?" Dalton asked as he wrapped the gelding's reins around a post and followed Aurora to another stall. She had put the big roan stallion in a larger stall that was separated from the other horses. She knew that the he was comforted having more space and less noise around him.

"What's his backstory?" Dalton asked quietly as she pulled two baby carrots out of her pocket. She shouldn't have been surprised that Dalton had known enough to ask that question, after all the man had proven to be very perceptive which was another reason she found him so damned attractive.

"I really don't know. The new owners purchased him a month and a half ago. They were told that he was five years old with an even temperament. They bought him sight unseen over the internet from an Arizona horse broker, then had him trailered straight to Sacramento. Aladdin had bloodied himself on the inside of that trailer. They had to call a vet and have him tranquilized before they could get him installed in their barn."

"Let me guess, when they called the previous owner, the telephone number was disconnected."

"Give the man a cigar," Aurora nodded. "All trace of their ads was gone from the equestrian web-sites. These are good people, they've hired a private detective agency, and haven't had any luck. They paid a lot of money for Aladdin, but that isn't what mattered to them. Their vet suggested he be put down, but the Beaumonts refused. They called me."

Aurora reached over the stall door and held out the carrots. Aladdin eyed Dalton warily.

"Come on Gorgeous, I brought these just for you," she coaxed. She tuned out everything and continued to croon to the big animal. Watching every twitch of his eyelid, every flex of his muscles. Finally, she saw him relax just a bit. "That's it, come here, you know you want to," she smiled softly when the red and gray stallion moved majestically forward and nibbled the carrots out of her open palm. She hovered her other hand over his muzzle. After a couple of seconds Aladdin lifted upwards and snuggled his nose into her hand so that she could scratch him.

"Aren't you a love?" she asked.

Carefully she moved her hands along the side of his face

toward his ear, stroking and lulling him into a sense of security. Each time she waited until he pushed against her hand so that she was confident he was ready for her next caress.

A loud crash sounded. Aurora yanked back her hand but before she could do anything else, Dalton had her around the waist and pulled away from the stall as Aladdin planted a powerful kick against the door, a plank shot at rocket speed across the aisle and embedded itself into the stall across from Aladdin's stall. If Dalton hadn't grabbed Aurora, she would have been maimed or killed.

Aurora strained her neck so that she could see what was happening to the terrified horse.

"Let me go," she demanded as she tried to twist out of Dalton's arms.

"Not until Aladdin is calm," Dalton said grimly.

"He's cowering in the corner. He's not going to cause anymore problems." She tried to push out of Dalton's grasp, but it was no use. "Are you going to let me go, or not?"

"Not. It isn't safe, Sunshine."

"This is my job. I do it day in, day out. I've been doing this since I was fifteen, Sullivan. You need to let me handle it." She tested his hold, there was no give. She went for a different approach and slowly relaxed her body. His hold changed too, one of his arms slid up her back and cuddled the back of her head, the other arm hugging her closer to his body. For a moment she reveled in the closeness. How could she not? Then she took advantage of his inattention and wrested herself away and went to a special bucket.

"Aurora, what do you think you're doing?" He was exasperated.

"I'm getting some herbs that he's going to eat. They're calming."

He took a look at the plants in her hand. "What is it?"

"Comfrey, dandelions, valerian and meadowsweet. You need to let me do what I do best."

"But that's the problem, you're not at your best. I saw you at breakfast this morning, you were pale and unsteady."

"I'll be careful," she said as she went toward the stall door. Dalton's hand was there to stop her.

"No," he said simply.

He was so damned frustrating. Great, now she had two stallions she had to soothe. For a second she considered offering him some of the herbs.

"Dalton, could you please look at Aladdin? Really look at him in there." She waited while he took a long look at the horse. "What do you see?"

"I see a very scared, two-thousand-pound animal that could easily kill you."

"Do you see him shaking?"

Dalton nodded.

"Look at his legs, do you see those crisscross scars? Did you know that their legs are their most sensitive area on their body because they have so little padding and it is right next to bone? Do you see how much scarring he has?"

Dalton squinted, then he nodded.

"Sometimes that's a sign of someone trying to train a horse to do different maneuvers for dressage. They've done a shit job, since nobody wants a scarred horse out in the arena."

"All of that abuse would be done for an equestrian event?" She could hear the disbelief in Dalton's voice. "Just how big are the purses for winning something like that?"

"They're nothing compared to winning the Kentucky Derby, they're pennies on the dollar. Most of this is about getting into the Olympics with your horse, and later competing nationally and internationally. There is a big community associated with this sport and more than a little prestige that goes with it."

"Yeah, but at the expense of this kind of abuse?" She liked hearing the outrage in his voice. She liked people who stood up for kids and animals, it was a big thing for her. "Still, it doesn't matter if it was for a little bit of money, or a lot of money, this is just sick," Dalton ended.

"Exactly," she agreed. "Now can I go in?"

"No."

She turned her head slowly so as not to scare Aladdin, but her glare was fierce. "I'm effing serious. I'm going into the stall. I'm never going to tell you how to be a SEAL, you're not going to tell me how to work with abused animals. This is my job. Are you going to be a bully and actually use force to keep me away from Aladdin?"

He gave her a calculating look. "Are you one hundred percent sure that you will be safe?" he asked.

"No. No, I'm not. But I'm ninety-eight percent sure that I will be, and I know how to protect myself. I need to get to him before he ends up working himself into another state and bloodies himself against the stall. I've seen him do it. You've got to let me work with him."

"Dammit, I wish there was a police vest or something that we could let you use. Can I go in with you?"

"No, that would just spook him. You're going to have to trust me."

She waited. Finally, Dalton nodded.

Aurora silently unlocked the stall and slowly entered it.

She was careful to lock the door in the same silent manner. It broke her heart seeing this proud stallion quivering in the back of his stall.

Aurora had no idea how long she whispered and crooned to the animal, waiting for his ears to finally perk up. There was no way she was going to move much closer when his ears were flat back against his head, but she wanted to be in a position to watch the stallion's tail. She moved two feet forward diagonally, so she could get a look at his tail which was still clamped down.

"Hey Handsome, I have some treats," she held out her hand, continuing to watch his ears and tail, waiting for signs of relaxation. She could feel Dalton's eyes on her, because her senses were wide open.

"Boo, can I come closer?" she asked the horse.

Nothing.

She started a wordless hum and started to slightly rock. Finally, his tail relaxed, and his ears began to perk up.

"We good?" she asked.

"Wanna treat?"

Aurora smiled when Aladdin took a deep breath in and nickered softly. He'd smelled the herbs and flowers. His nostrils flared, and he took a cautious step forward.

"Sunshine be careful." Dalton's tone was a very low whisper that didn't startle the stallion. She was impressed.

Aurora smiled. Two days, just two days and she was liking the concern that Dalton was exhibiting. Aladdin nickered softly and walked steadily towards her. He bent his big head and nibbled at the handful of plants, when he was done he looked at her and swayed his head. The big softy wanted a rub which she was happy to give.

Petting the side of his beautiful chestnut neck, she

praised him softly. He pressed into her hand, so she put more oomph into her strokes. She looked into his eye, on the right side of his head was getting droopy, between the excitement, the petting and the calming effect of the valerian flower, he was relaxed enough for her to look at his forelock and see how much damage he'd done when he kicked his stall.

Damn. She was going to need Doc Barnes.

She could still see some wood stuck in his flesh and automatically reached in her back pocket for her cell phone. She came up empty.

Smoothing her hand over Aladdin's silky coat, she spoke softly, "I'm going to have to leave now. Will you be a good boy?" She saw the effects of the valerian by the slight drooping of the big horse's eyes.

Aurora continued stroking his warm body until he finally nudged against her hand and blew a warm stream of air that ruffled her hair. "Okay, I'll take that as a yes," she smiled. "I'll be back."

She kept an eye on the stallion as she exited the stall. Dalton had the stall door opened as soon as she reached it. As soon as it was solidly locked, she slumped against it. Dalton shook his head and guided her to a spot further down the hall where she wasn't leaning on a stall door. Then he handed her his phone.

"How'd you know?" she asked tiredly.

"You would have asked for the first aid kit if you could have handled it on your own." He held up the kit that was normally on the center beam in the in the main walkway of the barn. "I figured you'd need to call the vet."

Aurora contemplated Dalton's phone then gave a rueful laugh. "What was I thinking, I don't know his number.

Everyone's on speed dial. I'm going to have to call Grandpa."

Dalton lips tilted upwards. "I understand. I only know five or six numbers, otherwise I would be S.O.L."

"What does S.O.L. stand for?" Aurora asked as she pressed in her Grandfather's number.

"Shit out of luck."

She gave a weak laugh as Gunnar picked up. She quickly explained the situation with Aladdin, noting Dalton's intent stare as he set down the first aid kit.

"What?" she asked as she handed back her phone.

"You were amazing with him."

"Grandad?" What was he talking about?

Dalton leaned forward and placed his hand next to her head, effectively caging her in, his face close to hers. "No, with Aladdin. It about killed me to agree to let you go in there. You know that don't you? He was enraged earlier."

"No, he was scared," she corrected as she looked into his Navy-blue eyes. "There's a big difference."

"Either way, he could have hurt or killed you." Dalton gave her a considering look. "But you weren't afraid. You knew exactly how to approach him. Handle him."

Was that admiration in his voice?

She swallowed. "Aladdin told me what to do. I just followed his cues."

"Can you explain them to me?" he asked in a smoky voice. It stroked her senses like velvet. His left hand touched her cheek, pushing a lock of her hair behind her ear. She nuzzled into his hand just like Aladdin had responded to her touch.

"Are you going to answer my question?"

Did he have any idea what he was doing to her? What was his question? Oh yeah.

"All horses have specific body language, you watch their ears, their tails. You listen to their breathing, you watch to see how they stand. It's simple really." Her voice trailed off as Dalton leaned closer. This close his eyes seemed almost indigo, they were mesmerizing.

"What cues am I giving off?" Dalton asked. She could taste the apple on his breath.

"I'm not sure."

He cupped her cheek, his thumb swiped her lower lip. "How about now? Is it coming into focus for you?" he rasped.

She shivered. He *had* to be able to hear her heart beat. He just had to.

"Then let me make it clear. Watching you in danger like that, brought out my protective instincts. Then seeing you beguile that stallion until he was literally eating out of your hands punched me in the gut. I've never seen anything like it. You are an enchantress, and I need to touch you. Hold you close and kiss you."

"Please," she whimpered. She didn't recognize the breathy sound of her voice. Dalton wrapped his arm around her waist and locked their bodies together. It wasn't enough. She twined her arms around his neck and delighted in his warmth. He bent his head and captured her lips. The taste of apples and Dalton exploded across her universe.

More.

So soft, her mouth flowered open.

More.

So luscious, her flavor tantalized his tongue.

More.

So willing, her body melted against his.

More.

Dalton couldn't ever remember aching like this, wanting like this. Ever. He needed to pull back. Then her tongue shyly met his and he was lost. He cupped the side of her face, then speared his fingers up through the silk of her golden hair. She arched into his hold and he felt her fingers digging into his shoulders. Molten heat and seared through his brain and gripped his body in a vice.

Dalton was on fire, he peppered kisses along Aurora's jaw.

"Sunshine," he murmured as he nipped her earlobe.

Her throaty moan shot a bolt of lightening to his cock. She must have felt it because she arched against him. He felt the wet heat of her mouth open against his neck, she sucked and bit, as she pushed her tummy against him.

His fingers bit into the plush globes of her ass and her long legs wrapped around his hips. Maple syrup, apples and Aurora filled his mind as he reveled in the fire of their intimate embrace.

The sounds that she was making were music to his ears, every breath, every moan. He was lost until a discordant squawk finally penetrated the symphony that was Aurora.

A distant car horn. Then it got closer.

"Easy." He kissed her neck. Inhaling the subtle scent of flowers.

She mewled and pressed harder, her fingers kneaded deeper into his back.

"Sunshine, someone's here," he whispered. "They're honking."

"No," she protested on a low wail.

He waited, knowing her innate pragmatism would kick in. Finally, it did.

She moved her fingers and sliced her fingers into the military short strands of his hair, pulling his head backwards so she could look into his eyes. "This isn't finished," she said as she slowly lowered her legs back to the ground.

He squeezed her ass. She had a great ass.

The car door slammed. He heard two men talking. Had to be the vet.

"I'm going to grab a shovel and make myself useful. I'll come introduce myself in a few minutes." Aurora's gaze dropped down to the front of his jeans. She gave a slow satisfied smile.

"You're not helping, young lady."

"Oh, I think I helped just fine," she smirked.

He liked her. Dalton admired her sway as she made her way to the front of the barn. He grabbed a shovel and went to one of the stalls and got busy.

5

"I'VE GOT TO SEE A MAN ABOUT A HORSE."

"Oh Lord, not that tired old line again," Aurora moaned. It was the second dinner they'd shared with Dalton and it seemed like her Grandfather was bound and determined to pull out all of his zingers. Aurora gave Dalton a surreptitious glance, it was only the forty-third in the last half hour. She needed to stop it. She would too, except she had noticed that three times she'd caught him looking her way when Gunnar was at the stove. Those three times when their eyes met were enough to keep her mind and her eyes on him.

"I can't believe that Johnny is finally thinking about selling, can you?"

In a heartbeat all her focus lasered in on her grandfather. "John Dunlap is thinking of selling Vertigo?"

"Yep," Gunnar grinned.

She pushed away her dinner plate and curled her foot up under leg on the seat of the kitchen chair, then rested her elbow on the table. Leaning in she gave Gunnar a long look. "We've been saving a long time for this. But are you really

73

ready to pull the trigger?" She studied his weathered face and saw nothing but excitement.

"Girly, this is it. Mae and I wanted Vertigo's sire. He was special, but Dunlap wasn't selling. After Heathen died I didn't think that any of offspring would be worth a damn, but Vertigo is the spitting image of Heathen." Her grandfather was practically rubbing his hands together.

Aurora bit her lip, she didn't want to ask her next question, but she had to.

"Why is Mr. Dunlap thinking of selling Vertigo to you, and not keeping him in the family?"

"Johnny thinks his brother's two boys are worthless. There's not a chance in hell he wants Vertigo to go be passed down to them."

Aurora sat up straighter. "Is something wrong with Mr. Dunlap?"

"Cancer," her grandfather said succinctly. "Stage four liver cancer. I'm going to drive up to his ranch and stay a few days with him. We're going to talk over some old times, and then I'll load up Vertigo and head home. Your Uncle Tate will be by each day riding fence while I'm gone. He was planning to start today, but one of their boys at the Dressler Ranch broke his arm and Tate had to take him into town to the hospital."

"There's nothing wrong with our fence," Aurora sighed in resignation.

"Fine, then Tate can cook for you and Dalton while I'm gone."

"What if I were to say that Dalton and I can cook for ourselves?"

"I'd say good, because Tate hates to cook." Gunnar glowered at her from underneath his bushy white eyebrows.

74

"Live with the fact that he's going to be out in the field while you're riding around. You got a problem with that?"

Aurora whipped her head around to glare at Dalton. "Just how many people do you think is warranted for the 'Protect Aurora' project?"

Dalton forked carrots into his mouth and chewed, his blue eyes weren't flirting now, instead she could tell he was considering how to answer her.

"I want the truth."

Dalton swallowed and took a sip of his iced tea. "More than I did yesterday."

"Why?" she demanded.

"Because I found two sets of hoofprints next to the orchard that looked a lot like the ones next to those shell casings. We need another set of eyes here at the ranch. Your grandfather has been keeping watch here at the house, but with him leaving we especially need someone new."

"I still don't have the slightest idea why I would be the target of anything."

"And that's something we're going to have to work on," Dalton agreed. "Because we can be damned sure it isn't about two pre-teens who were throwing apples against your barn."

"Well Dalton, I see that you were right, I was worried about nothing."

She gave her grandfather a sharp look. "What do you mean?"

"I thought you would give us a hell of a lot more trouble for bringing Tate over to the ranch. Dalton thought you would be more amenable."

"Still noticed you were willing to put up with my wrath," she sighed.

"Aurora, you mean the world to me. If a trained SPECOP soldier has a hunch, it behooves me to listen to him."

She grinned.

"Make up your mind, you're either mad at me, or your happy. Why are you grinning?" Gunnar demanded.

"You're the one who combined a whole lot of sweet with a whole lot of gruff in one sentence. How could I not grin? I love you too, Grandpa." She untangled her leg and leaned over and kissed the old man on his cheek.

"Got dessert," he smiled.

"None for Dalton," Aurora scowled at the Navy SEAL who was trying to stay unobtrusive. "He doesn't deserve a reward for stirring up shit."

"Are you kidding, he's getting extra ice cream to go with the apple brown betty." Gunnar pushed up from the table to get the food from the oven.

Dalton looked up from his empty plate and gave her a smile that would melt more than just ice cream.

"WE NEED TO TALK," she whispered outside his door.

Even if he had been soundly sleeping, Dalton still would have heard the moment her bedroom door opened, and there wasn't a chance in hell he would have slept through her softly worded command outside his door. He listened as she drifted down the hall toward the kitchen. It was still pretty cold for her to be going around barefoot, what was she thinking?

He pulled on his jeans and a flannel shirt which he didn't bother to button. Did he do that on purpose? Maybe, he admitted ruefully. It was the middle of the night and a gorgeous woman wanted to talk to him. A woman who had caught fire in his arms, damned right he was going to see if he could talk her into a little bit of play. Grinning, he pushed through the swinging door of the kitchen.

"Get rid of the smirk, Sullivan." Even in the dim light he could see her chocolate brown eyes sparking.

The scent of cinnamon, apples, vanilla and Aurora permeated the room.

The microwave dinged, and she pulled out a single serving dish of left over dessert.

"Only one bowl? That's not very friendly," Dalton was unable to keep the laughter out of his voice.

She slid the bowl onto the table and got a spoon. "I asked you in here, so we could talk about you keeping things between me and you going forward. I don't want grandpa worried about this situation more than he has to be."

He leaned his shoulder against the cupboard, enjoying how she moved around the kitchen. The sweatpants hid all her charms, but he sure loved the way her breasts looked in her thermal. Aurora should never wear a bra, it was a crime against humanity.

He watched her get a spoon out the silverware drawer. "Aurora, I gotta tell you, he seems in great shape to me. Part of my job is to keep an eye on the health of my teammates, and for his age, your grandfather seems in peak condition."

"He's seventy-six years old, he doesn't need the stress," she frowned.

When he watched her fold the paper towel and put it underneath her fork beside her bowl he realized she was a woman after his own heart.

"You know, it's not very friendly, inviting me into the kitchen and then only serving yourself."

"If you want something, help yourself," she said as she bent to the freezer drawer.

As he watched her bend over he reassessed his earlier position. Even in sweats, she looked delectable. Dalton moved across the large farm kitchen and put his hand on her hip and peered over her shoulder.

"What are you doing?" she asked throatily, continuing to rummage through the contents of the freezer.

"Helping myself."

"Stop it, we have to talk." She made an attempt to wiggle away from him, but that only pressed her fanny against his crotch.

"Do that again," he pleaded.

Aurora jerked around with a tub of vanilla bean ice cream in her hands and took a deep breath. He saw her eyes dilate and color suffuse her face. When she bit her lower lip, he was lost. Dalton covered her mouth with his, sliding his hand around her hip so that it dropped lower. She tasted so good.

He swept his tongue against her lips, begging for entry. It took an eternity for her lips to part, but when they did, he hurtled into a whirlwind of pleasure. Of need. Dalton slipped his hand from her hip to the tempting swell of her fanny. Everything about this woman called out to his senses, telling him that she was his.

"What the hell?!" Dalton jerked and looked down at the smear of vanilla ice cream that was dripping down on his abdomen. He looked up at eyes that were spitting fire. He couldn't tell if she was angry, frustrated or laughing, maybe it was a combination of all three. When she lifted her hand and licked her fingers, he groaned.

"I told you we needed to talk."

Dalton shivered as rivulets of melted cream slithered down his stomach toward the waistband of his jeans. He continued to watch Aurora's tongue delicately lapping up the sticky white dessert. Then she had the audacity to look down, and he knew there wasn't a chance in hell she could miss his erection.

"It's your fault. There's no way I can talk now," he rasped.

"You're a SEAL. I've read up on you guys, you're trained to handle any situation, no matter how *hard* it is."

Shit, this time it was obvious that she was laughing.

"Sunshine," he began.

She turned away and wet a washcloth in the sink then threw it at him. He wiped up the mess. And buttoned his shirt.

"You're a mean woman."

"You shouldn't go around flaunting your hot body and making advances when it's time for a serious conversation." She plopped the container of ice cream down on the table and gave it a considering look. "Dammit, I had my hand in that. Now only I can eat it. Granddad's going to be disappointed."

Dalton grabbed a spoon and put a big scoop on her apple brown betty, then pulled the container in front of him as he sat down. "I don't mind eating it, I'll enjoy the extra bit of sweetness," he said as he took a spoonful. "What's our topic of conversation?"

"You keeping all of this stuff just between the two of us. I don't want Grandpa worried."

Dalton looked at Aurora as she savored her food. He

appreciated a woman who ate in front of him. Lacey hadn't. She was constantly on some fad diet or another, her temper flaring from lack of food.

As soon as he thought that, he shut it down. He didn't like thinking about his dead wife. Ever. Certainly not when he was admiring Aurora. The two women shouldn't ever occupy the same part of his brain.

"Dalton? Are you listening to me? Or are you watching me eat again. This time I'm not licking my fingers." Her smile was wicked as she sucked on her spoon.

"My God woman, you are putting out so many mixed signals, if I were a ship in the night I'd crash on the rocks."

Aurora's laugh was like a stroke of velvet. "Yeah, I know. I'm sorry. You mix me up. I've never wanted a man as much as I want you." She immediately put out her hand, palm up. "But...before we get all hot and bothered, I have a couple of questions."

"Shoot," he smiled.

She looked him dead in the eye. "How old are you?"

"Thirty-three."

"How long have you been in the Navy?"

"Since I was nineteen. I've been a SEAL since I was twenty-two," he answered slowly.

She stirred the contents of her bowl until it was apple sludge. "Give me some more of that," she nodded at the ice cream. He gave her another hefty scoop. She stirred some more, then took a big bite, swallowed and sighed. "You've been here for three days now, can you think of any reason why someone would target me? Are you sure this is actually happening?"

"'Fraid so."

"If I'm in the cross-fire, what about Granddad?"

"He was taking precautions before he left. That's why he hadn't gone into town. That's why he extended the hours of Hal and Erwin."

"Well at least now I know why I wasn't allowed to sit on the porch swing," Aurora said wryly.

Dalton lifted an eyebrow.

"I'd bet my bottom dollar that Granddad has his rifle hidden underneath the seat cushion."

He winced. "Yeah, well I'm thinking that might not be the best hiding place."

"Ya think?" She scooped up more apple mixture, eyed it, then dumped it back into the bowl. "I don't even think this is going to make me feel better. Dammit Dalton. What the hell is going on?"

"I don't know. But we'll keep you safe."

"I don't care about me, I worry about my grandfather."

Of course, she would. "I think him going to Sacramento is the best thing for him."

"But what about when he comes back?" she asked worriedly.

"Sunshine, this is probably about something that happened in your past. I'm going to want to go through your employment records for the last five years."

"Those are confidential."

"I spoke to Hal and Erwin, both of them said it was great working here, but that you've had to let at least two people go since they've been here at Valhalla."

"It was for cause," she sat up straight in her chair, her eyes bright.

"I didn't doubt it for a minute," he assured her. "But a disgruntled former employee is definitely different than some kid who you chased away from throwing rotten apples at your barn, don't you think?"

"Neither one of the made a stink." She jammed her spoon into the mush of dessert. "Not that they had a chance to," she qualified. "They should feel damned lucky they got their final paychecks. As far as I'm concerned they should have been run out of town on a rail." Aurora stirred the apple mixture so hard that some of it flew onto the table.

Dalton put his hand over hers. "You can stop now, I think you've killed it. It deserves to be buried in the garbage disposal." He pulled the bowl away from her and picked up the melted carton on the table in front of him and took both to the sink. When he came back to the table, he pulled his chair close to hers and sat back down.

"Tell me what happened with the two men that were fired. Did you terminate them, or did Gunnar?"

"I did," she bit out. "I didn't want granddad to know what happened. If he did he would have gotten out his shotgun and plugged their asses. Especially Darryl."

He didn't like the sounds of that. "Tell me."

She rubbed her forehead, then winced in pain. "I keep forgetting about the bump on my head," she admitted with a half-smile. She continued to probe the bruise.

There was nothing about this that he was finding amusing. He tugged her hand away from her head and then stared at her bruise. "You could have been killed that day, you do realize that, don't you? This isn't a game."

SHE LIKED the feel of his fingers against her skin. She liked it too much. There wasn't anything about this man that she didn't adore, and it had only been three days. Shit, was she staring again? She saw a flare of fire in his eyes. His fingers trailed down her cheek to her jaw. Who knew that she was an erogenous zone?

"Tell me about Darryl."

Well that stopped all the tender feelings.

"It was nothing." As soon as the words were out of her mouth she saw him scowl and knew she was in for an argument.

"Aurora." Nothing more, just her name.

"Dalton."

"Enough with the bullshit. Tell me what happened."

"Number one, I handled it." She moved her face away from his hand, and stood up, then placed her palms against the table. "Second, it's not him. Do you know how I know? Because he's currently doing time in Folsom for assault." Her legs buckled and fell back into her chair. "He hurt someone, and it's my fault." Her gut twisted just thinking about it.

Dalton was around the table in an instant, he crouched down beside her, one hand on the top of her chair the other on the table, effectively blocking her in. "Tell me," he coaxed.

"Darryl hurt someone on my watch. He hurt a girl while he worked for me." She bit her lip, attempting to hold back those old feelings. She started again. "I tried to get Renee to press charges, but her mom talked her out of it. I told Brody about it, but he said without her filing a complaint, his hands were tied. That left Darryl off to do the same thing in California."

"I don't understand. Tell me what happened."

"The Henderson family is one of our clients. Darryl was

supposed to deliver their horse. Renee was the only one that was home. She was seventeen at the time. After the delivery, I called to make sure that the mare was settled, and Renee sounded funny. I asked if everything was all right, and should I come over. She freaked at the idea that I would have Darryl come with me, which just set me on red alert. He'd always seemed a little smarmy with me, but nothing to overt. I immediately went over to see her."

"What did you find?"

Aurora pushed Dalton out of the way as she jumped out of the chair. She charged to the sink and clawed the remains of the dessert down the garbage disposal with her fingers, but she didn't' turn it on. Even with the door closed to the kitchen she was afraid the noise might wake up Gunnar, instead she looked out the window. The night was pitch black. She couldn't look at Dalton to answer his question, but she could speak the truth into the vast inky night sky.

"I found a teenager with all of the doors and windows locked. It was in the middle of summer, and she had on a t-shirt, hoodie and jacket. It took me fifteen minutes to convince her to open the door."

Aurora jumped sideways when Dalton touched her shoulder. "Shhh, I'm sorry I startled you."

"It's all right," she said. She looked up at him wearily.

He stared down at her. "How bad was it?"

"Not as bad as it could have been. When Darryl was making a grab for her, the mare got fractious, and Renee took off at a run."

"That's really good."

"Nope." She shook her head, then pulled at the hair that caught in her mouth. "It should have never happened. I should have been there."

84

Dalton put his hands on her shoulders. "Did you know that he was delivering the horse to a house where a teenage girl was alone?"

"Of course not. When I'd set things up the day before, Lowell had said he'd be taking delivery. That day he got called into work on an emergency and he figured Renee could handle things."

"Lowell should have called and given you a heads up," Dalton bit out.

"No!" she glared up at him. "This was on me. I should have had better instincts."

"Did you check his references? Did you have any other complaints before this?"

"Of course, I checked references," she whispered fiercely. "There had never been any complaints. And if there had been one whiff of a complaint I would have checked it out. But Dalton, I should have done something about the fact that he made me feel icky." She rubbed her arms, trying to fight off the cold.

Dalton grabbed her up in his arms and she snuggled into his heat.

"Unfortunately, that isn't cause for any kind of employee action," he sighed.

"But still-"

"Uh-uh Sunshine, you've got to stop beating yourself up about that. Tell me what you did when you got to the Henderson's."

"It took me about twenty minutes to coax Renee to open the door." She said into his flannel shirt. She took a breath and took comfort from being wrapped in his strength. "It made my heart ache when I saw her all bundled up. It was summer, and it had to be eighty degrees in the house. I got her to the couch, and it took me another twenty minutes and a glass of lemonade before I could talk her into taking off her jacket. She was in shock. It wasn't until I said I had to call her parents and get her to the hospital that she started to talk."

Aurora could picture the young girl. She'd looked like the awkward teenager she was, tear streaked face, glasses and long brown hair that she used to hide her face.

"Tell me," Dalton prompted.

"She didn't want to take off her hoodie. I was so worried. When she finally did, I could see his handprints on her arms. They were already bruising."

"What else?" Aurora appreciated the warmth in Dalton's eyes, the softness in his voice. She really believed he cared. He made it so much easier for her to talk.

She wrenched out of his hold, and he let her go. "I don't know why I'm acting like a victim. For God's sake, it was that poor little girl. Her mother was out of town." Aurora took a deep breath, then continued in a steady voice. "It took me almost an hour for her to tell me that Darryl had grabbed her arms and held them above her head, shoved her up against the horse trailer and rubbed himself against her. She said it went on and on, and if it weren't for the horse kicking the side of the trailer, she wouldn't have gotten away."

"Aurora, you wouldn't be human if something like that didn't affect you."

She shook her head. Again, her hair went flying, and she grabbed it up in a tight fist, enjoying the slight bit of pain. "Anyway, I finally got her dad's number, and called him home. He was great with her, but no matter what I said they refused to call the sheriff. As soon as I was sure he handled it. I went straight to the sheriff's office. I wanted this asshole locked up, but because Mr. Henderson wouldn't come forward because he didn't want Renee upset any further, I was...what did you call it?" She looked up at Dalton.

"Shit out of luck."

"Exactly."

"So, what did you do?"

Aurora thought back to that day and a feral smile passed her lips. Seriously, she hadn't wanted her grandfather anywhere that mess, because she knew that whatever he did would end up be reported to the sheriff.

"It was the good luck to be a Friday. He always hung out at this dive in town. I called Erwin and said that he should suggest that he and Hal should invite Darryl out that night. I also said that should make sure the booze kept on coming."

"I think I'm going to like how this ends."

"I pulled in two of my Dressler cousins. One was a tight-end another was a blocker. I told them what had gone down, and they met me at midnight out behind the bar."

"Except for the part that you were there, I'm really liking this." He pried her fingers apart, so she wasn't gripping her hair, then held her hand so that their palms were pressed together. "Tell me what happened. I'm assuming your cousins held their own."

"Suffice it to say, that in under two minutes, Darryl was screaming for mercy. He promised never to touch another girl or woman against her will. Hal and Erwin eventually came and took him back to the cabin he was staying in. I was pounding on his door the next morning at dawn."

"You had back-up, right?"

She loved how concerned he was, for some reason his worry felt like caring and didn't chafe like when other men said something like that.

God, she really was one of those psycho broads.

She knocked her head against Dalton's chest.

"Ouch," she yelped.

"Ah, Sunshine, don't hurt yourself."

"Yes, I had back-up," she looked up into his eyes. "Erwin and Hal were both with me. I stood over him with my shotgun while he packed up his cabin and we followed behind him until he was off the property. But it still didn't stop him from hurting some other girl."

"That wasn't on you."

She gritted her teeth so hard she thought they might shatter.

"It *wasn't* your fault," Dalton reiterated. "You did everything you could. Hell, even the police's hands were tied. You couldn't very well follow him around every day, now could you?"

"I about died the day Brody told me. Apparently, the assistant DA in California who was handling the case called Brody to find out if there were ever any problems that didn't get reported. To find out if there was some kind of pattern. The attorney wanted to get an idea of what kind of sentencing to go for."

Dalton nodded for her to continue.

"When Brody found out Darryl was successfully put behind bars, he told me. He wanted to make sure it was a done deal, before he told me."

She curled her left hand, the one he wasn't holding, into a fist and hit him half-heartedly on the chest. "Logically I know it wasn't my fault, but Dalton, it just kills. You know?"

HE LOOKED into her brown eyes that shimmered with tears that she was holding back. Fuck yeah, he understood. He cuddled her next to his heart and looked off into space. It took him far too long to pull himself together, but eventually he did.

"Tell me about the other guy."

"Ned Little. He only worked for us for two weeks. Again, I checked his references, but it turned out that he had us call a cell phone number that didn't belong to the ranch where he'd had worked. If I had talked to them, I would have found out he had been tossed out on his ear. Instead I was totally duped."

He heard the weariness in her voice.

"So, I hired him. His first assignment was to work with one of our new horses. We were slammed, that's why I hired him. After a week I could tell he didn't like taking orders from me because I was a woman. I didn't have time for his bullshit, so I just put Hal in charge of him. He was working with to break a young and eager filly. Yeah, she was a little rambunctious, but it should have been easy."

"I take it, it wasn't."

She shook her head. "I don't know why I was doing a walk through the barn one night, but I did. I couldn't find Lily in her stall. I checked the corral, but she wasn't there. I finally checked the horse trailers, and that's where I found her. The bastard was actually hang-tying her, so she'd be more malleable when he went to train her."

"What's hang-tying?"

"It's when the halter is connected to a chain hooked into the ceiling and the horse's neck is forced upwards. It's like they are on their tiptoes. It's barbaric."

Her rage was palpable.

"Let me guess, she'd be so tired and sore, she wouldn't put up a fight the next day."

"You got it one," Aurora agreed. She pushed out of his arms. "After I took care of Lily, I got my shotgun and rousted him out of bed and kicked him off our land."

He grinned. Seemed that Aurora liked her shotgun. Then he frowned. "Wait a minute. Didn't you get Hal or Erwin to back you up?"

"I was too pissed to think of it. The little shit refused to open the door. He was a little scaredy cat. I used the key to let myself in."

Dalton's blood ran cold at the thought. "Jesus Aurora, he could have had a gun trained on you."

"The little fuck picked on young horses, he would be too scared to pull shit on me. I knocked him upside the head with the butt of my gun. He ended up crawling around half the time to grab his shit. I actually kicked him in his ass out the door," she said with a laugh.

Dalton didn't care if she found it funny, it made him sick to his stomach. God knows what could have happened while she was alone in that cabin with that man.

"The next day I put the word out to everyone I could think of about the little shit. I faxed and e-mailed his ID around to make sure nobody would hire him. His name is mud in the horse community."

"Do you know where Ned Little is today?"

"Not a clue." She yawned, it pushed her breasts into prominence. He needed to keep his mind on task, and not focused on her body. But what a body.

"I need to get to bed." She peered at the clock on the stove. "Only three more hours of shut-eye," she sighed woefully. "I'll see you in the morning."

It took everything he had not to offer to tuck her in.

What the hell was he thinking? He only hooked up with women who didn't want relationships, and Aurora screamed white picket fence. He needed to stop thinking about her.

He shifted his stance. Maybe staying here hadn't been such a good idea, but he just hadn't been able to stomach the idea of Aurora being unprotected.

He strode back to his bedroom and snagged his cell phone. Kenna was going to hate him, but that didn't stop him from texting Dex. If the man wanted to mother the Western Hemisphere, then he was just going to have to start mothering Aurora too.

Dalton threw the phone down next to him on the bed and peeled out of his shirt and jeans. He waited for Dex's call. He started to get pissed when twenty-five minutes passed by.

"Is everything okay? Is everyone safe?" Dalton asked when Dex finally called him back.

"Yeah, everyone's good," Dex answered.

"Then what the fuck? What took you so long to answer? I said it was important."

Was he being an irrational, impatient prick? Definitely. Was it because he was a horny asshole? Most likely. But he was worried about Aurora too.

"I was in the middle of a delicate operation," Dex said with a smile in his voice.

The way he said it just pissed Dalton off more. The man had been getting lucky.

Dammit!

"Whatchya need? I figure since it's three in the morning it's important." The man was laughing at him.

"It is," Dalton bit out.

"Does this have something to do with a beautiful blonde? I heard she knows her way around disgruntled animals," Dex teased. "By the sounds of things, that's probably for the best."

Dammit. Dammit. Dammit. Nothing was fucking sacred with Dexter Evans. And he knew that Zed hadn't spilled the beans.

"Somebody's out to hurt her."

"What are you talking about? I need details." Dalton calmed down a little when he heard the concern in his friend's clipped voice.

"Somebody took shots at her. It wasn't that professional, otherwise she'd be dead, but still, they targeted her. The locals are insisting it was some poacher who mistook her for big game. My happy ass it was. They're idea of policework is handing out speeding tickets, seeing if granny is tilting a slot machine to make it pay out or worrying about someone peeing in their pristine lake."

Dex let out a big laugh. "What has your tail in a twist? Usually this level of pissed-offed-ness is left for the spooks in Langley who give us the wrong intel for an op."

"They've let Aurora down twice now. If I wasn't on a time schedule to come back home, and I didn't have to track down the bastard who has her in his sights, I'd have you get me info, so I could dismantle the sheriff."

Dalton was surprised to find himself pacing around the small bedroom. When had he gotten out of bed?

"Calm your shit down. Tell me what you need and it's yours," Dex said soothingly.

"Cut it out Evans, you're never going to be a horse whisperer." A picture of Aurora burst into his mind. She'd looked so tiny compared to the mammoth stallion. Even now his mouth felt like it was filled with cotton when he remembered her going into that stall with Aladdin.

"Tell me how to help your lady," Dex said. Again, he was calm and steady. It helped. Maybe he was a Navy SEAL whisperer.

"I need you to get me all the info you can on a guy named Ned Little. He used to work at this ranch, it's called Valhalla. He only worked here at the ranch for a couple of weeks. He worked as a horse trainer. Look, I've met her and her grandfather, plus the two hands who've been here forever, she just doesn't have any real enemies. This has got to be the guy. I need you to track him down."

"Do you have anything else? Can you get his employment file?"

"I'll get it tomorrow."

There was a long silence. "Ned Little, huh? His real name is probably Edward. I'm on it. I'll get you something by noon."

6

AURORA WATCHED HIM RIDING SIREN IN PEARLESCENT afternoon light and her heart jumped into her throat. The blue Henley shirt molded to his chest, shoulders and arms. The sun glinted in his blue-black hair. Dalton was the embodiment of every warrior in history. But what made her want to cry, was what he was doing.

A crisis had happened today, and Hal and Erwin had their hands full going to Reno to pick-up another abused horse that had been fraudulently purchased. Gunnar left about the same time, and she had screwed up by not calling and telling Crystal that she wouldn't be able to take Taylor and Mark for their lesson.

When they showed up at three o'clock she was devastated at the thought of turning them away. Crystal was the boy's foster mother, and Aurora's oldest friend. Both boys scored high on the autism spectrum scale and they had been coming to Valhalla for over a year to do Equine Therapy. It was because of Crystal that she'd gone to Torrey

Pines for ten days a year and half ago for training. After identifying two horses that would be perfect for the boys she'd worked with Erwin and the horses for three months before inviting Crystal, Taylor and Mark over for a test run.

"What's going on Sunshine?" Dalton had asked when Crystal's SUV came up the drive.

She'd explained and watched his thoughtful expression. "My friend Dare Stanton has a son named Georgie, he's eight years old. Georgie's great, when you can get through to him. It takes a lot of patience, he's severely autistic."

Aurora wished she had time to be subtler in her questioning, but Crystal and the boys were getting out of their vehicle. "How much time did you spend with Georgie? Was it just a one-time thing, or do you have a relationship with him?"

Luckily Dalton didn't take it bad. "Georgie and I seemed to hit it off at a couple of team barbeques," he said quietly. "I went and visited him at his house a couple of times. He soothed me. Rylie, Dare's wife, said I calmed him."

"Okay, you're hired to help me. I've seen you with the horses, I'll have you work with Mark, he normally works with Erwin."

Now here she was, leaning on the corral fence, watching Dalton like a besotted fool as he rode behind Mark.

"Dalton's nice," Taylor said.

Aurora looked over at the thirteen-year-old boy who was almost as tall as she was and smiled. "I think he is too."

"Is he a cowboy?"

"He's a soldier."

A grin split the boy's face. "Does he have a gun?"

What was it about testosterone and guns? "I don't know. Did you enjoy riding Pepper?"

Taylor looked off into the distance, then he bent down to climb through the fence rail. She put her hand on his back. "Taylor, I need your help to groom Pepper. Crystal's going to be back here soon."

He shrugged her off and was inside the corral before she could stop him. She'd lost him, he was off in his own world.

Shit, he didn't have his helmet on. Aurora grabbed him, and he started to howl and fight. Soon he was on the ground.

"Shhh, Honey." She knelt down and cupped his cheeks, out of the corner of her eyes she could see that Dalton was steering Mark and his horse to the gate.

"Calm down Honey. You'll get to play with your brother and Dalton in just a minute. But you need to remember not to go into the corral when there is a horse in there, them's the rules. Remember?"

She looked at his tear-streaked face. He finally nodded. Then he grinned. He yelled over her shoulder.

"Do you have a gun?" Taylor yelled to Dalton.

Dalton was helping Mark off his horse as Taylor ran toward them. Dalton kept the horses under control even with Taylor running awkwardly hell-bent for leather and yelling. She was impressed. She moved quickly to join them, so she could help the man. As soon as she had the horses, he had his arms around each boys' shoulders and was patiently answering their questions.

Aurora was grinning as she took Pepper and Lightening to the barn. He was fantastic with the kids, they'd be talking about him for months. By the time she got the two horses into their stalls, Crystal was there, and Taylor and Mark were getting into the blue SUV, still hollering questions at Dalton.

"Aurora can I talk to you for a second?" Crystal asked.

Her friend practically dragged her up onto the porch.

"What's wrong?" Aurora asked. "Did you find more info about Siren and Aladdin, because I think Erwin and Hal are bringing in another abused horse today, so that makes three."

"We can talk some other time," Crystal waved her off. "This is more important. Who's the hunk?"

"I don't think Danny's going to appreciate it if you bring a man home. He doesn't strike me as someone who's into a ménage." Aurora teased. She knew the types of romance books her friend read.

"I'm not thinking for me, I'm thinking for you, you idiot. Oh my God, the way he fills out that shirt. The way he fills out those jeans. You've been celibate for five years. You do realize that your hymen has probably grown back, don't you? I hear that happens."

Aurora started to cough, then choke. Crystal whacked her on the back.

"He's looking this way. Don't make a spectacle of yourself. Do you have any kind of toy? Have you been taking care of business? If you haven't, you might have forgotten how to orgasm. If that happens, you might have to fake it the first few times until you get back into the groove. Just saying."

Aurora glared at her former best friend. "How 'bout you just send Danny over, so I can have a couple of practice runs?"

Crystal's eyes twinkled. "You're not ready for the advanced class." Then her gaze shot over Aurora's shoulder. "Of course, if I'm not mistaken, that man could help you earn your PhD."

Heat suffused Aurora's entire body, it was almost like she could feel him.

"Crystal, you've done a great job with those boys." Dalton's voice rumbled like distant thunder at midnight, it made her shiver. Crystal gave Aurora a knowing grin, she didn't miss a trick.

"Thanks Dalton. Danny and I were blessed when they came into our lives."

"How long have they been living with you?" he asked.

"Taylor came to us when he was five. Mark has only been with us for four years. Aurora's therapy has done wonders for them."

Dalton's big hand slid up under Aurora's hair and rested on the nape of her neck, giving her a subtle squeeze. "She's a special lady."

"Gunnar left today, didn't he?" Crystal asked. She had the subtlety of a freight train.

"Nona! You promised us McDonald's," Mark yelled from the SUV.

"Duty calls," she shrugged. She jogged down the porch steps, then looked back at the two of them. "Don't do anything Danny and I wouldn't do. Dalton ask Aurora what that list entails, it's pretty extensive." She lifted her hand and waved. She was laughing all the way to her vehicle.

"I like your friend," Dalton said as he shifted so he could look down at Aurora. She swallowed nervously. "I take it Danny is her husband?"

"Yep."

"So how extensive is their list?"

The man had a killer smile. Crystal was right, she should have invested in toys years ago.

PULLING the porkchops out of the oven, Dalton listened for Aurora's footsteps. He tried to throw off his nervousness, but it was impossible. He'd realized midway through glazing the meat that the last time he'd cooked dinner for a woman had been for Lacey. Did his past have to color every aspect of the present?

"What smells so good?" she asked as she opened the refrigerator and pulled out the pitcher of lemonade.

"I bought wine, if you're interested," Dalton said as he cut into one of the porkchops to see if it was cooked through. "It's there on the table."

When she didn't answer, he turned to get a good look at her. "What's wrong?"

"I didn't realize that this was going to be a dinner, dinner."

"What do you mean?"

She held out her arms and looked down at her jeans, then up at him. "Fancy."

"Sunshine, I'm wearing jeans."

"You bought wine," she said as she tilted the bottle. "It's really good wine too."

Dalton left the stove and put his arm around her shoulders. "I'm glad you like it." She'd washed her hair, it smelled like strawberries and vanilla. "Why don't you tell me where the wine glasses are."

"I'll have to rinse them."

"I'll take care of it, just point me to the right cupboard."

She pointed, then he held out her chair, and she sat down. He watched with amusement as she practically vibrated in her seat. The woman had trouble sitting still.

"I can help," she offered after three seconds.

"It's handled."

"I could-"

He slid the plates of food on the table, then dried off the wine glasses and set them down as he picked up the bottle of wine and uncorked it. Dalton sat down and poured them both a glass.

"This looks amazing."

"Hopefully it'll taste good too." He'd tested the peach glaze to be on the safe side. It hadn't been too bad, even though he hadn't made it in years. He watched her close her eyes after taking a bite.

"This is heavenly. I see you went against policy and used peaches, I love it." Dalton felt a bone deep satisfaction as she savored her bite.

She was quiet as she cut into more of the pork. When he started to talk about the boys, she waved him away. "Quiet. Eating zone."

He watched as she demolished two thirds of the meat, then she grinned up at him. She picked up a sprig of asparagus and swirled it in the peach glaze then licked off the sauce before biting into the vegetable. It took everything he had not to groan.

"Do you do that on purpose?"

"Huh?" She looked genuinely perplexed. He thought about the fact that she normally just ate with her grandfather and decided that she probably didn't.

"Never mind. I'm glad you liked the meal." He topped off her wine.

"Liked is too mild a word, adored is more appropriate. Grandpa and I usually do roast beef or chicken, this is a wonderful change."

"I'm glad you adored it then. I have to admit, when I get back home, I'm going to have to detox for a month."

"What?"

"The food here has been pretty rich."

"Don't let Granddad hear you say that."

Dalton took another bite of his asparagus. "Don't you worry about him?"

"When I introduced him to turkey bacon, you would have thought I had poisoned him, even though I swear to God it tasted the same," she looked up at him and giggled.

"It's been in the last three years we introduced chicken into the mix three times a week. He can even identify a vegetable now."

"Corn is a carb, not a vegetable. He uses a lot of butter." As soon as the words were out of his mouth he regretted them.

"Don't be snarky, it's not attractive." Aurora glared at him. "If you don't think I take this seriously, you're out of your mind. I want him to live forever. I don't know what I would do without him. I've busted my ass changing his diet since Doc Barnes told me what's what."

She shoved out of her chair and yanked open the refrigerator and pulled out the carton of Vitamin D milk and slammed it onto the counter. Then she bent to the freezer drawer and pulled out the tub of vanilla bean ice cream and damn near threw that onto the table so that it slid over to Dalton who had to stop it before it fell onto the floor. Then she went to the freezer again and dug through bags of frozen vegetables until she pulled up a tub of non-fat frozen vanilla ice milk.

"Look at this. Do you see this?" She held it up triumphantly.

Dalton nodded, knowing that was the only response to give. She whirled to the cupboard and pulled out a glass and poured a glass of milk. "Drink this," she said as she pushed the glass into Dalton's face. He was doing everything in his power not to grin. She was beautiful when she was this worked up.

"I said drink it," she said as she waved the glass at him again.

"I don't drink milk. I drink Soy milk."

"Figures," she sighed. "Well, this is non-fat milk."

He took the glass from her and looked at the carton on the table. Looking at the milk in the glass he could see it wasn't nearly thick enough to be vitamin D milk. He gave her a slow grin. "You're faking him out."

"Damn right I am. First, I started changing the milk out with two percent, then I changed it out with one percent, this year it's non-fat milk."

"And the ice cream?"

"Same thing. I just keep refilling this high-fat vanilla tub of ice-cream with the non-fat vanilla. He thinks he's getting his real treat, and he's none the wiser. He still bitches about the chicken and the vegetables. There's no way I can trick him on that."

Dalton pulled out his chair and pulled her disgruntled butt onto his lap. "You're brilliant," he pushed his nose into her fragrant hair.

She giggled.

"I don't know about brilliant, but I am concerned."

"You're an evil genius." Dalton was having trouble paying attention to his words, she felt so good in his arms.

She turned around, so they were eye to eye. "Thank you, that means a lot."

Her lips were so close, a whisper away from his. When he'd gone shopping for dinner he'd bought condoms. He wanted this, he needed this. Did she?

"You're over thinking this, Handsome." Aurora pressed a kiss against his temple. Then she kissed her way down his jaw until her lips hovered over his. "Ah Dalton, I want this. Don't you?"

Dalton looked into her eyes and felt his heart expand. How could he hurt and feel so good at the same time? He shoved the question away, not wanting to face what it might mean. Instead he focused on the beautiful woman in his arms. She was the embodiment of joy, generosity and heat. For the first time in years he felt alive. This was real. She meant something.

His muscles tensed. Was he doing the right thing?

"Dalton? No second thoughts allowed, you seduced me with food. I'm a sure thing."

He laughed. Dalton cupped her cheek, sighing in relief when she molded her mouth to his.

Sparks blazed behind his eyelids. He tangled his fingers into her wealth of blonde hair, luxuriating in the silky texture. The softness of her lips, combined with the flavor that was all her, was a heady magic that spoke to his soul. Deeper and deeper he fell under Aurora's spell. He swept his hand down the elegant length of her spine and felt her tremble. Gently, Dalton broke their kiss.

"Are you all right?" he asked softly. He continued stroking her back.

"No. If I don't have all of you soon, I'm going to be one of those people who spontaneously combust," she said huskily.

"That's just a legend, like bigfoot."

She bit his lower lip.

Hard.

He liked it. Still... "That hurt," he couldn't help but tease.
"You big baby."

Aurora's eyes gleamed. She bent backwards and snagged the container of ice cream and popped the lid. She came away with a dollop of cream on her finger and ran the cold treat along his wounded lip. Then she swept in for an even deeper kiss. Now he was going to be the one who was going to go up in flames. The woman was dangerous.

He stood up with her in his arms.

"What?!" She wrapped her arms around his neck. "You're not supposed to be able to pick me up like that. That's too difficult."

Dalton grinned and headed toward the hallway.

"Wait!"

"What now?" He looked down at Aurora.

"The ice cream will melt all over everything."

He sighed. She was right. He let her slide down his body, it was pure torture. Her breasts felt so good against him. She moaned. Then the imp had the gall to wiggle against his erection, and he groaned.

"Be good," he admonished.

"I'll try," she said as she ducked her head and went to the table. She had things put away in under a minute. It took a moment for Dalton to realize that she had been less than confident. That surprised him. Everything about her was sexy as hell, and she caught fire in his arms, how could she doubt herself?

"Aurora?"

She turned to him, a bright smile on her face. Too bright. He stepped forward and tucked her hair behind her ear.

"You do realize I've been fantasizing about you since I the first day in the woods, don't you?"

"Same goes," she grinned up at him.

The smile still hit him as false. He laced his fingers with hers and tugged her down the hall toward his bedroom.

"My room," she whispered.

"Depends," he whispered back.

She stopped in front of the door to his room. "What does it depend on?"

"Are your walls pink? Or do you have horse themed wall paper?"

She let out a laugh. Good, she sounded more relaxed. "I just have to clear the stuffed animals off my bed."

That deserved a kiss, and Dalton gave her one. By the time they were done she was holding onto his neck and he wasn't sure that he was going to be able to keep them both standing. "Tell you what, you go clear your bed, and I'll go grab the protection." He opened the door to his room. He'd done a lot of shopping while he'd been in town. He wasn't absolutely sure where tonight would lead, but he'd had hopes.

When he got to Aurora's room Dalton was enveloped in a universe of soft greens and blues. She was standing at the foot of the bed, her golden hair and white chambray shirt a beautiful contrast. Dalton hated to see that slight look of insecurity. How was that even possible considering there had to be a scorched spot in the hallway from where they had just been kissing?

Enough. His lady was not going to feel this way. Not on his watch.

"You're beautiful, you know that don't you?" He queried gently.

"Sometimes. Sometimes I do."

He prowled toward her. "Tonight, we're going to change that." He slid his palms against hers, he felt the callouses, and even those were sexy. Seeing her ride, a horse was a thing of beauty, and those slight ridges were a testament to her abilities. He entwined their fingers, and pulled her arms wide, taking note of the thrust of her breasts.

"Gorgeous."

"Crystal ogled you," she blurted out.

It took a half second for him to process her words, then he responded. "The only one I care about is you. Have you ogled me?"

"Oh yeah. A lot," her breath came out in a puff of air.

Dalton saw the rapid pulse at her neck and pressed a kiss to the hot flesh.

"What are you doing?" she asked, her voice quivering.

It was different than in the hallway. She still seemed nervous. Instead of the conflagration he had been expecting, Dalton realized he needed to seduce. He turned them around so that he was sitting on her bed and she was standing between his legs. "I don't know if I can take this slow. At least not the first time," he admitted.

Dark brown eyes stared down at him. "You really want me that much?" she asked wonderingly.

He wrapped his arms around her waist and tugged her close. "Oh yeah," he breathed. "Sweetheart, you're exquisite. Everything about you calls to me, your beauty, your grace, your passion and joy, they're like a siren song. But more than anything it's your heart that seduces me."

He watched as her eyes widened with delight and wonder. "I...I...you..." She cupped his cheek and her thumb softly brushed over his bottom lip. "You'll never know Dalton. You can never know how much your words mean to me," she whispered.

Aurora's hair fell around them both as she bent down and took his mouth in a slow, passionate kiss. Dalton felt like he was ensconced in a golden dream. He gloried in her heated seduction, until he couldn't wait another minute. He rolled them over so that she was beneath him on the bed, then he slowly divested her of her shirt and found himself staring at a plain white cotton bra that left him breathless. How could such a serviceable piece of underwear turn him on?

He propped himself up on his elbow and traced the upper swell of her breasts. Aurora's breathing became more rapid. He unclipped the front clasp and they both gave a sigh of satisfaction.

"You're perfect," he whispered. He loved seeing how her nipples swelled under his gaze. He needed more though. So much more. Dalton had taken the time to shave just for this moment. He smoothed his cheek against the delicate flesh of her breast a moment before he lashed her nipple with his tongue. She gasped his name as she jerked upwards.

Dalton slid his hands along her arms and clasped her hands above her head, then continued discovering the exquisite texture of her skin, of her responses, of her desire.

"Dalton?" she mewed.

He licked.

She sighed.

He suckled.

She moaned.

He nipped.

She begged.

Sweat popped out on his forehead. He'd never had a woman more passionate in his arms before. He didn't know if he was going to survive.

Aurora bucked against him. "Clothes! Off!"

He grinned. Apparently, Miss Shy was gone. He liked it. Oh, who the hell was he kidding? He liked any flavor of Aurora that she was willing to give him. He just adored Aurora Chance. He knelt up on the bed and she scrambled backwards and undid her jeans.

She scowled at him. "What did I say? Why aren't you undressing?"

"Sorry." Dalton's lips twitched as he stood up and undressed. He pulled condoms out of his jeans pockets and put them on the nightstand, then he looked over at a naked Aurora, she was the stuff of dreams.

Her hand headed straight for his cock, but before she could touch him, he stopped her.

"Nuh-uh. Me first."

"You already tortured me," she pouted. "It's my turn."

Using his superior strength, he pressed her down onto the bed again.

"No fair," she whispered.

"Who said anything about playing fair?" God it felt good to lay naked on top of her. She might be long and lean, but she was soft in all the right places. Dalton shifted downwards before she could make anymore protests and spread her thighs, once again delighting in the feel of his cheek brushing against the softest skin imaginable.

"Dalton, please don't do that," she said quietly. He looked up, her eyes were filled with unease. He needed to respect her wishes, so he kissed his way up her taut stomach and enjoyed her sighs of pleasure. As he once again worshipped her breasts with his tongue and lips, he eased his hand between her legs and found her wet folds.

His name came out in a long sigh. This she approved of. Ever so slowly, she parted her legs more, granting him more and more access to explore. Dalton shoved his hand under the nape of her neck and ground his mouth to hers as he gently thrust a finger into her tight sheath. He needed to taste this woman any way he could. Their tongues tangled, the kiss fierce as she arched against his hand.

He didn't even realize she had grabbed his head until he felt the sharp sting of his hair being pulled. Dalton could feel the pulsing of her core, the need rising up in her body. He pushed a second finger in with the first and Aurora shuddered.

She yanked her mouth away from his and whined, "Please."

He knew what she needed.

Dalton smoothed the silky essence of pleasure up and over her swollen clit.

"More."

He loved the breathy shriek. He circled and teased, wanting to hear that sultry tone again.

Aurora's eyelids fluttered. He saw the cords in her neck strain as her head arched back, and she shouted his name. Then she slumped back against the pillow. Finally, she opened her eyes, and they shimmered like black diamonds as they stared into his. He was lost.

Aurora couldn't catch her breath as she stared into eyes that were as deep and mysterious as her beloved mountain lake. This man made her believe in herself, and now she needed more. So much more. She wriggled.

"Where are you going?" Dalton's arms tightened around her.

Her arm stretched out to grab a condom and she giggled when most of the others fell to the floor. "How many did you bring?"

"Not enough," he said as he kissed behind her ear. That felt so good.

"You're probably right." She pressed the packet into his hand, then as soon as he started to put the condom on she immediately batted his hands away.

"What the hell?"

"You've got more of them. I haven't played yet." She had no idea what she was going to do but watching him touch himself had made her mouth water. She needed to feel him. He watched her through hooded eyes as she gently grasped his shaft in her hand. Dalton shuddered, and she smiled, it was wonderful knowing that she could evoke such a response out of man like him. It was as if she had never been intimate with a man before, and when she truly thought about it, had she? This moment in time transcended any experience she'd ever had before.

"Harder." His voice was rough.

She gave him a wicked smile and delighted in the feel of the velvet strength of his cock, her core ached at the thought of him filling her.

He tipped her chin so that he could look at her. "Enough playing. I see your need."

Her breathing roughened. He was right, but she didn't want to stop. Remembering the pleasure, he gave her, she smoothed her cheek against his hard flesh, and lashed her tongue against him.

She didn't know what happened next. One moment she was savoring his taste, then suddenly she was on her back again with Dalton was pressing against her entrance. She twined her legs around his thighs, trying desperately to bring him closer, needing him deeper. He pushed in further and they groaned their pleasure in unison.

He pulled out then pushed back in and it was rapturous. Then he stopped, his body vibrating. She could see the tension coiling in him. He was so close.

"Fuck!"

He pulled out of her.

She stared at him, not understanding. He lurched toward the nightstand and grabbed a condom and quickly sheathed himself. "Sunshine, you make me lose my mind."

"Hurry. Please, just hurry." She'd never felt this level of need before. Her hands stroked along his wide shoulders, her legs wound around his lean waist, she would do anything to pull him into her, to make them one.

Their eyes meshed as he thrust slowly inward. Would this man ever be anything but a caretaker? She was determined he go back to moments ago. She dug her nails into his skin, but it didn't make a difference, he continued his careful penetration.

"Please," she whined. Was that her voice?

"So good. You feel so good. Ahhh Sunshine, what you do to me." His lips touched hers. The kiss was reverent. She had to blink back tears. Never had she felt so close to someone. She savored the feeling. Then Dalton looked at her and gave her a wicked smile.

"Are you ready?"

Was she? She swallowed and nodded.

He started slowly, a rhythm as old as time, smooth and languid, it started a slow burn deep inside her.

In her body.

In her heart.

In her soul.

She couldn't look away from him, his eyes trapped hers, telling her things she couldn't begin to understand, let alone believe.

His thumb brushed back a damp tendril of hair from her forehead as he surged again and again. How could she possibly survive this dazzling assault on her senses?

"Don't close your eyes. Please, Aurora, I need to watch you." Dalton's voice was a thunderstorm of passion. She forced her eyes open and was rewarded with brilliant blue sapphires focused on her.

"Ahhh."

She was past the point of being able to contain her sounds of pleasure. It had never been like this before. He was everywhere. His chest hair rasped against her nipples, sparking an erotic yearning that triggered even more pleasure where they were merged. She shifted against him, but it wasn't enough, she began to undulate.

"Jesus! You're killing me." He rasped.

But she wasn't, because nothing stopped his mind-numbing thrusts.

"Please Dalton," she begged right before she lurched up and bit into his shoulder.

She thought she heard her name, but she was lost in his eyes, then all sound stopped. She couldn't breathe, it was as if the earth fell away.

Beautiful sapphire blue fire, so much joy, all wrapped in layers of ecstasy. Her last thought was that nothing would ever be the same.

7

SHE WAS A SNUGGLER. HE WOULD HAVE SWORN THAT IT WOULD have irritated him having a woman burrowing against him. Aurora slept like she loved, her hand over his heart, ensuring that he was cared for. Lacey, meanwhile, had always rolled away from him, insisting that she needed her space. Even when Reagan had snuck into their bed after a bad dream, his wife had always pushed their daughter into his arms. He knew deep in his gut that Aurora would never have done that.

As he eased out of bed, he brushed the softest of kisses against her temple and pulled the covers around her. He pulled on his jeans, then grabbed his other clothes and boots then left the bedroom. Dalton knew that the backdoor and all the windows were secure when he locked the front door behind him as he left the house. He stood on the top porch step and took a deep breath, loving how the scent of the pine and bitingly fresh air help to clear his mind. After long moments he heard a noise, not surprised to see Tate

Dressler walking up the stairs toward him. There had been a question that had been niggling at him.

"You serve?" he asked Aurora's uncle.

The man's smile shone brightly in the night light. "Marine. Eight years."

Dalton looked him up and down.

"Raider?"

"If I answered, I'd have to kill you," Tate smiled blandly.

"Out of Pendleton?" Dalton pushed.

Tate walked up the porch steps and was almost eye-to-eye with Dalton when he asked, "What's with all the questions?"

"Ned Little's cousin, Ricky, spent six months in the Marines before he was dishonorably discharged."

"For what?" Tate asked.

"Got into a fight over a pool game and broke the cue over the other player's head and killed him. The bet was five dollars."

"Are you shitting me? So besides being booted out of the Marines, I take it he did time?" Tate asked.

"A nickel in Chino for manslaughter. It's a case of dumb and dumber working this operation. Both of them were seen in Reno together ten days ago."

"I'm taking it that your info is solid?"

Dalton leaned back against the porch rail and stared at Tate.

The man held up his hands. "Okay, stupid question. Did your source get anything else?"

"Since Aurora sent him packing, Ned's been floating around the Western United States, mostly picking up part-time work under an assumed name."

"If he was using an assumed name, how did your guy figure it out?" Tate asked.

"It wasn't hard. He called himself Ned Small."

Tate let out a laugh but stifled it quickly. He tilted his head and they both started walking away from the house. They stopped at the corral and Dalton rested his foot on the lowest rail as he stared off into space. "Turns out that in his late teens and early twenties he was in the rodeo circuit but was kicked out for cheating. He's blown every opportunity he's ever had."

"Still doesn't explain why he would suddenly turn on Aurora now. Hasn't it been two years?" Tate asked.

"My guy is trying to sort that out. Our job is to find his happy ass and shut this shit down."

Tate gave him an assessing look. "Seems to me you and my niece have gotten pretty close, you still planning on leaving on Sunday?"

"I can put in for more leave if I need to, but I'm always on-call. My preference is to get this shit with D&D sorted before I leave."

"D&D? Oh yeah, Dumb and Dumber. I'm going to call in my boys and have them start patrolling too."

"The football players?" Dalton asked.

"Yep," Tate said proudly. "Rhys is studying to be a vet. Luke is thinking about joining the Marines next year."

"Maybe a better idea is to have her go to your ranch for a day. Then we can lay in wait."

Tate turned away from the rail so he could look directly at Dalton. "I might be reading this wrong, but I'm not."

Dalton waited for the man to continue. He knew what was coming.

"There isn't a chance in hell that Aurora is going to be

leaving you for the little time that you two have left together."

Dalton worked hard to keep his face impassive. Tate couldn't be right, could he? He and Aurora had only known each other for four days. Granted the chemistry was off the charts. Hell, it was on no known chart that he'd ever seen or heard of, but it didn't matter, he didn't do relationships. Full stop. End of story.

Tate frowned. "It's like that, is it? So, you're toying with my niece?"

"No."

"Explain yourself."

"The only one I have to explain myself to is Aurora," Dalton bit out.

"Then you better fucking do it." Tate's eyes narrowed. "In the meantime, I'll stay here with Hal and Erwin, tomorrow you and Aurora can spend the day at my ranch with Rhys and Luke."

Dalton pushed away from the rail and started to head toward the house, then he hesitated. Turning back, he looked at a man he respected. "I'm not going to hurt her."

Tate sighed. "Yes, you are, but you're also making her happy, so Gunnar and I are going to see it as a wash."

AURORA WAS half asleep when Dalton crawled back into bed. He was cold. When she went to put her arm around his lean waist he stiffened and eased away from her. She rolled against him, so that she could at least warm him up, but again he pulled away, that was when she realized it wasn't just his body that was cold.

"Dalton?"

He went still. "I didn't mean to wake you," he whispered.

Aurora had to strain to hear him, since he was facing away from her and he didn't turn over. "Were you outside? I thought I heard the front door," she said.

"Yes."

She waited for him to elaborate, when he didn't she finally asked, "why?"

"I thought I heard something."

It was obvious he didn't want to be touched, but to hell with it. She tugged at his shoulder and he rolled to face her. He looked grim, almost as if he was carved out of stone.

"Did I do something wrong?" Aurora finally asked.

She watched as the strong line of his neck bobbed as he swallowed. "No. It's not you."

"But it's something," she guessed.

His eyes looked black in the moonlight, she had to imagine the navy-blue color as he looked down at her. "I don't want to lead you on," he finally said. "I'm going to be leaving soon."

His words hurt. They were so final, and they sliced through skin and twisted into her guts. There shouldn't be any pain. She'd known. She'd known that this was just a moment out of time, but after the way they'd come together? It had felt like so much more.

Suck it up, Buttercup.

She plastered on a smile.

"How could you possibly be leading me on?" she asked. "Dalton, you live five hundred miles away from me, I always knew this was a one off."

"Four hundred and fifty."

"Huh?"

He cleared his throat. "It's four hundred and fifty miles between Tahoe and San Diego."

She pushed upright in her bed and looked down at the man who had, just hours before, taken her to the heights of ecstasy. Dalton's entire body was rigid, like he was expecting a blow. He was not some man who was just playing fast and loose with her, she knew it, he had too much honor. But looking at him, he reminded her of Aladdin. Who had abused him?

"Look, I don't need a geography lesson, so don't play semantics. It doesn't matter if it was twenty miles or two thousand I always knew this was going to be finite."

His impassive face twisted, a deep pain was etched across his features. "It's not you, it's me," his normally smooth voice sounded like it had been scraped over glass.

Her lips twitched, and he frowned. Long moments passed.

"I didn't mean to hurt you," he growled.

Aurora bit her lower lip until she was afraid it would bleed, just to keep herself from smiling. "I know you don't want to hurt me," she finally said.

"Are you smiling?" he demanded to know.

She looked at him helplessly and shook her head.

"Why are you smiling?" He was clearly frustrated.

"You know that's the oldest brush-off line in the world, right?"

She saw the light dawn and he sighed. He sat up and pulled her hand into his and twined their fingers together.

"I didn't mean to demean our time together," he said softly.

With her free hand she touched the underside of his jaw, tracing downward to the rapid beat of his pulse. God, he looked so solemn. Who had hurt him, she wondered again.

"It's okay." This time her smile was weary. "I know it's not true, I know that you didn't mean it."

His hand squeezed tight, "I did mean it. I am leaving."

"I know that," she assured him. "You didn't mean to hurt my feelings and give me the time honored 'it's me, not you' line."

His thumb brushed tenderly over her knuckles and she all but melted. "How can you know me less than a week and read me so well? My-" His lips clamped shut.

She wasn't going to press him. The man had secrets, that'd been clear from the get-go, and the last thing she wanted to do is to be intrusive.

"Dalton let's just enjoy the time we have left, okay?"

"I don't want you to get the wrong idea. I don't want to lead you on."

"You're not. You didn't. I promise." She stroked her fingers down his neck, over his sternum. Now his skin felt hot. "Dalton, when you leave here, we might not be lovers anymore, but this is always going to be a safe place for you. A haven. You're always going to be welcome back."

———

HE HAD NEVER MET another woman like her. She was beyond his comprehension. She deserved him to be as honest as possible.

"I'm not coming back."

She continued to stroke his chest. "Okay, but know that if you change your mind, the gate will always be open."

His forehead tipped in surrender to touch hers.

"You need to know why," he said hoarsely. He hated talking about this. Only his team knew, and now Zed.

"You don't have to tell me anything, especially if it is going to bring you pain," she reiterated.

"I'm a bad bet. The worst bet you can imagine." A tiny cream casket floated behind his closed eyelids.

Warm arms slid around his neck. How did she know what he needed, even if he didn't deserve it?

"I failed my daughter. She died because of me."

A soft feather of fingers fluttered through the short hair at the nape of his neck.

"Tell me," she whispered. He heard no judgement.

"Lacey had been out of rehab for the third time. She'd been sober for three months, but that didn't matter, I knew better. I fucking knew that this time wasn't any different, but did I listen to my gut? Hell no." How often had he replayed that last morning in his mind?

Aurora moved so that her head lay on his chest. He soaked in the comfort.

"Lacey had opened two credit cards while I was overseas and hid them from me. I was furious. I didn't want to yell because Reagan would hear and get upset, so I just left to go to the gym. Then I grabbed a burger with Hunter and Dex and bitched."

The next words felt stuck in his throat, but he forced himself to push them out.

"I was gone for hours."

He could picture it so clearly. It had looked like their apartment had been hit by a hurricane. Lacey and Reagan were gone. He'd found a half-filled suitcase underneath the dining room table, and then more clothes strewn in the kitchen. When he'd lifted a tiny pink sundress of Reagan's that had been left on the kitchen counter, he'd found an empty wine bottle.

Where there was one, Dalton had known there would be more. He yanked open the cabinet under the sink and found two more in the trash bin. He broke into a cold sweat and lunged for his cell phone. Lacey didn't pick up. He'd raced to the parking spot where Lacey's hatchback had been parked, the stall was empty.

He stopped talking, thinking about those awful moments when he had realized that his drunk wife had driven off with his child.

"I knew where she was going," Dalton finally continued. "Her mother's house. When I called Norma, she wasn't picking up either."

He was aware of Aurora pressed against him, but he didn't feel any heat, he felt frozen.

It was the longest and shortest drive of his life. As soon as he saw the slow down on the highway he knew what had happened. It was a nightmare. He flew down the bicycle lane in his truck, honking the entire way. He had to get to the accident. He saw the flashing lights, so many emergency vehicles. Then he saw the silver that matched Lacey's hatchback. He heard a sound pummel through his truck, it took a moment for him to realize it was a moan coming from his throat.

The car that he had just washed yesterday was upside down, he couldn't even make out a roof let alone windows. Where were the windows? The doors? How could it have collapsed like a pancake? Dalton swerved, missing a highway patrolman by less than a foot.

"I thought I would rip through my seatbelt as I got out of my car. The guy tried to stop me from getting to Reagan. He didn't stand a chance. I mowed over him and three others and got there in time to see them zipping up my baby girl into a body bag. I don't remember what happened next. I went crazy."

Aurora's cheek was now pressed against his, and he didn't know if it was her tears or his that he tasted.

He didn't know if he could finish it. How could he? It wasn't finished. It never would be. Aurora wheezed, that was when he realized he was squeezing Aurora so tightly that it was amazing she hadn't popped.

"I'm sorry," he rasped.

"I'm not."

He could barely understand her. She was shaking. So was he. Eventually he remembered holding his daughter's tiny body in his arms. Reagan's face had looked like she was asleep, but when his hand combed through her curls they came away wet with blood and...

For a moment, there on that California Highway he thought he was back in Afghanistan, amidst the blood and gore of war. But then he saw his daughters' dark eyelashes, then he howled. Dalton literally howled her name as if he could call her soul back down from heaven.

Lost, his baby was lost. Gone forever.

Aurora was on top of him, her hair a tangled jungle blocking out anything but her tear-filled eyes.

"She's not lost. Not with you as her father, she can never be lost. Do you hear me? Are you listening to me Dalton?"

She wasn't making sense, but her tears were. The anguish on her face made perfect sense.

"She's gone forever."

"Sweetheart, she's in your mind. Every time you think

about her, she's here with you. She's in your heart. You need to talk about her. You need to share her."

He couldn't. It was like a serrated blade ripping through his gullet every time. He didn't realize he was shaking his head until Aurora gently grasped his skull and held it straight. "Tell me what she looked like. I bet she had the sweetest smile. Did she giggle?"

"I can't."

"Yes, you can, Dalton. Talk to me. Tell me about your baby," Aurora's words flowed over him. It took him back in time.

"Daddy! Daddy! Daddy!" Reagan's voice would shout out as she'd practically tumble across the grass of the little grass patch of yard to get to him when he got home. He swung her up into a huge hug, amazed how such a little package could hold his whole heart hostage.

"High. I wanna go high," she shouted. Her little purple dress flowed in the breeze when he zoomed her up in the air, her shrieks of laughter were heard all around the apartment complex.

"Again, Daddy!" Her smile dazzled him as she looked down upon him. Dalton imagined that every single person who lived there couldn't help but be touched by his little girl's happiness.

"You're right Aurora," Dalton said. "Reagan had the best giggle in the world."

"What a beautiful name."

"Reagan Elizabeth. Elizabeth was my mother's name," Dalton explained.

Aurora laid a reverent kiss on his temple and then flashed him a soft smile. "I'm hungry. I'll make some French toast and you're going to tell me all about your wonderful daughter. I'm betting you have a picture or two in your phone, don't you?"

God, when was the last time he'd shown anyone pictures of Reagan?

His heart felt a little lighter.

"You're on."

8

"ARE YOU REALLY THAT WORRIED?"

"I'm just naturally cautious," Dalton said as he pulled Aurora into his arms.

She smirked at him as she wrested away. "Yeah sure, that's why Rhys and Luke said they'd be sleeping in the barn tonight, because you're cautious." Dalton grinned at her. "Your uncle brought over five of his horses for training, he wants you to teach your cousins how to break them. It's a compliment."

"That was only after I nixed the idea of spending the day with my Aunt Leah over at their place. Then suddenly they had that wonderful idea and all the males decided to come this way," she scoffed. She pulled her sleepshirt off over her head.

Aurora liked how husky Dalton's voice was as her breasts came into view. The fact that she could make a man like Dalton so aroused amazed her. Still, she wasn't going to let him bullshit her. After the last two nights of lovemaking he had made her feel confident enough in her body to seduce the truth out of him. She sat down on the bed and put her legs out straight, then started to push down her panties.

"Why are my cousins really here?" she asked.

"What?" Dalton's eyes were glued to her thighs and she loved it.

"Did you ask them to come?"

"Tate did."

She kicked the pink silk off onto the floor, then traced patterns along the tops of her legs. "Are you watching?" she asked quietly?

He nodded.

"Are they here to keep watch?"

He nodded. Then his head snapped up, his gaze sharp. "Where in the hell did you learn this interrogation technique?"

"So, you admit they're here to keep watch."

Dalton knelt in front of her, his hands brushed hers away and she trembled. "It isn't a big deal, and we'll talk about it later." He pressed his thumbs on the inside of her thighs, seeking to part them.

She shoved at his shoulders and he looked up into her eyes and sighed. "I'm not going to get my way on this, am I?"

"Not until you tell me what is going on."

His hands trailed upwards, ruffling the curls at the apex of her thighs. "Really?" His eyes glimmered, but she knew he would respect her wishes. The man had honor seeping from his pores.

"Spill it."

"Ned and his cousin have been spotted near here. His-"

Dalton's head jerked sideways, and he flew to her bedroom window. She'd heard a distant sound of thunder.

Aurora scrambled across the bed to join him. "What is it?" The night sky was clear. "That wasn't thunder, was it?"

He put his hand on her shoulder and pulled her around, so she was facing him. "Stay here."

"No."

"Aurora, stay inside and call nine-one-one."

"What's happening? I don't see anything."

"It's an explosion." He said as he pulled on his jeans.

Come on Aurora, snap out of it. She went to her nightstand and grabbed her phone as Dalton left her room.

She could hear him on his phone, but she couldn't make out what he was saying. Then the attendant picked up and she explained her emergency. The front door slammed. Within seconds she heard the roar of Dalton's truck as he peeled out of the gravel drive.

"WHERE ARE YOUR BOYS?" Dalton asked as Tate sat stone faced in the cab of his truck.

"They're on horseback on their way to Hal and Erwin's cabins."

Dalton could see the fire now, it clawed at the night sky. His powerful truck bounced over the field, easily eating the distance to the flame.

There were four cabins, two hundred yards apart, it was the structure on the far left, closest to the forest, that was on fire. He saw horses and men. Dread licked down his spine as they pulled near, he only saw three men battling the blaze.

"Only three," Tate muttered.

Dalton eased off the accelerator as he got closer so that

he didn't spook the horses. Tate was out the door before the truck even came close to slowing down.

Dalton was in mission mode. There was no way he believed this was an accident. No way in hell this was some kind of gas leak or kitchen fire. He slammed the brakes on his Chevy then shoved up the invisible piece of the front bench seat that housed the high-tech gun safe. He pressed in the security code and pulled out a pistol, rifle and night vision scope. Ned was not going to get away with this. He was going hunting.

Dalton ran to where four men were fighting a losing battle to put out the flames. Erwin was almost dead on his feet. He needed medical attention. Dalton realized this wasn't his cabin it was Hal's.

Pulling the hose out of Erwin's hands, he shoved it at Rhys.

"I've got to try to get in there again," Erwin shouted.

Dalton looked the haggard man over. It was clear that he had at least second-degree burns. "Have you already tried to get into the cabin?"

"Yeah, but the fire was too hot. I thought I heard Hal yelling for help," Erwin sobbed.

"He was dead as soon as the explosion hit." Being harsh was being kind in a situation like this.

Erwin dropped down onto the ground, his head between his knees, hands over his head.

"He was my best friend." Erwin's shattered words were broken by fits of coughing.

"I need to leave you here, are you going to be all right?" Dalton asked.

Erwin waved him away. "Go find the fucker who did this and kill him." He started coughing again. Dalton looked up and saw that Rhys and Luke were working hard to make sure that the fire didn't spread to the forest beyond. Tate jogged over to Dalton.

"You're loaded for bear," Tate observed.

"You and I both know that Dumb and Dumber are probably watching. I'm going to go gather them up," Dalton snarled.

"Not without me, you're not." Tate held up a rifle he'd gotten from God knew where.

"You need to be on watch to ensure that nobody takes pot shots at your boys or the first responders. Aurora called them, they should be here soon." Dalton looked over toward the ranch. He still couldn't see another horse headed this way, but he figured she'd be coming soon. "I told Aurora to wait at the ranch."

"Like that will work," Tate said in disgust.

"Exactly," Dalton agreed.

"Be careful," Tate called after him as Dalton headed for the tree line. His heart ached for Aurora, know how much she would hurt when she realized her friend Hal was dead. After that he concentrated on the task at hand. He melted into the forest and immediately felt at home. Dalton had already been all over the ranch, including this forest. He knew that it was at least a mile back before it butted up to a rural highway.

The noise of the fire blocked out any kind of sounds that the men might have made, so it was up to him to just check out the woods for signs of disturbance. It didn't take long to see the broken branches at shoulder height.

Sloppy, it was just plain sloppy to leave such an obvious trail. But then again, they probably didn't expect anyone to come after them. The dipshits probably thought everyone would be fighting the fire. Dalton heard the faint sound of a siren. He felt a sense of relief, they would be able to focus on the blaze and Tate would be able to ensure that Aurora stayed out of the forest.

He leapt over a dead tree and silently landed on the other side. Despite some of the rain that they'd had lately, the undergrowth was still dry. As Dalton got closer to Ricky and Ned's trail it was easy to spot where they'd gone because of all the snapped branches, twigs and sticks. Ideally, he'd like to get in front of them before they reached the road.

Dalton took off to the right of their trail and then started to run parallel. He was now far enough away from the fire that it was just the sounds of the forest, soon he would hear the two men, and he knew for sure that there was no way they would hear or see him.

"Ned, you need to move faster."

The man wasn't even trying to be quiet.

"I'm going as fast as I can," the second man panted.

"Well go faster, otherwise I'm leaving you behind. You're not worth a lethal injection."

"Ricky, California doesn't have the death penalty." Ned sounded pompous and oily.

"We're in Nevada, you idiot! We're dead men walking." Ricky shouted.

"Oh shit, I never thought of that. I'll keep up, I promise," Ned said.

Dalton heard the racket they were making, but he easily passed them. They had flashlights and he saw where their trail was leading. Hell, he had time to pass them, do his nails, get a facial, then climb a tree and get into position.

When he was two hundred yards before the highway, he got into position behind a Ponderosa pine and pulled his night scope off his rifle and watched for their arrival. As they came into sight he could make out Ned from the picture that his teammate Dex had sent to his phone. Dumbshit and Dumbshitter were making it easy for him. Ned was walking ten feet behind his cousin and he was sweating profusely.

Fish in a barrel.

Ricky was within four yards of Dalton when he walked by, he didn't notice a thing. Thirty seconds went by and Ned walked by, Dalton hit him in the temple with the butt of his pistol. It was just a love tap. He grabbed him and lowered him behind a bush. He picked up Ned's gun and put it into his pocket. It was three minutes before Ricky spoke.

"Ned, you need to pick up the pace. Ned are you listening to me?"

Ricky whipped around, but it was too late for him, Dalton was there.

"What?" Was the only word he got out before Dalton had him down to the ground his knee digging in his chest, his razor-sharp blade to his throat. Ricky's eyes narrowed.

"Go ahead and kill me, it beats waiting around for a lethal injection," the man spat out.

"I'll slice your stomach open and leave you with your guts hanging open for the bears to get you, then you'll be begging for the state's mercy."

Ricky trembled. "What do you want?"

"Did you try to kill Aurora?"

Dalton moved the knife down and shoved up Ricky's coat and flannel shirt. He nicked him with his blade.

"No, I swear to God, I didn't. I blew the shot on purpose the other day," Ricky stammered. "Ned was pissed as hell."

"Why now? Why is he coming back at her after all this time?" It was a question that had been gnawing at Dalton.

"He just got fired again. He said all his real troubles began when she fired him two years ago. He hadn't been able to pick up a decent job since he left this ranch. He promised to pay me good if I helped scare her."

"You mean kill her," Dalton said harshly. He threw down the knife, not wanting that kind of evidence. He knew the perfect thing. He dragged Ricky three feet to a sharp rock that was protruding from the forest floor. He pushed his cheek against it.

"Owww."

"Too bad about your fall," Dalton said fiercely. "The slower you are answering my questions, or the more you don't tell me the truth, the closer you are to having your face split open on this rock. We clear?"

"Okay, okay."

"Where'd Ned get the money, if he'd been fired again?"

"I don't know."

Dalton pressed him down harder.

"I swear," Ricky shrieked, "I don't know."

"You knew you'd have to kill her, didn't you?"

He didn't say anything, so Dalton pressed his face into the rock until blood trickled over the stone.

"Yes, I knew."

"What was tonight's plan?"

"We wanted to get her away from you and all of her protection. We'd been watching the place. We knew men were ready to help her. If we provided a distraction, we thought I could pick her off. I was ready with my rifle."

Just because he was pissed, Dalton picked up Ricky's head and slammed it into the rock, not hard enough to make him pass out, or that any bones would break, he still needed to talk more, but enough that there would be a lot of pain.

After the screaming died down, Dalton heard a twig snap. Dalton let go of Ricky and lunged for his knife. He picked it up by the hilt, and out of the corner of his eye saw Ned holding a rock over his head. Dumbershit should have thrown it while he had the chance.

Dalton swung his knife in a wide arc and it caught Ned across his thigh and he went down in a stream of curses.

"You should have stayed put," Dalton said grimly as he watched blood start streaming down the man's leg. He turned back to Ricky who hadn't moved a muscle.

Dalton didn't hear anything but Ned's crying and Ricky's heavy breathing, but he waited, he just knew what was coming. He looked off into the woods and nodded when Tate materialized. Yep, the man had definitely been a Marine Raider.

"Can you use a hand getting these two back to the scene of the crime?" the older man asked.

"Almost." Dalton turned to Ned.

"Where'd you get the money to pay Ricky?" he demanded of Ned.

"I stole it before I left my last gig."

Figured. Dalton turned to Tate. "Let's get this trash to the sheriff. Looks like Aurora is finally safe."

"I need to go and change," she said as they walked into house. She barely glanced at the big country kitchen that normally gave her a sense of peace.

"Honey sit down. You haven't eaten a thing since last night. There's plenty of food," Gunnar said.

"I'm not hungry."

"Sit," Dalton said.

She was seated in a kitchen chair before she even realized it. She pulled down at the stretchy black skirt of her dress. Gunnar magically put a piece of cheese and broccoli casserole in front of her.

"It's warm, how'd you do that?" she asked listlessly.

"Mrs. Sanderson kept it in a thermal pouch for us when she dropped it off. Now eat, it's one of your favorites." Gunnar wrapped her hand around the fork.

She put it back down on the table.

"Don't make me feed you. I've done it before," he warned.

"I might just throw it up."

He got up and poured her a glass of milk and set it in front of her. She looked at the watered-down milk. She really wished it was whole milk. She picked up the glass and took a sip. Then she took a small bite of the casserole. Soon she was actually eating. She looked up to see Dalton's concerned face. They'd been right, she was hungry.

"It was a nice service," she said. Her voice broke. "God, I'm going to miss him so much. I loved him, do you think he knew that?"

Her fork clattered to the floor. Dalton bent and picked it up.

"He did Baby Girl, I promise." Gunnar stood up and kissed the top of her head. "Let me get you a new fork."

"I'm done eating."

This time her grandfather didn't push.

"You need to talk it out," She looked at her grandfather helplessly.

"I need to go change."

"It's not your fault," Dalton said quietly.

"How do you figure?" she asked bitterly. "Hal died because they wanted to flush me out. I'd say that was my fault. Erwin is hurt and it's going to take over a month for him to recover. Again, that's because of me." Her grandfather tried to cover her hand, but she wouldn't let him. Instead she got up and rushed to her bedroom. She tugged off her dress and flung it into the corner of her bedroom. Then she pulled on her clothes, so she could go to the barn. Her Grandfather was putting the food that had come from the neighbors into the fridge, and Dalton was standing by the door.

"I need to go check out Lucky and Vertigo," she said quietly.

"I'll go with you," Dalton said as he pulled his jacket off the peg by the door.

"Stay with grandpa," she said quickly and practically ran out the front door. She didn't want company. If one more person told her that Hal's death wasn't her fault, she'd go for her grandfather's gun and shoot them. Lucky wouldn't try to feed her a line of bullshit. Hell, that poor mare was as traumatized as Aurora.

She was at the bottom of the porch stairs when he called out to her.

"Wait up." She hated that voice of his. It was all comandereey. She shot a glare out over her shoulder. "Aurora." He said her name like she was a petulant child. She stopped and whirled around, with one hand on her hip, and the other hand up and out.

"Don't. Just don't. I don't need to hear from you. I've heard enough."

Dalton stepped into her personal space and grabbed her outstretched hand, he rubbed it against his cheek. It was the wrong thing for him to do. It made her start to feel even more, and it hurt. She tried to yank her hand away, but he wouldn't let her. Instead he turned his face and pressed a kiss into her palm. Oh God, he was breaking through her flimsy defenses.

"Please Dalton, I'm begging you." She tried her best to keep her voice even.

"You gotta bend before you break."

"You were supposed to leave yesterday," she reminded him.

Liquid blue eyes looked at her compassionately. "I'm not leaving you like this."

"The danger is over. You need to leave." This time he let her hand go when she pulled.

She turned back toward the barn. It was seven o'clock, nobody else was there except the horses. Siren and Aladdin were doing better. Vertigo was settled, but the new horse Lucky who Hal and Erwin had just brought in, needed a lot of tender loving care. The mare would bring her solace.

Dalton stayed as close as a tick as she strode past the corral. She made one last attempt. "I really want to be alone."

"Not happening."

What a bastard.

She strode down the center aisle toward the stall that was across from Aladdin's and was the mirror image. Lucky needed the extra space. She was a young mare who bit and kicked, at least she did when she wasn't cowering in a corner.

Before she got halfway to Lucky's stall, Dalton was in front of her blocking her way, she tried to step around him, but he was like a moving wall. She looked into his face.

"Leave me alone."

"We're going to talk."

"No, we're not," she said vehemently.

"Okay, I'm going to talk, and you're going to listen." His big body herded her against a wall, effectively pinning her there.

"Just say your piece and leave." She stared at his chest.

Dalton put his knuckles under her chin and tenderly tilted her head up. She'd never seen his eyes that color, they shimmered like the midnight sky. "Sunshine, I know exactly how you feel, and this is never, I repeat, never going to leave you. One day it might just become a dull ache, if you're lucky, but you're always going to know that this happened on your watch. You're always going to know you made a decision that ultimately resulted in a man's death. Everyone will tell you that Ned was the one who lit that fire, but you'll never be able to shake the fact that if it weren't for the fact you made the choice to get rid of Ned and told others not to hire him, Hal would be alive today. I really want to be able to tell you something different, I really do Baby, but I can't." He looked desolate.

Her shoulders slumped. "That was a shitty pep talk," she whispered hoarsely.

The corner of his mouth lifted, and he stroked her cheek with the back of his knuckles. "I'm always going to speak the truth to you Aurora, always." His thumb captured the tear that trickled down her face.

"But I should have known. I should have been able to guess what he would do." How often had she told herself that over the last four days?

"I've been telling myself the exact same thing for five years. But we have no alternative but to live with the consequences of our actions."

She heard the raw emotion in his voice, and the pain in his eyes eclipsed hers a hundred-fold. Holy hell, he was talking about Reagan. No wonder. She shook her head to clear it. He wasn't being insensitive, he was really trying to help. And maybe, just maybe, if she asked the right questions she could help him.

"How do we live with it?" she queried softly.

"By doing," he answered. "You get up, every day, put one foot in front of the other, and squeeze as much happiness out of the day as humanly possible, but this underlying agony will pop up when you least expect it."

"Is that how've you coped? Since Reagan?"

She watched the strong man in front of her swallow and nod.

"You just live your life as best you can."

She shuddered, as a terrible thought occurred to her. Is that what he had been doing when they had come together? Was that all their lovemaking had meant to him, coping?

He wrapped his arms around her and answered her unasked question. "But occasionally you get little pockets of peace, even joy. Like I did with you. Those are moments more precious than gold."

She melted against him. "So, I'll find joy? Please tell me I'll find joy."

"There will be times," he assured her sadly.

She looked up, trying to see his expression, but his eyes

were hooded. "Dalton, there's got to be more," she insisted. "It can't color every aspect of your life forever."

He rested his forehead against hers. She felt enveloped by him, like she was in a cocoon of safety.

"For you Sunshine, it won't color every aspect of your life. You will be able to move on, I promise."

Her heart broke. She wrapped her arms around his waist and squeezed as hard as she could. "Isn't there any possibility of more for you?" she asked. "More than just these small stolen moments?"

He didn't answer.

"Dalton?"

"I just can't." His voice was like a lone eagle's call in the wilderness. "I'm incapable of loving like that again." He lifted his forehead, his eyes searched hers. "There's a part of me that died that day. I'll never be able to love like I did."

"But-"

He shook his head. "I'll never offer more than I can give. I would never be that cruel." His brow furled. "Tell me you didn't expect more than a few nights," he practically begged.

Aurora gave him the best smile in her arsenal. "Dalton, I always knew that this was temporary. But you have to know...I want you to know...I wouldn't have traded it for the world."

She twined her fingers into the hair at the base of his neck and pulled his head down to hers. He didn't resist. His mouth slammed onto hers, their desperation was equally matched. There was a deep growl emanating from Dalton's throat as he ground his mouth against hers, forcing her lips to part. She needed him. Deeper, she lured his tongue to mate with hers. If this was all she could have, then she would take it. She wanted it with every fiber of her being.

Aurora arched up against him, wishing that there was no cloth separating their bodies. She needed to feel her breasts rasped by the dark hair on his chest. Dalton grabbed her hair and pulled her away from his ravenous mouth.

"No," she wailed.

He licked downwards, igniting flames along her jaw to the pulse of her neck, then he bit. Aurora felt it in her core, moisture flooded the folds of her sex. He let go of her hair, and hoisted her up by her legs, she immediately wrapped them around his waist, grinding herself against his erection. She whined in frustration.

"Not close enough," she whimpered. She looked frantically around the barn. "Tack room," she panted.

Dalton nodded. He kept her in his arms as he strode toward the spotless room at the back of the barn. She shivered with anticipation when he kicked the door shut behind them.

"Let me down," she commanded.

"Nuh-uh. Like you where you are." Dalton's big hands squeezed her ass and she thought she might explode.

Aurora let out a sound of complaint when Dalton moved one of his hands. Then she heard a thud as he threw a saddle on the floor. She pointed toward a shelf. "Clean blankets." He grabbed two and threw them down on top of the saddle, then let her slide down his body, but even then, he kept one arm firmly clamped around her waist.

"Let me," she struggled to bend down and spread out the blanket.

"Nuh-uh. I've got it." One handed, he grabbed the corner of the blanket and sent it into an arc so that it landed softly over the saddle. He did the same with the second, and they had a spot to lay down.

She saw him frown as he looked down, then he grabbed three more of the horse blankets from the shelf. "I like that you're anal about cleanliness," he grinned. She watched as he mounded the blankets into a nest. "There, now it's soft enough for what I have in mind."

Aurora squeaked as he picked her up then smoothly laid her down onto the makeshift bed. But as much as she wanted this, needed this even, she had to know that he was in this with her. Mind, body and soul. She cupped his cheeks and when he bent down she pressed kisses to his forehead, his temple, his jaw and finally the tip of his nose. He gifted her with a smile.

"This will bring you happiness?"

"Right now? Sunshine, this means everything to me," he promised her.

9

EVEN STUCK IN A TREE, OVER FIVE MONTHS LATER AND thousands of miles away from Aurora, and he still couldn't get her out of his mind. The first seven hours he had been able to concentrate on the mission, but after that his mind started to wander. Here he was on hour twelve, and blonde hair and brown eyes floated through his brain, even as the weather changed from a category two to a category four hurricane.

His receiver wasn't working. As the storm had increased in power, his SEAL team's communication devices had gone to shit. Half the time it was nothing but static. The rain was now hitting Dalton sideways as he clung to the high limb of the Encenillo tree.

Was Aiden signaling him? His second in command was a hundred meters away hidden beneath the jungle floor, but Dalton was almost positive he had seen him hold up a hand, or was it a fist?

Yep, there it was again. He must have gotten some kind of communication from someone else saying that they were going to make a move. It was about damn time. They'd come to Columbia to extricate Angel Restrepo from the jungle drug cartel's hacienda. That's what the drug dealer who owned the place, liked to call his fortress. Restrepo was a DEA informant, and if they didn't get him out in the next twenty-four hours then an entire network of operatives was at risk of being exposed.

Dalton flinched when gunshots sounded in his ear. Was that Wyatt who grunted? Goddammit, he better not have gotten shot. He could hear the pounding of boots, then more gunshots.

"Be ready, we have a fan club," Gray whispered. That was his, Dex and Aiden's cue. The team was coming out with their man.

"I can walk," Wyatt Leeds said loudly.

"Keep it down," Hunter hissed.

Yep, Wyatt was injured, and Dalton would bet his last dollar that Hunter was carrying him.

Shit, what a cluster.

It had been decided that a four-man team would go in for the rescue.

Dalton knew that Dex was also outside the compound, waiting to pick off anybody trailing the members of Black Dawn if they came out the front entrance. Aiden was covering the side entrance, and Dalton was covering the roof and back.

"Which way are you coming out?" Dalton queried.

"Not sure yet," Gray answered.

More shots were fired. Dalton hoped they were coming out the back. He knew that being positioned up in the tree gave him the best ability to take out the bogeys.

"Back! We're coming out the back!" Griffin Porter yelled.

It seemed like forever before the back door was flung open, and Griff flew out. He held it open. Hunter had Wyatt over his shoulder in a fireman's carry. Wait, he wasn't holding his left leg, that was dangling uselessly.

Not good. Not good at all.

A barefoot man came out, followed by Gray who immediately picked him up and started to run to the left side of the building. Men swarmed out fifteen seconds behind them. Dalton started shooting.

One down.

Another down.

Then a third.

He saw more going down. It was either Aiden or Griff.

"What's the status on transport?" Gray demanded. For once their lieutenant sound stressed. Wyatt must be in bad shape.

"Still waiting for a response," Dex answered over the comm.

They needed to get the hell out of there. The hurricane was a blessing and a curse. There were two helicopters positioned meters from the compound. One of them was already tipped so that the rotors were embedded in the sodden dirt. What was once a road leading up to the huge stronghold ten hours ago, was now a muddy river. There was no way that anyone inside was going to be able to follow them except on foot.

Dalton was going to make another bet that the Black Hawk helicopter they were supposed to take out to the aircraft carrier was not going to be able to land at their extraction spot.

"Black Hawk is cancelled," Dex communicated. "We're hoofing it to the coast."

"I'm staying," Dalton said into the mic.

"Roger that," Gray responded. "We'll give you an update on Wyatt ASAP. Let us know when you think it's smart to follow."

"Will do," Dalton responded.

He lodged himself tighter against the tree branch. Was the rain letting up?

Dalton gave a bitter laugh when a wave of water hit his face. Served him right for thinking that things were getting better. He raised his scope and scoured the back and roof of the compound to ensure that nobody was moving. There was no way he was going to let anyone get by on his watch.

He looked at his watch. It had been two hours since his team had left. It should take them three hours to get to the extraction spot in ideal circumstances. Lightening lit the sky, exposing eight dead bodies. Still no word from his team and it was killing him. Why couldn't they at least give him an update on Wyatt?

More thunder, but then he heard something else. Dalton realized it was the sound of an engine grinding. Someone was trying and failing to start a car. He shimmied down the tree and took off at a dead run for the front of the building. He rounded the perimeter of the huge compound but stopped before he got to the courtyard gates.

The loud grating noise was clearer, then he heard shouting. He thought it might be Spanish, but who knew over the rain? Thunder boomed, then lightening flashed and Dalton took that moment to move. He dove into the mud and pointed his rifle into the flagstone courtyard. He saw the problem. The four gigantic decorative palm trees that were in massive pots had toppled over onto the two Land Rovers.

He saw three men. Wait, was there a fourth bent under the hood of the SUV?

What the hell were they thinking trying to start the SUV's? They wouldn't be driving anywhere, anyway. He kept trying to apply logic, and realized it was useless.

Dammit, it would be best if all of them were clear, so he could just rapid fire on the bunch of them.

Thunder boomed again. An instant later the sky lit up with lightening.

One of the men froze as he spotted him. He yelled, and Dalton took the shot. The three men went down. The man who had been dicking around under the hood was gone. Dalton was done with this happy horseshit. He was taking him out, then clearing out the rats' nest inside. He didn't want one more person following his team, especially when Wyatt was injured. He wanted his friends safe.

He gave a feral grin when the man started shooting his way. He saw the muzzle flashes. Perfect. Now he knew where he was. It was just a waiting game.

More bullets came his way. Dalton crawled backwards in the mud on his elbows and lodged himself behind the terra cotta wall of the hacienda. He adjusted the muzzle of his rifle and scope so just a little bit was showing as he took aim and fired shot after shot at the Land Rover's gas tank.

Score!

He watched with satisfaction as a fireball of flames burst up and out. He heard a scream, then the man launched himself toward the middle of the courtyard. Metal fell from the sky and landed on him and he joined his compatriots, sprawled in dead silence.

Dalton was not going to rush things. This explosion was

a perfect time to wait and see if more people were going to join the fray.

Fifteen minutes passed as rain bombarded him. It felt like he was in the ocean, not on Terra Firma.

Nobody showed. Okay, time for reconnaissance.

He threw his sniper rifle onto his back and put his assault rifle to his assault to his shoulder for the close quarter work.

With all the noise from the storm he could probably sing the national anthem and not be heard, but still, Dalton took pains to be silent as he entered the hacienda. For twenty minutes he checked every nook and cranny of the first floor. He even found the trapdoor hidden under a jute rug in the dining room. Nobody was in the cramped space.

He headed upstairs. After long minutes, he headed for the last door at the end of the hall. He heard muffled crying. He slammed it open, his gun ready. He found a terrified woman frantically hugging two small children to her bosom.

"Hands behind your head," he commanded in Spanish. It took her and the children long moments to comply. He couldn't take this at face value. He just couldn't.

He checked the room, the closets and under the bed. When he was satisfied that they were the only three occupants, he crouched down and gently patted down the women and even the children for weapons. He hated, absolutely hated, having to do so.

The woman was fighting back tears and the children were sobbing with fright. He saw the little girl was wearing a Hello Kitty shirt. His heart clenched, she couldn't be more than five. The little boy looked to be about seven.

"Please, please don't kill us," the boy sobbed in Spanish.

The woman immediately reassured the children that he was a friend. He didn't know how she could be so confident, but he thanked God that she was. He pulled at the bedspread and wiped the mud off his face and smiled. The little girl's tears started to abate.

"You're right, I am a friend," he said to the woman. "I'm here to help. Who are you?"

She quickly explained that she was the housekeeper, but she didn't hold his gaze. If he had to guess she was probably more than just a housekeeper. He also took in the dark bruise mottling jaw.

"I need to get you out of here."

She shook her head wildly. She scrambled under the bed and pulled out a cell phone and lifted it high as if it was a prize.

"Please, please, let me call my father. Please, please let him come and get us." Tears welled in her eyes.

"Where did you get that phone?" Dalton asked in amazement.

She trembled and didn't answer him.

"Where-" he cut himself off. He looked at her bruised cheek and realized there were bruises on her arms from a man's grip. What was he thinking come at her as an angry male?

"What's your name?" he asked in a soft voice.

She gave him a wide-eyed stare.

"My name is Dalton Sullivan. I'm an American."

"You're a soldier. You're going to save us!" The little boy grinned.

"He killed people," the little girl shoved her face under her mother's arm.

"Ma'am? Can you tell me your name?"

"Carmelita Hernandez," she whispered. "I stole the phone from Rodrigo's body."

Rodrigo was the drug lord who'd overseen the whole operation. Dalton was pretty damn sure that he was the man who had roughed her up.

"Please can I call my father?" He watched a single tear run down her cheek.

He nodded, knowing she wouldn't get a signal. Not in this weather.

He watched as she fumbled with the phone. She pressed buttons, her eyes welling with tears as she tried again and again to no avail. It was heart-wrenching.

"Papa!"

Dalton figured it was his training that kept his jaw from hitting the floor in amazement. Really? She really got through to her father?

The Spanish was rapid fire. She tearfully explained he had grandchildren. And she was beyond thrilled when the man told her he was on his way. That was as far as the conversation got before the line went dead.

He got up and walked across the room, leaning against the wall so he could watch the small family. Dex had tried to contact him during the firefight out in the courtyard, and again while he was checking the house. He'd indicated that he was okay but couldn't respond, so now he took the time to check-in.

"About damn time you responded," Dex practically yelled.

"How's Wyatt?"

"He's going to make it."

Dammit, he could hear a 'but' in Dex's voice.

"What?"

"He needs surgery for his leg. Aiden is trying to work his magic."

Dalton's gut clenched. "Saving his life is the most important thing," he replied. "You better not be waiting on me. I'm good. I've cleaned out all the rat's nest here, nobody will be following us. I have three innocents that I need to ensure are safe, then I will get to you."

"We're having Griff circle back to you."

"No need, I'll be fine." He hated the idea of Griff exposing himself to more time in the hurricane than necessary. He should just stay with the team and keep heading to the coast.

"Sullivan, this is protocol," Gray Tyler said through his receiver. He his tone brooked no argument.

"Got it, Sir."

"Good."

"Now tell me who these innocents are." Gray asked.

"Woman who is the housekeeper and two small children. She's been abused. My guess is she was kept here against her will. Her father is on his way to pick her up."

"I'm not going to ask how the hell that's going to happen," Gray said. "I trust that you've got things under control, so get your ass here as quickly as possible."

"Yes, Sir."

There was a pause, then Dex came on the line. "Griff should be there in less than an hour."

"Tell him to be careful, it's always possible there was someone outside the compound that I missed."

"Thanks for telling me how to do my job, Sullivan. Any other words of wisdom?" Griff said with a laugh.

Even over the howling of the hurricane, he could hear

the others chuckling. Damn, he was tired if he was sticking his foot in his mouth like that.

"Yeah Griff, stay dry."

"Shut it," Aiden said harshly. "We need to get Wyatt moved now."

Dalton waited for Griff to respond, he knew the situation with their wounded comrade and where the team was located in correlation with the coast.

"Depending how long we have to wait for the housekeeper's family, we should be able to catch up with you before you hit the midway mark," Griff said.

"Good," was Aiden's clipped answer. Dalton knew they were done. He also knew that Aiden must be pretty damned worried about Wyatt, because his Second-in-Command didn't normally come off so grim. Dalton turned his entire focus to the little family.

"How long will it take for your father to arrive?" he asked in Spanish.

"Not long." She dislodged herself from the children and went over to the shuttered window. She started to open it.

"No!" Dalton was across the room with his hand on shutter before she could unlock it. "It's not safe, leave it shut. Why did you want to open it?"

"I wanted to point to where my village is."

"You don't have to. Can you just tell me how long it normally takes to get from your village to this hacienda?"

"A little less than an hour."

Dalton's hopes were dashed. If they usually made it by truck in an hour than hour, then it was going to take five to six hours to get here in this mess. The only good thing was that the storm seemed to be abating.

"When they get here, you'll need to stay, you understand that, right?"

"He is bringing many men from the village. They will be here very fast."

Sure, they would.

"Normally they walk when they come here, instead they will run. Even in the mud, they will come fast. Two of my brothers have been killed trying to rescue me." Her chin trembled. "I am his only daughter. Their only sister." She shoved her face into her hands.

"Mama?" The little boy pulled his little sister with him. The little girl stared up at him for just a moment, her brown eyes now curious, not filled with fear.

"Come here baby," Carmelita said. Then the three of them wrapped their arms around each other and gave one another comfort.

"You are good children. Soon you will meet your grandfather," Carmelita said as she peppered them with kisses.

Dalton had to look away from the touching family scene. Why couldn't Lacey have protected Reagan the way this woman cared for her children?

"I'm going to keep watch. You and your children stay here, okay?"

"Yes." She didn't look up, she just nodded, holding her kids close.

Dalton went outside the room and took position at the end of the hall. He crouched down and settled in along the inside wall right before the ornate bannister. From that location he could still see anyone who might start to come up the stairs. There was something soothing about having higher ground.

He looked over his shoulder at the closed bedroom door. The elephant in that room had been the little girl, maybe not an elephant, more like a little Hello Kitty. She hadn't been much bigger than Reagan.

Did every single thing, every single time, all circle back to Reagan? He blinked rapidly, his eyes getting gritty, probably from all the sweat and grime. But the little girl hadn't had blue eyes, they'd been brown, not quite like Aurora's but similar.

Dalton rested his head against the wall, three days with barely any sleep came crashing down.

"Suck it up," he growled under his breath.

Aurora. Her name and face played through his mind like a siren's song.

For five long months he'd done everything in his power to keep his mind on the present, on anything but that small oasis of time that could never amount to anything. Hell, he'd even volunteered to do an assignment with Zed and his Night Storm team in Virginia.

He heard a subtle sound, and in seconds, he made it to the room where Carmelita and her children were. Was that a giggle? Was that even possible?

He slowly opened the door and peeked in. Yep, Carmelita had her son smiling and her daughter laughing. He quietly closed the door and went back to his post.

He surveyed the bullet ridden first floor, ensuring that there was no sign of movement.

He looked at his watch. Only ten minutes had passed since Carmelita had called her father. Twenty minutes had passed since he'd been informed that Griff was on his way. He figured he had another forty-five minutes of waiting for his teammate.

A picture of Aurora, soothing Aladdin flashed, unbidden, into his mind. She was magical, the way she could soothe and bring comfort. He let his head drop against the wall, enjoying the small hurt. He'd been able to bury so much of their time together for months, but not today, why not today?

He smiled grimly.

Gee, could it be the way that Carmelita's family had died trying to rescue her? Wasn't that like the Dressler's, Erwin and poor Hal? Then there was the fact that the little girl's eyelashes were as long as Aurora's. God, he had it bad.

Great. He wasn't really happy about all this alone time in his own head. Even the five months since he left Tahoe he'd done everything possible to keep busy so that he didn't have to think. And he sure as hell hadn't wanted to feel.

Fat lot of good that had done him. And now, after seeing Carmelita with all that compassion and bravery, how could he not think of Aurora? Dalton took a deep breath and repositioned his rifle so that he was ready if anyone made a move downstairs. He kept a keen watch on everything, but his thoughts turned inward, back to his last time intimate time with Aurora.

10

AURORA'S HAIR SMELLED LIKE IT LOOKED, SHADES OF fragrant honey. Dalton lifted a silky strand to his face.

"Are you sniffing my hair?" her laugh was languid.

"Busted." Not that he cared, she smelled delicious and he wanted to savor every moment of what little time they had left together. He looked down at her.

He saw the same need reflected in her eyes.

"When are you going?" she asked.

He shook his head. He didn't want to talk about it now. She rested her cheek against his chest. If he could, he would make a habit of sleeping on a hard floor so that Aurora would always end up sleeping on top of him. He enjoyed having a blonde blanket. That was the problem, he liked her, this, too much.

He swept his hand down under the blanket and cupped the swell of her bottom. She looked up at him underneath her dark lashes. "Are you looking for an encore?"

"We need to get back to the house. Your grandfather is going to send out a search party."

"I think granddad knows what's going on," she said wryly.

He winced inwardly, he really hadn't wanted to consider that. Thank God for the man's discretion, he'd done absolutely nothing to indicate that he'd noticed anything. Still, it made him feel lower than pond scum.

She shifted, raising herself up so that she was leaning on her crossed arms, her breasts a plumped feast.

"You're looking pensive. What's wrong?"

He tucked a thick lock of hair behind her ear. Then because he couldn't resist, he lifted and kissed the pulse point that he'd revealed.

"You really have a thing for my hair. I heard you breathe in, don't even deny it Sullivan." God love her, she was trying to lighten the mood.

"I'm leaving tomorrow," he said baldly, answering the question she'd asked before.

"I was pretty sure, since I was the one who folded your laundry," she sighed.

He couldn't figure if that made him feel better or worse. Better that she knew, or worse that she'd figured it out without him talking to her first.

She cupped his face in her calloused hands. Hands he reveled in. "Dalton, listen to me, you never once made a promise. We covered this, okay?"

"But tomorrow?"

Shit, why was this hitting him so hard? Hell, he'd had a couple of relationships since Lacey. Well, not relationships exactly. Now that he thought about it, he really couldn't pretty it up that much, a relationship inferred emotions were involved, and he never let one emotion get past his walls. How in the hell had Aurora gotten past every single one of his barriers?

"-life."

"What? I'm sorry I didn't get that." Shit, now he wasn't even listening to her.

"I said I understood you had to get back to your normal life."

"Did I ever tell you how much I love coffee?"

She stared at him like he'd grown a second head. "Well no Dalton, you've never mentioned that you were a coffee connoisseur."

"Chocolate too. I love chocolate."

"Okay." She bit her bottom lip, and it turned a deep red.

"Raspberries. I fucking love raspberries. Shit Aurora, your eyes, coffee and chocolate, and your lips are like the sweetest, ripest raspberries. I don't know how the hell I'm going to be able to drink another cup without thinking about you."

He clamped one arm around her waist and fisted his other hand into her tangle of honey hair, forcing her luscious lips down to his. She twisted against his naked body, grappling for his erection, making him groan against the devastating power of her kiss. He bucked up, needing more, needing so much more of this woman.

Ah God, did he taste salt?

He pulled away.

"Ignore it. I need this." She slammed her mouth onto his and straddled him. He felt her wet core stroking up and down his cock. He heard denim being dragged across the cement floor. She reared up, she had a foil packet from his jeans pocket, she tore it open with her teeth.

He didn't think he would last when she sheathed him.

She pushed down, enveloping him in the tight depths of her body. He pushed back her hair, so he could see the glittering emotion in her beloved eyes. She held him enthralled. Dalton traced his fingers up the ladder of her ribcage until he cupped the bounty of her breasts. Aurora mewed her pleasure as his thumbs circled the beautiful tips, then plucking them to tight nubs.

He did a partial sit up as she continued to ride him. He had to taste her. He took a nipple into his mouth and suckled.

"Dalton," she shrieked softly. He squeezed his eyes shut as her core tightened around him, she was strangling his dick. He'd never come close to feeling such pleasure. He carefully bit down on her nipple, and her body gripped him tighter. It was too much.

He stopped teasing her, he looked into her eyes. "Are you with me?" he gasped.

"Now." Tears dripped down her face.

"Aurora?"

Her rhythm faltered. She moved her hands and gripped his short hair, then whispered in his ear. "Fuck me."

He reared up and grabbed her ass. He slammed upwards.

"Yes," she panted. Her short nails dug into his scalp, her teeth bit into his neck. "Harder."

He couldn't go any harder, he didn't want to hurt her. Instead he twisted, moved his hand just a little so his thumb found her clit.

"Yes," she hissed as she slumped. He held her up and she trembled.

"It's too much."

Joy washed over Dalton as he grunted out a laugh.

"Harder," she gasped. He circled the nub of flesh again. "Too much," she panted.

He thrust up, pressed and circled, watching her as he tortured her. "Which is it, Sunshine?"

"Both. It's both," she breathed out. "Keep doing it."

She thrashed and squeezed.

"Ahhh. So good." Her smile outshone the sun. "So good," she cried as she found her bliss.

She was right it was so good he thought, as he found a joy he never thought he would again.

"WE HAVE COMPANY," Griff's voice whispered into his receiver.

It took a split second for Dalton to comprehend that Griff said 'we' have company, indicating they had additional incoming. He looked at his watch. Thirty-five minutes had gone by. He gave his head a swift shake and spoke into his mic.

"Could be friendlies," Dalton cautioned as he stood up and took another visual sweep of the foyer. "I have a woman and two children in here with me, she called her father and others from her village to come and get her."

"I'm checking them out," Griffin Porter said.

It seemed like a long time, but according to Dalton's watch it was only three minutes, Griff spoke again. "These are amateurs. They're talking loudly about someone named Carmelita. Is that the woman?"

"Affirmative." Dalton was relieved to think that Carmelita's family was arriving so quickly, that meant that he and Griff could hotfoot it to the team and Wyatt. His jaw clenched at the idea of just how bad the younger man's injury could be. Aiden could sometimes be an angry son-of-a-bitch, but he always kept it together when he was dealing with a patient. If he let even a tiny bit of emotion show, that meant it had to be bad.

"Shadow them Griff, I want to make sure they get here safe, and we can hand off Carmelita and her kids. I want to get back to the team ASAP."

"Ditto," the other man said grimly.

Shit, shit, shit. Nothing sounded good.

It was ten more minutes before a ragtag group of six men proceeded Griffin Porter through the front door of the hacienda. Two of them were carrying rifles that had probably been manufactured fifty years ago, however all of them had wicked looking knives.

Before he could go down and start a conversation with the oldest man, a younger man pushed him aside and bounded up the stairs.

"Carmelita," he yelled at the top of his lungs. "Carmelita! It's your brother, Jose!" he shouted in Spanish.

"Griff," Dalton yelled out. Then he darted down the hall as the door to the bedroom swung open.

"My brother Jose is here?" Carmelita cried. "Take me to him," she demanded. "Please take me to him."

Dalton sighed. He wanted to ensure that everyone was who they said they were, but really, was there any doubt?

"Carmelita, have your children stay in the room until we're sure everything is safe, okay?"

"I want to see my brother. I want to see my Papa."

"Tell your children to stay in the room and not come out until you come back for them, got that?"

"But-"

"Carmelita, do what I say." She still hesitated. "Now." His voice was a low roar. She winced, then ducked back into the room. She came out and glared at him. He bit back a smile. It made him happy to see someone who had been so sorely abused not afraid to go head to head with him.

"Stay behind me."

They went to the top of the stairs where Griff and the man named Jose were waiting. It was then that the waterworks started. Dalton had always thought his command of the Spanish language was excellent, but there was no hope of him keeping up with the two siblings. They literally fell into one another's arms. Then came the father. Now that man he could understand, but that was because he was mostly talking about defiling a dead man. Dalton understood vengeance.

"Wait. Wait." Carmelita held up her hand. At last she was speaking clearly, and Dalton and Griff could keep up. She grabbed her dad and brother's hands then tugged them down the hall. Shouts of delight were heard as they were introduced to their young relatives. Griff and Dalton were left staring at the other four men who had accompanied Carmelita's family.

"Everyone is dead, eh?" A man with dead eyes asked.

Dalton couldn't get a read on this man who held such a huge knife.

"Everyone but Carmelita and her son and daughter," Dalton answered.

"You kill them?" Another, younger man, asked.

"Who are you?" the first man asked as he looked over his shoulder toward the front door. "There's a big mess in the courtyard. You do that?"

Griff looked at him too. "Yeah, did you?"

Dalton gave his friend and exasperated look.

"We're Americans." Dalton said answering the first man with the knife. "We're with the United States Navy, and yeah, some of what happened out in the courtyard was my fault."

The man's blank expression finally turned fierce. "Those motherfuckers have killed many of my people. They should have died slow." He easily stuck the knife into his belt and stuck out his hand for Dalton to shake it. He had a firm grip and looked him straight in the eye. "Thank you. From the bottom of my heart and for all the people in my village, I thank you."

"You're welcome," Dalton said solemnly. "My teammate and I need to leave now. Are you going to be okay?"

"Yes," the man said firmly. The other three men around him nodded in agreement. "Thank you again." He turned and shook Griff's hand, then all four of them headed up the stairs as Griff and Dalton took the stairs two at a time so they could head toward their team.

"Bout' time you got back." Wyatt waved.

He was under a makeshift lean-to that someone had fashioned. Aiden O'Malley was underneath with him. Even through the rain, Dalton saw that he was grinning with Wyatt. Apparently, his big blonde friend only kept his shitty bed side manner for everyone else, for Wyatt he was all smiles.

Dalton also saw that Aiden was administering fluids and Wyatt was feeling no pain whatsoever. Hell, a tenth of whatever drug Aiden had administered to Wyatt would have

Dalton on his ass drooling and moaning in his sleep for Aurora.

"Come 'ere." Wyatt motioned with his whole arm for Dalton to come to him. Aiden gave him a warning look.

Dalton wiped the rain from his eyes and slicked the hair off his face. He leaned in to smile at his wounded teammate. "So, you just had to find a way to get a little more attention from the ladies, huh?" Dalton teased.

"Always looking for an angle my man. You should try it. You need to get laid," Wyatt waggled his eyebrows at him. "Come closer. Gonna tell you a secret."

Dalton exchanged a worried look with Aiden as he ducked further under the tarp. He could see that that the huge bandage above Wyatt's knee still had blood seeping through.

Please God no.

Dalton knew what this meant. He had seen this kind of thing before when a soldier's limb was packed like this. He could lose it.

"Okay Wyatt, I'm game. What wise piece of advice to you have to offer me to succeed with the ladies?"

"Gotta whisper it to you." Dalton crouched down beside the youngest member of Black Dawn.

"I'm listening," he said gently.

"You gotta lead with your heart. I know everyone thinks I lead with my dick, but I really don't. I wanna have what everyone else does. When the women know that I value them and I'm seriously considering them for the long-term, that's why they stick around. Ya know? I just wish I could find the right one," he slurred. He looked up at Dalton with big soulful hazel eyes, "I'm so lonely."

Dalton felt like he'd been kicked in the chest. Thank

God Wyatt took that moment to pass out. Hopefully he wouldn't remember what he'd said. He turned to escape the lean-to and his eyes met Aiden's. His friend had heard. He looked as torn-up as Dalton felt.

"I think the rain's letting up," Dalton said. "I'm going to check with Dex on the status of the Black Hawk. Maybe we'll get lucky."

Aiden gave a choppy nod. "You do that."

Dalton looked around. Griff was talking to Gray, probably filling in their lieutenant as to what had transpired back at the compound. He saw Dex and Hunter engrossed in a conversation. He went over to them.

"Why are we staying here at the evac spot? Why not move to the coast?" Dalton asked. "You can't tell me that anyone is going to approve the Black Hawk to come out in this weather."

"Talked to the Black Hawk helicopter pilot. He and Gray go way back. He's chomping at the bit to fly in, no matter what the weather is like. He said that he can make it," Dex informed him.

"I'm sure his commander is all ready to sign off on that," Dalton said sarcastically.

"His commander is Liam MacLure, so don't be so sure," Dex responded. "Hell, knowing MacLure, he just might fly the Black Hawk himself."

Hunter's low whistle could be heard even over the rain. "That man really doesn't give a damn, does he?"

"I think after everything that went down, he's about done. If he can make a difference for us, that's what he's going to do," Dex answered.

That was the reason Gray had Dex on point for communications. Besides the fact that he had an unnatural relationship with his military grade laptop, Dex knew all the rumor, scandal and scuttlebutt in the Pacific Fleet. Dalton sure as hell hoped that the rumor was right, because Wyatt needed to be evac'd now. Logically he knew that his teammate could live a good life even if he lost his leg, but Dalton knew that having to leave the teams would gut him.

Dex didn't say anything, he just took his baby into the lean-to, so he could fire it up. It might be rugged, but all its little electrical parts still didn't like the rain.

Gray and Griff joined them.

"Sounds like everything went really well from what Griff said," Gray said.

Dalton nodded. Then all four men looked over to where Wyatt lay passed out. Aiden was staring over Dex's shoulder at his computer.

"You know the Black Hawk pilot?" Hunter asked Gray.

"Yep. Edge is a good man. He was the pilot for the first three years I was on the teams. We're lucky he's attached to the Roosevelt."

"Edge?" Hunter asked.

"It's a nickname. Never play poker with him," Gray smiled. It was the first time Dalton had seen him smile since getting here. "I'm going to leave you ladies and see if I can do some final persuading along with Dex and Aiden."

Griff and Hunter were looking too damn positive for Dalton's taste as Gray walked off.

"Come on Dalton. You need to think happy thoughts," Griff admonished.

Dalton gave his friend a world-weary stare.

"No, I'm serious. You've been in a shit place for months. Right now, Wyatt needs all of us pulling for him. Believing in him. And the fact that Liam MacLure is on the USS

Roosevelt, and so is this pilot friend of Gray's, I'd say things are shaping up pretty good."

"He's right you know," Hunter said as he adjusted his hood and moved out of a mud puddle. "Even the rain has let up in the last two hours."

What, were they expecting a rainbow and a unicorn to come prancing out of the jungle? He looked at the two men staring at him. Then he realized they were right, he needed to pull his head out of the dark depths of wherever and see some semblance of light. It was almost like he was in mourning again.

"Gray did it!" Dex shouted from the lean-to.

Hell, even Gray was grinning. Mr. Cool had done it.

"There you go, did it kill you?" Hunter bumped his shoulder.

"Huh?" Dalton didn't understand what Hunter was saying.

"You're smiling. I knew you had it in you."

WELL THE SMILES hadn't lasted for long. Nor had the decent coffee. He'd been in dry clothes for a day in a half, but even that didn't make him feel better. He and his team were here in San Juan, Costa Rica. They'd missed their flight home... again. As they waited for Wyatt's surgery to be done. Gray was going to catch hell for allowing his team to stay in Costa Rica so long just to hang around a waiting room, but he didn't give two shits.

The doctor on the aircraft carrier had done what he could, but he knew that it was above his pay grade, so they had flown in a surgeon to the closest decent surgery center that a Black Hawk could make from the USS Roosevelt. Every single hour counted to save his leg. Again, it was Liam MacLure who pulled every string imaginable to get things done.

So, an orthopedic surgeon from Walter Reed was flown down to Costa Rica. Liam and Gray were down in the cafeteria. That left the rest of the team in the waiting room. Dalton was standing away from the rest. He'd tried, he'd really fucking tried, to have more of a positive outlook. He wanted it for his friend. But Hunter was right, it was almost like he expected shit to go wrong these days. Which in a sense made him an Uber SEAL, he was seeing shadows behind the shadows, and the only thing he took for granted was that his teammates had his back. But Wyatt coming out of this whole? God, he so fucking wanted to believe. But instead he was building contingency plans in his head as to how he could help him build a life without a leg.

"Goddammit, stop it." Dex glared at him as he plopped down in the chair next to him.

Where had he come from? Dalton hadn't even noticed him move away from the group and cross the room.

"Stop what?" Dalton asked.

"You need to hire an exterminator and get them to kill that bug that crawled up your ass. It's been months now, we might have to tent you."

"I don't need to listen to this. Don't you need to go make love to your laptop, or have phone sex with Kenna?" Dalton pushed out of the chipped plastic chair and started to walk away.

"Quit deflecting. You're in need of a personality transplant, and it's due to Aurora Chance."

Dalton winced with pain when he whipped his neck

around to stare at his ex-friend. "Aurora is a closed subject. Finished. Done. Are we clear?"

From over Dex's head, Dalton saw Hunter coming toward them.

"Did you hear something?" Dalton asked.

"Still nothing. Remember, they said this kind of surgery can last up to eight hours, it's only been four," Hunter answered.

Great, then he just came over to bust his balls.

Hunter's eyes darted to Dex who shrugged his shoulders.

"Guys, it's not that bad," Dalton defended himself.

Hunter looked him dead in the eye. "Actually, it is. You don't want to hear this, but it's like you've lost Reagan all over again."

Somehow, he managed to stay upright, even though he felt like a brother had just taken a battering ram to his chest. Dalton didn't reply, he just stared at Hunter, willing his friend to take back his words.

Finally, Hunter rubbed the back of his neck. "Maybe I'm reading the situation wrong."

"You are," Dalton said grimly.

"But you are in mourning," Hunter said as his hand fell to his side and he took a step forward. "Dammit Dalton, you're one of my best friends, and your pain is palpable. There was nothing that could be done last time, but there is this time."

"Stay out of this, Diaz," Dalton warned Hunter as he took a step closer.

Dex was suddenly there pushing his way between the two men. "Okay, enough with the testosterone display. We get it. The nurse over there is sufficiently impressed."

"Nurse? Does she have news?" Hunter asked.

"No, she was talking to another family. Who by the way, was also sufficiently scared. You both need to dial it back," Dex admonished the two men. "I'll help. Dalton, Hunter is right, suck it up."

Dalton felt his head literally pound. It was a damn good thing he was in a hospital, because when he had a stroke they might be able to save him. "You two don't understand shit."

"Explain it to us." Hunter sat down in the chair Dalton had vacated. He stretched out his legs and crossed his arms. "Tell me a story."

Asshole.

"I met a woman. She's up there with Kenna and Aliana." Hunter sat up a little at the mention of his fiancé's name. "You know me. Hunter, you of all people *know* me. I can't do the whole relationship thing, and I sure as hell can never do the husband thing ever again. I'm a bad bet for a woman. Especially one like that. She deserves someone who's whole."

Dex snorted. "This from the man who likes romance novels."

"What?" Hunter sat up even straighter in his chair.

"Yeah. Kenna told me that she and Dalton discussed books and he was even able to name one of her favorite romance novelists."

"That's bullshit," Dalton protested. "The series she's talking about is a female cop in the future and her rich husband. It's a crime thriller series. She thinks it's romance, but it's categorized under thriller."

"Nope, Kenna definitely said romance," Dex rubbed his

hands with glee. "Admit it Dalton, you want what Hunter and I have."

For a second he flashed back to what Wyatt had said. But Dalton didn't feel lonely, he felt like a part of his heart had been ripped out of his chest. But it was for the best. Aurora deserved better.

"Who is the woman?" Hunter asked.

"Aurora Chance, he met her in Tahoe. She's the reason he's been acting like a wounded bear for the last five months."

Hunter slid his gaze over to Dalton and grinned slyly. "Finally, the pieces fall into place. Tell me more Dex."

"No, how 'bout you don't." Dalton clipped out.

"Silly me I thought you'd like to know when your girl was in trouble."

"She's not my girl-" Dalton started, then he realized what Dex had just said. "Trouble? What the fuck do you mean she's in trouble?"

"Ah-ha, so you *do* care."

"Cut the shit, Evans, and explain yourself." Dalton used the three inches he had on Dex to tower over the man. Dex turned serious. "It's about damn time you started using your head for something other than a butt plug."

"I'm fucking serious, if you don't fork over whatever information you have Dexter, I am going to wipe the floor with you."

"I've been monitoring things up there. I wasn't sure that it was anything. If I had actually been sure there was a problem, you know I would have told you, you know that."

Dalton looked at Dex, really looked at him, and nodded. "Okay, so what happened?"

"First thing was that little fricking piece of shit that you had me do a check on? Ned Little? Well he was shanked in the little county lock-up where they had him. First murder they'd ever had there. Totally pinged with me."

"When was that?" Dalton asked.

"Three months ago."

"What about his cousin, Ricky?" Dalton asked.

"He demanded witness protection, which he didn't get."

"Why in the hell would he want that? What the hell kind of information would he have to give up?"

"Funnily enough, that was what the authorities asked. He said that Ned had been working with some people, and he knew too much. Ricky said that he needed protection, they had to explain to him if he didn't have information to exchange, he wasn't eligible."

Dalton snorted. Yep, definitely dumbshiterest. "So, he had no idea who was pulling Ned's strings?"

"Nope. That man would have sung like a canary if he had the slightest song," Dex sighed.

"You said first thing, what else was there?" Dalton asked.

"The second thing seemed unrelated too. One of the horses that Aurora had rehabilitated was fatally injured on the way back to its owner."

"Do you know what horse?"

"No, I didn't pay any attention. The horse was on its way back to Sacramento. There was an article in the Sacramento Bee that mentioned Aurora Chance's name. I have Google alerts on her."

"Was it a stallion?" Dalton persevered.

Dex tilted his head. "I'm sorry man, I really don't remember."

Dalton pushed back his concern for Aladdin and focused. "How did the horse die?"

"Somebody tampered with the brakes of the horse trailer, and the damn thing flipped on the freeway. An SUV crashed into it from behind killing the horse. It was a miracle that nobody was killed. After an investigation it was determined that the tampering had been done at a rest-stop in Placerville, which took Aurora and her folks off the hot seat."

"They actually thought someone from Valhalla might have something to do with hurting a horse?" Dalton asked incredulously.

Dex nodded. "I dipped into the highway patrol report. But the couple who were hauling the horse vouched for Aurora and her grandfather, so they immediately started looking for other suspects."

"Did they find one?"

"They got some footage of the man who did the tampering, but they still don't have anyone in custody."

"Those two things really seem suspicious," Dalton admitted.

"Especially with what I saw on the aircraft carrier this morning."

"There's more?" Dalton practically came out of his skin. Dalton couldn't respond fast enough. "It better be something minor."

Dex winced, then put his hands on his shoulders. "She's fine, that's the important thing."

The world stopped. He gripped Dex's forearm. "What do you mean? What happened."

"Her car was run off the road. But she wasn't hurt, just shaken up."

Black edged his vision. Dex's face swam in front of him

from a far-off tunnel. "How? How do you know that for sure?"

"I checked the EMT report. They didn't even need to take her to the hospital or anything. There was just a little bit of paint exchanged."

"Paint exchanged? You mean somebody hit her car? Where? Those mountain roads are treacherous."

Dex's eyes slid away from his. Dalton hit his friend's hands off his shoulders and grabbed him by the front of his t-shirt. "Tell me how the hell you knew what happened. Then you tell me exactly what occurred. Don't leave out one fucking detail."

Dalton shook his head, it felt like a train was roaring through it, he needed to clear it to be able to hear anything that Dex would say.

"I got an e-mail from Brody in my personal account. He knew I was keeping tabs. He knows my relation to you. She's good. She's fine. No hospital. Not a scratch on her. As a matter of fact, Brody said she was pissed as hell."

Dalton's breath hissed out.

"Are you sure?" He asked again thinking about when the sleepy driver had run her off the road and she'd been hurt.

"Man, I wouldn't lie to you," Dex said passionately. "Trust me. Your woman is fine. But somebody was out to get her."

Relieved, Dalton could breathe now. Then rage roared. "When did this happen? Did they find the fucker who did it?"

"Four days ago. I would have known sooner except we were in the jungle. Now in answer to your next question, nope, they haven't gotten him yet. She identified a black truck with California plates. They found it abandoned. It was stolen. Guess where from?"

Dalton slumped. "The rest stop in Placerville."

Dex nodded.

It had been years since he'd felt so torn. He needed Wyatt to be okay, and despite all the shit that his team had given him, he couldn't leave his young teammate. Never leaving a man behind wasn't just a motto, it was a deeply ingrained belief that was tattooed on his soul. Somewhere in the inside of his lizard brain, Dalton didn't think that Wyatt would come out of this whole without his ass planted here in the waiting room.

That stopped him up short.

"You need to leave? Want me to go get Gray?" Dex asked.

Dalton eased into the chair next to Hunter. "I'll talk to Gray after we hear the good word about Wyatt."

Hunter gave him a slow smile.

"Good man," he said. "You being here will make a difference."

Those words felt right. He'd changed. When had that happened?

178

11

Once again, she felt like she was in a trance. Mornings were no longer her friend. She pushed her hair out of her face, too tired to even throw it into a pony tail. On auto-pilot, she stretched past her grandfather for the coffee pot, then the smell reached her, and she shuddered.

"Honey sit down before you fall down." Gunnar guided her to the kitchen chair and Aurora plopped down, resting her head on the table. Last night she couldn't get to sleep, and this morning was awful. Suddenly, the wonderful aroma of ginger filled the air as her grandfather put a mug of tea in front of her. She heard the toaster ping, and she soon had some dry toast set beside her. She missed butter, but it was her enemy.

Slowly she sipped and chewed until her stomach settled and the fog lifted.

"Better?" Gunnar asked.

She smiled. "Much. Thanks for all of the T.L.C."

"I love taking care of you, Darlin'. You remind me of your

grandmother. She was still throwing up until the last month of her pregnancy."

Aurora looked at him in horror. The idea of being big as a house as she heaved over the toilet made her want to cry. "Please tell me that's not true."

"Sorry, but it is. Each morning, I was on basin patrol, because she couldn't make it to the bathroom." Aurora felt sick to her stomach just thinking about it. "That's why you need Dalton here to take care of you, Aurora."

She looked at her Grandfather's resolute expression. This was a familiar refrain, and despite all her attempts she hadn't been able to change his mind.

Deflect.

Deflect.

Deflect.

"I can handle it if you want to eat some bacon today, the smell won't bother me, really," she smiled at him.

"Don't you mean my turkey bacon?" he asked slyly.

She barely stopped herself from cringing. "What are you talking about?"

"I'll tell you what I'm talking about. When I went to pick up supplies at the Safeway, Kim wanted to know why I wasn't buying turkey bacon. She was also curious as to why I was buying whole milk, when you normally buy non-fat milk. You care to explain that to me?"

"Kim must be confusing me with another customer."

"Nope, when we went to coffee, she and I had a long conversation. There was no confusion at all."

Kim and Granddad were way too friendly, that's why she avoided her line and checked out with Barb.

Really? Did Kim really have to spill the beans? Fu-Fudgenuggets.

Aurora sighed.

Heck, she even had to start thinking in kid friendly terms. Aurora's hormone addled mind soon had her smiling dreamily.

"What are you grinning about?" Gunnar asked tenderly. "I've been snookered for a year and a half and you can't have coffee. I don't see why we're both over here grinning."

Aurora lovingly smoothed her hand over the swell of her stomach and beamed at her grandfather. "Because we are both softies. In just under four months we're going to be able to hold this little guy."

"It shouldn't just be us holding him. You need to call Dalton." Gunnar pushed away from the table. "It isn't right Aurora Dawn, you know better than this."

Aurora winced. It wasn't often that her grandfather threw down with her dreaded middle name, but when he did, he was dead-set serious. She opened her mouth to explain, but her mouth wouldn't work. She tried to swallow but couldn't. Finally, she eked out words.

"I do know better. But you don't understand. Having another child will break him," she whispered hoarsely. "I hate the idea of putting the man I love through that kind of pain."

"Another child?" he said slowly.

Gunnar was crouched in front of her before she could even blink. "Tell me, darlin'. Help me understand."

"Dalton lost his baby, his little girl. He showed me pictures of her holding her little stuffed baby seal. She was beautiful. So beautiful. Black hair and blue eyes, she was the image of him. She was only three years old when she died." Her lip trembled. "Oh Grandpa. He doesn't have room in his heart for another child."

Gunnar gripped her shoulder. "That doesn't sound like the man I know."

Aurora blinked back a storm of tears. "Grandpa, he doesn't believe in himself. He thinks he would fail to love another child. But I'm like you, I can't believe it's true either." She hiccupped a sob, and leaned forward, cradling her stomach with both arms. She looked up. "But what if he's right? What if he tries and fails? How can I put Dalton through that? How I could I set him up for that type of failure?"

God, just saying it about killed her. Night after night she'd cried as she caressed her tummy. Her little boy was precious, he was going to be loved to the moon and back, just maybe not by his daddy.

Aurora fell forward into her Granddad's waiting arms. She didn't even know what she was saying, only what she was feeling. She pictured Dalton as he'd told her that he could never love another child, that he had nothing left to give. He was so damn guarded. She'd held him when he'd cried as he'd said that he'd buried his soul with Reagan's body. When he'd told her that she didn't know who hurt worse, him or her as she realized that there was never a possibility of a shared future.

Gunnar finally got her sitting back up in her chair and gave her a napkin to blow her nose. When Aurora's trembling finally stopped, he sat back down and took both her hands in his.

"He knew me Grandpa, he didn't say the words, but they were in his eyes. He knew I was the type who was going to want a corral full of kids."

"One thing I don't understand, why did he leave you when he didn't know you were pregnant?" Gunnar asked.

Aurora sighed. "It took me a while to figure that out. It's guilt. He doesn't think he's worthy of being happy. He thinks he's responsible for Reagan's death." Tears threatened, and she blew her nose again.

They sat there for a long time and she took in the comfort that her grandfather offered. Then she felt her son move. The little flutters had just started in the last week.

"He's moving?"

"Yep." Aurora bit her lip, willing herself not to cry again. She so wanted to share this with Dalton. She wanted him to have joy and love in his life. Nobody deserved it more.

"When are you going to tell him?"

Aurora gave a watery laugh. She was so lucky to have her grandfather. He knew her inside and out.

"So, you knew that despite all my big protests I was going to tell him, huh?"

"You always do the right thing," he smiled with pride.

"I have to figure out the way to tell him in the most loving way."

"You know he's going to love him because he's Reagan's little brother, have you thought of that?"

She nodded. She thought of the pictures she'd seen of the little girl and imagined how their son would most likely look like her.

Gunnar leaned forward and kissed her forehead. "If you want me to be with you when you tell him, I will."

Aurora laughed. It felt good.

"I'm serious," Gunnar said.

"I know you are. But I think I can manage that on my own. I just have to figure out what to say."

"And even if he doesn't want to be in his boy's life, you have all of us who'll be here for him."

"I always knew that," Aurora smiled.

"Good, because tonight Tate and your other uncle Zebadiah will be here for dinner along with all three of your cousins. We've invited the good sheriff to join us."

"Three? You mean Lindy too?" Lindy Dressler worked in Los Angeles on the SWAT team.

"Yep, Lindy too. Can't imagine why she might have taken some vacation to visit her family, can you?" He raised one bushy eyebrow.

"But-"

"What did you expect?" Gunnar's blue eyes were the color of steel. "There is something going on around here, and it didn't end with Ned Little going to jail."

AURORA WANDERED into the barn and her eye immediately went to the end of the aisle and saw the closed door to the tack room. It called to her. It was the last place she and Dalton had made love, in the hour before he had left the ranch for good. Maybe if she could just untangle what he'd said that afternoon, she'd figure out the right way to tell him about their son.

She walked purposefully down the long aisle and opened the tack room door and was immediately transported back in time.

"Sunshine, you stay here," Dalton smoothed his hands down her arms. "I'm going to talk to your grandfather."

"I'm not twelve," she huffed in amusement.

His hands came up and cupped her face. "We've been in the stables for three hours. He's going to know why. I need to talk to him, man to man."

"Dalton, my grandfather has eyes, he knows we're lovers. And if he didn't, Uncle Tate has told him."

"I still need to go and talk to him." Dalton was resolute.

It took everything she had not to roll her eyes. Then he stroked her bottom lip with his thumb. "Please Aurora, I have to do this."

He was so damn solemn, how could she do anything but say yes? She nodded. Dalton dipped down and gave her a toe-tingling kiss. She whimpered when he lifted his head.

"Give me twenty minutes, and then come to the house, okay?"

She watched as he left the tack room. She looked around and realized she would never be able to come into this room again without thinking of Dalton, of the gentle and passionate storm they had created together in one another's arms. Of course, he'd already put the saddle back up on the wall and helped her fold up the blankets. And, of course, being a guy, he thought the blankets could be put back onto the shelf with the other clean ones. Silly man.

She set those on the grain bin, then went over to Vertigo and gave him some love, as well as Troy, Siren, Lucky and, of course, Aladdin.

"So, would you also insist on going and talking to your girl's grandfather?" she asked the big stallion. She grinned when he shook his big head. It was almost as if he could understand her. Maybe he could.

"I like you Aladdin. You're my kind of horse."

Vertigo whinnied from the stall over. She looked at him and he snorted. "What, are you saying you would do what Dalton's doing?" Vertigo stamped his foot.

"God save me from hard-headed males."

She went down the row and gave pats and scratches. She

should be monitoring to see if they were all in good health, but her mind was on what was possibly being said at the house.

"Bloody hell." She pulled out her phone from her back pocket and checked the time. Fourteen minutes. She hustled and grabbed the blankets, so she could throw them in the wash, as she reached the barn door she paused.

"Really? You're really going to rub Grandpa's nose in it?" God she was an idiot. She was not going to bring the soiled blankets that smelled of sex into the house.

She rushed back to the tack room and shoved the blankets into the laundry bin, and then launched herself toward the house. When she noted that Gunnar's car was missing from the drive she slowed down.

Was he that mad?

She tried to picture what had gone down between the two men and for the life of her she couldn't. What could have made her grandfather leave? She took the porch steps two at a time and opened the screen door. She found Dalton sitting at the kitchen table.

"What happened?"

"Everything's fine," he assured her.

"It's not fine if my Grandpa isn't here."

Dalton held out her hand and she grasped it. He tugged her onto his lap. "He left to give us some privacy."

She sat down on one knee, she couldn't bring herself to relax into his hold. "You're leaving, aren't you?"

He made a move toward her hair, as if to push it behind her ear, then pulled back. "Yes," he agreed.

"Tonight."

He nodded.

"Now," she whispered.

He leaned his forehead against hers. "Yes," his voice was low.

She couldn't stop the next words. She tried, but they spewed forth like a lava from a volcano. "Could I come with you?"

His eyes were indigo again. "I'm going to miss you so much."

That was her answer. She tried to hold back the tears, and she did, barely.

His eyes turned heavenward, then he looked back at her. "Aurora-" he started

"It's okay," she interrupted. Then she swallowed and gave a wan smile. "Just remember, you always have a safe place to come back to, I need you to know that, okay?"

He gave her a half smile back, and she knew he never intended to return. He was so buried in grief he was never going to break free.

"I'm so sorry, Aurora. Please say I didn't hurt you."

She finally relaxed in his hold and cupped his cheek, then whispered a kiss over his sculpted lips. "I don't regret one moment of our time together." She was content, knowing that she had spoken the truth.

"You're a special woman."

"I hope you know that you're special too." God, how she wished she could tell him that she loved him, but she knew that would just be a burden.

"I'm glad you think that, Sunshine."

She got up from his lap and tugged at his arm. "Do you need help packing?"

The corner of his mouth kicked up. "You're just trying to get your hands on my skivvies."

"Always," she might have grinned, but she died a little on the inside.

SHE USED the soft brush around Aladdin's face. She'd started working with her favorite horse after she finished crying in the tack room. These pregnancy hormones were going to be the death of her.

She dropped the brush and Aladdin jerked when her cell phone rang. She looked at the display.

"It's okay Baby. It'll only be a minute. It's Grandpa," she reassured the horse.

"I'll be on-time for dinner this time, I promise. I thought everyone was arriving at six-thirty. It isn't even six yet."

"Thought I'd let you know that there are two trucks coming up the drive. One I recognize and one I don't."

"Okay, give me five, and I'll come in and help you get dinner on the table," she reassured her grandfather.

"Hold up. The first truck is a beat-up baby blue Chevy."

As soon as the words were out of his mouth, her blood turned to ice, and her left hand spanned her stomach. What was Dalton doing here? Worse. She hadn't figured out anything to tell him.

"Aurora, you still there?"

"I'm here. Just considering all of my options."

"Seems like fate has taken a hand."

Her eyes narrowed.

"Grandpa am I hearing glee in your voice?"

"No baby girl, you're not," Gunnar sighed. "Just know that in fifteen minutes there will be a house full of Dressler's as well as one big Olsen who'll have your back. So, I want you to wait before you come up to the house."

"That's not-"

She heard what sounded like a knock on the front door. "Just do what I tell you and sit tight. Play with your horsies little girl."

She snorted with laughter at her grandfather's long-ago refrain. He hung up, and she turned back to her horsie.

"What do you think, Aladdin? Should you and I play?" She bent down and picked up the soft brush off the ground. Aurora did long sweeping strokes along the length of Aladdin's body, she didn't know who she was trying to soothe more, the stallion or herself.

She'd expected to be the one to determine when they'd see each other again. What was she going to say? How was he going to react? Please God, let him be happy.

SHE LOOKED AT THE TIME. Six-forty-five. She breathed deeply as she passed the corral and made her way to the ranch house. She counted five trucks and the sheriff's SUV parked in front.

Great.

She thanked all the powers that be that she'd grabbed her grandfather's shearling coat on the way to the barn. It hid her swelling stomach better than her own coat. Aurora climbed the steps just a little more slowly than she had five months ago, her breath fogged in the cold air. She opened the door and saw Lindy waiting for her in the kitchen. Her cousin's eyes immediately lowered to her stomach, then they lifted with a twinkle.

"Hiding something?" she asked as she opened her arms.

Aurora's eyes darted to the closed kitchen door. "They all in the living room?"

Lindy nodded, then waggled her fingers. Aurora walked around the kitchen table and stepped into a big hug. "I've missed you," Aurora said.

"Missed you more." Lindy pulled back and looked at her. "Why am I just hearing about this bullshit now? I should have been told as soon as that weasel was offed."

"Because you would have just rushed up here, is why." Aurora whispered. She really didn't want any of the testosterone in the other room to hear her. "I wanted you to burn your time off for when the baby arrived."

They stood there staring at one another. Aurora took a deep breath.

"Oh God, I need a Tums."

Lindy laughed.

"That's not nice. You're not supposed to pick on me." Aurora glared at her cousin as she went to the cupboard and got down the bottle that was recently her best friend.

"Your baby daddy is gorgeous. Is that supportive enough?"

Aurora grimaced at Lindy, then spilled out three tablets instead of just one.

"Aurora, this is going to be okay," Lindy said as she put her arm around her. Aurora leaned her head against Lindy's shoulder.

"The other men he brought with him are fine too. Find out their status for me, will you?"

"What other men?"

"Your guy brought in reinforcements. Seems like he's taking this as seriously as I am."

"Oh God," Aurora moaned. She shook out two more Tums.

Lindy laughed and gave her one more supportive hug.

"All we need is Crystal here, and it will seem like old times," Aurora gave a sickly grin.

Buck up girl, you can do this.

"Do you want me to go in first? That way you and the bump will be less noticeable?"

"I've got Grandpa's coat," Aurora said. She pulled it tighter around herself.

"Sure, Gramps keeps it one hundred and ten in here and you're wearing that, I'm sure nobody will think it's odd. Come on kid, follow me." Lindy gave her one more side hug, then pushed open the swinging kitchen door.

All conversation stopped as eight sets of male eyes turned to look at them. Nope, make that nine. There was a big quiet Hispanic man sitting on Grandma's loveseat, he was watching everything. Meanwhile poor Brody was literally cornered by Uncle Tate, Dalton and one other man she didn't recognize.

"We've been waiting for you," Gunnar said. He got up off the sofa where he had been sitting with Rhys and Luke. The other man stood up from the loveseat. "Let me introduce you to our new guests," her grandfather said. "They're teammates of Dalton's."

That was as obvious as the nose on her face.

Dalton and the two other men moved forward. They didn't invade her personal space, but it felt like she and Dalton were the only two people in the room.

"Hello Aurora," his voice had every one of her nerve endings flaring to life. She opened and shut her hands in reflex.

"Hi Dalton." Could he hear the longing in her voice?

"We've heard about some of the problems you've been having. It sounds like they didn't die down with the capture of Ned Little. We're here to help."

Her heart plummeted. Gunnar's arm was immediately around her waist to help keep her standing up. Somehow, he'd known that her knees had turned to jelly. Once again Dalton wasn't here for her, at least not really, he was just here because of his sense of chivalry.

Dalton frowned at her. "Are you okay? They said you weren't injured."

"I'm fine," she said quietly.

He moved forward, and she shrank backwards. Dalton looked like she had hit him. "Aurora?"

One of his friends pulled him back. "Why don't you introduce us?"

She watched as Dalton gathered himself. She liked that he was affected by their reunion. "Aurora, these are two of my teammates." He nodded to the man on his right, "this is Hunter Diaz," then he pointed his thumb at the other man with the lighter hair. "This is Dex Evans."

It took a moment for her to put two and two together. "I suppose I have you to thank for Dalton's presence?" she asked.

Dex opened his mouth to answer, but Dalton spoke first. "I haven't been able to get you out of my head," he said baldly.

Her grandfather's arm squeezed her gently as she waited for Dalton to continue, but he didn't.

Dex and Hunter shared a look, then Dex sighed. "I was the one who was feeding Dalton information about Ned

Little and his cousin Ricky. After Dalton came back to San Diego his mind was still hung up on you."

Her eyes cut to Dalton. He was looking at her like his life depended on her. Dex continued.

"After Ned's death in prison, Brody and I kept in touch, that's how I knew about you being run off the road."

"We would have been here as soon as it happened, but we were on a mission. Communication was practically non-existent," Dalton said tightly. "Brody said you weren't hurt, is that true?"

That was the first time she really looked at him. He looked awful. Awful and beautiful. She'd only ever seen him clean-shaven or with five-o'clock shadow, now he had scruff. He had bruises under his eyes from lack of sleep, and he'd lost weight.

"I'm fine."

"You don't look fine. You're flushed." He stared at her intensely. Then his eyes traveled downwards. She saw the exact moment he realized what she'd been hiding.

12

PREGNANT!

Aurora was pregnant. In a trance, he moved forward. He speared a dark glance at Gunnar who gave back as good as he got. "Let go of her," he Dalton growled at Gunnar.

"Calm down," the older man growled back.

He saw Aurora blanch. She already had a sheen of perspiration on her forehead and seeing her face drain of color scared the piss out of him.

"Are you all right, Sunshine?" He was torn between gentle, frightened and angry. His friends read him, and Hunter put his hand on Dalton's shoulder. He shrugged it off and took a step forward.

"Answer me. Are you okay? You look like you're ready to fall down."

He winced when Aurora grimaced.

"I'm fine Dalton."

A woman he didn't know pushed in front of Aurora. "Why don't we take this into the kitchen? We can get her some ginger tea."

"I don't need any tea," Aurora said irritably. Then Dalton saw her swallow convulsively.

"Come on Honey, I'll get the kettle on." Gunnar said as he started turning Aurora toward the kitchen, which was when she threw up her hands.

"Enough. I can walk all by myself like a big girl. I can also make my own tea. I just need out of this damn coat." Dalton was riveted as she pushed off the man's shearling jacket and her newly shaped body was exposed. Where she was once long and lean, she was now beautifully rounded with life. "Dalton, follow me, I don't think we need an audience."

She was ramrod straight as she held open the swinging door for him. After he entered, she started toward the stove.

"Sit down before you fall down," he said as he pulled out one of the sturdy wooden kitchen chairs.

Aurora contemplated it, then looked up at him, nodded and sat down. "The tea's in the cupboard to the right of the sink."

Dalton went over to the front door and opened it, leaving open the screen door. He heard her sigh of contentment.

"That feels wonderful."

"You only get five minutes worth," he warned. "What the hell were you doing wearing that coat around a house that feels like a sauna?" He wasn't surprised when she didn't answer. He filled the kettle with water, pulled down the tea, spotted the bottle of Tums on the counter and got her a glass of ice water. He set the water and bottle of Tums on the table in front of her then sat down in the chair across the table from her.

Aurora took a sip of the water and then shook out a tablet and ate it.

He waited. Was he waiting for her to feel better, or was he was he trying to figure out what in the fuck he could possibly say? She bit her lip. "Dalton," she started.

The kitchen door opened. It was the dark-haired woman. "Everything okay in here?"

Aurora whipped around in her chair. "Go away, Lindy. If I needed the police I'd call nine-one-one." Her voice cracked. Lindy looked helplessly over Aurora's head at Dalton.

"Everything's going to be just fine," he assured her. The door eased quietly close behind her.

Dalton saw where Aurora's hands were trembling. Dalton knew he what he was going to do. Then the kettle sounded. He got up and made her tea and brought it back to the table and set it in front of her.

"Thank you," she said softly, she made a grab toward the mug, but pulled back because her hands were shaking. Enough already. He picked her up out of her chair and sat down in it with her in his lap.

"Leave the tea."

"I can't seem to stop shaking so I might as well."

"In that case, tell me a story, Sunshine."

She blew out a breath and gave him a helpless stare.

"Okay, I'll start. Is it safe to say we're having a child in a little less than four months?" he smiled solemnly.

She placed her small, capable hand on his heart. "Yes. Our son."

A son. A son. A baby boy. He looked down at her stomach and tried to wrap his head it. Wrap his head around him. Five months. Five months that he had missed. Had Aurora-?

"Have you picked out a name?" Dalton asked.

"I wouldn't choose a name without you."

The relief that crashed through him was like a wave at Waimea Bay. His arm clutched her close and his head found the hollow of her neck. "When? When were you going to tell me?"

"I was going to tell you this month."

"Why did you wait so long?"

She looked at him sadly, her diamond black eyes filled with sorrow and hope. How was that even possible? "Dalton, I know you didn't want another child after Reagan, but I couldn't have your son and not tell you. That wouldn't be right. Even if you were never planning on coming back."

He could barely hear her over the pounding of his heart. When his head cleared her words registered.

He looked at her beloved face. "Aurora, I was coming back to you."

She didn't answer, he could see the doubt in her expression. He cupped her cheeks.

"It's true, Sunshine. These last five months have been hell for me. You have been on my mind constantly. You've never been out of my heart. I was coming back." He needed her to believe him, but she didn't respond.

"Aurora, I know everything I said before." He softly raked his fingers through her hair and kissed her temple. "The guilt that I lived with shadowed every day of my life until the moment you fell at my feet."

"I felt your guilt. I felt your pain." Her was subdued and now she wasn't even looking at him.

He had to get through to her. He had to.

"Aurora, I met a woman on my last mission." Aurora's lashes flew upwards, her eyes clashed with his. "She was a mother protecting her children."

"Oh," she said in understanding.

"I needed to make sure she and her little boy and girl were safe, but all the time I couldn't help thinking of you. How you would be just as strong and fierce. I had been longing for you, and then God put a sign in front of me, that even *I* couldn't ignore. I was coming back for you. There was no way I was staying away 1 second longer. I love you, Aurora. You're my life."

Aurora's smile was bleak.

"What? Don't you believe me?"

Her hand stroked upwards and circled the back of his neck, massaging his nape. "But it's not just me anymore." Her eyes were wet with tears. Then she shivered, and he realized the door was still open.

Dalton pulled her hand away and kissed her palm. He eased her up, and then sat her back down on the chair and went to shut the door. When he got back he saw her sitting there, hunched over, holding her tummy. He knelt down in front of her and pulled her cold hands into his. He blew on them, then gently put them back down to rest on her swollen stomach.

"Can you look at me?" he asked.

She looked up. "I love you, Dalton. I was falling hard for you when we walked up that hill that first day, but when I saw you with Taylor and Mark, you were it for me. I wanted you in my life forever. But that wasn't what you wanted." Her voice quaked. "So, I took what happiness I could, and hopefully I gave some back."

"How could you doubt that?"

He watched as a lone tear dripped down her face. "At first, I wanted to break through those walls of yours, but then I realized they were your protection from pain. I never wanted you to hurt."

"Fuck that," he said vehemently. "I needed to feel that pain, walk through it, and find the courage to embrace the beauty of you." She opened her mouth to say more, but he gently touched her lips with his fingers. "And don't think I didn't hear you, Love. I did." His fingers lightly traced down until they rested on top of her tummy.

His. His boy.

His large hand spanned over both of hers, she moved them, covering his with hers. He felt the warmth emanating from her womb. He trembled.

Dalton had so many emotions roiling around inside of him. Despite everything there was still some resentment that she hadn't told him, that he'd had to find out this way. But he knew that she also felt abandoned by him. But, this was his woman, Aurora would be able to handle each one of them. They would be able to work through everything, because there was love. But right now, he needed to tell her what she most needed to hear.

"Never doubt that I love our son. The only regret I have is that I haven't been here for the last five months while you nurtured him under your heart."

"Really?" Her voice was nothing more than a puff of air.

He leaned forward and kissed her raspberry red lips.

"Really."

She hesitated, then asked, "What about Reagan Elizabeth?"

Feeling the pulse of life under his palm there wasn't a doubt in his mind that his beloved daughter wasn't beside him, wanting this child for him. He closed his eyes and swore he could hear chimes. Yes, his daughter would adore having a baby brother.

"I want our son to know about his big sister," Dalton said.

Aurora let out a huge sob and grabbed him around his neck. "I wanted that too. I wanted that too."

As he held her, he whispered in her ear. "I'm scared Sunshine."

"I know. I know, Honey. But it's going to be okay. I promise."

She couldn't make that promise, but maybe between the two of them they could keep their son safe. And for damn sure, he knew their son would always feel loved.

"Seriously, I don't want tea."

"Crackers?" Dalton said holding up a package of saltines he found in the cupboard.

Aurora shook her head and fought back a smile. She watched as he went to the fridge. She followed him and put her hand over his. "Seriously, I'm fine now. Are you stalling?"

He looked down at her. "I have five months of caretaking to make up for."

She heard the disquiet in his voice. "And that upsets you, doesn't it?"

"Aurora, I get why you waited. Hell, I would have done the same thing in your shoes if I had heard all the shit I spewed." Dalton dragged his hand threw his blue-black hair. "But it still doesn't..."

"Just say it."

Instead he wrapped an arm around her neck and drew her close. He slammed his lips over hers. Heat. The power and passion of this man hit her like a tsunami. She opened her mouth and his tongue dipped in, mating with hers.

He was conveying every one of his emotions, his pain was raw, and she wrapped him close to her, but she felt his anger too, even though his kiss did nothing but evoke heat and hunger. One hand cupped the back of her head, positioning her so that he could mold their mouths together, while the other hand snuck under her sweater. When he touched the swell of her abdomen, that was when everything changed.

His rough and powerful kiss turned languid. She tasted wonder. He stroked her hair and sipped at her lips. She clung to him, undone by the reverence in his touch. Finally, he pulled away.

"I'm sorry," he whispered.

It took a full minute for her to compute his words. "Why are you sorry?"

"I was angry when we started."

"Oh."

He looked at her for a long moment and then laughed. "Come to think of it, there was a little bit of angry kissing going on, on your side too."

"Huh, you're right. There was." She hadn't really realized she'd been pissed off at him, she'd thought she'd been feeling sad and sorry, not angry.

He put his knuckles under her chin and tilted her head up. "I'm not sure this is going to be all solved today, but we can agree on the fact we love each other, and we love our son."

She sagged against him. "Oh yeah. I do love you. So much."

He stroked her cheek. "I have the world here in my arms."

It took long moments for Aurora to rouse herself out of this state of bliss. She realized that Lindy would be checking on them soon, if not Gunnar himself.

"We need to go into the other room. This whole little party is about me."

"I know it is. That's why I brought reinforcements."

"I still don't understand how you were watching over me, if you only just decided to come back to me. Care to clue a girl in?"

"His name is Dexter Evans, aka the housemother. He's the one I tapped to get information on Ned in the first place. He did a lot of the digging." He tried to open the refrigerator, so she leaned against it.

"That still doesn't explain why the Scooby Gang is here."

She didn't miss him wince. "If I tell you that I was coming no matter what, will you believe me?"

"Absolutely," she said, and he frowned.

"Dalton. You've never lied to me. You're the most honorable man I have ever met."

She watched as he relaxed. "Thank God you think that, because this just seems a little too coincidental, I would be questioning it."

"You're a cynic," she grinned.

"You're an optimist. You believe in fairytales and happily-ever-afters."

She went up on tiptoes and pressed a long kiss against his sexy-as-sin lips. "Damn right I do, and they're coming true."

"My teammates, who by the way don't want to be referred to as the Scooby Gang, are here because we're going to take down and pulverize whoever is out after you. Dex knew that you were important to me. He believes in happily-ever-afters and knew you were my woman before I got it through my thick head. Therefore, you were part of the Black Dawn family. He just keeps an eye on all of us, and when things started pinging, like Ned Little dying in jail, Dex started to get concerned."

She was going melt into a puddle of goo. "He thinks of me as a part of your team's family?"

Dalton kissed the tip of her nose. "You are a part of our family."

"Okay, I won't call them the Scooby Gang."

"That'd be for the best. Let's go face the hoard."

13

THE SCOOBY GANG, LINDY AND UNCLE TATE WERE THE FIRST heads to turn when the kitchen door silently opened. It must be a training thing. She saw there was a distinct delineation in the room, 'The Professionals' and the others. She couldn't help but grin, because Brody hadn't made the cut. Uncle Tate, Hunter, Dex and Lindy were standing in the farthest corner from the big bay window. She approved of the way that Hunter and Dex immediately zeroed in on Dalton. They were good friends to her man.

Gunnar, meanwhile, had been waiting by the kitchen door.

"Everything good?" He asked as he looked her up and down. He broke into a bright smile. "Oh yeah, everything's really good." Gunnar swept her into a huge hug, careful of her tummy. She knew her grandfather was probably grinning like a loon at Dalton, over her head.

"So, you're here to stay?" he asked Dalton.

Damn.

They hadn't discussed logistics.

"First thing is stopping whoever is behind the attempts on Aurora's life. Then Aurora and I need to talk about our future. But, rest assured, it will be together. Nothing will ever tear me away from your granddaughter. Nothing." Aurora felt like a rock was lifted off her shoulders, one that she hadn't even realized was there.

Gunnar gave her one last squeeze, then released her to Dalton's embrace.

"Let's get you sitting down," Dalton said as he guided her to the sofa.

"You know I'm not an invalid, right?" she teased her Irish hero.

"I know that you looked like you were going to fall over only forty-five minutes ago, so humor me. Anyway, you're the leading lady so people need to congregate around you."

"Great," she muttered. In an 'Eagle Scout Gentleman' fashion, he settled her onto the couch. When he remained standing, she yanked on his hand.

"Hmmm?"

"If I'm the leading lady, your butt is seated next to mine," she said sotto voice.

He looked ready to protest, then she smoothed her hand over her tummy and raised her eyebrow. He immediately sat down beside her. She figured she had about three days where she could pull this crap, so she'd take advantage while she could. Dalton put his arm around her and kissed her temple.

"It's going to be all right, Sunshine."

Somehow, Dalton performed magic, because the youngest, tallest and broadest SEAL suddenly crouched down in front of them. He looked a little scary, until a dazzling white smile illuminated his face.

"I don't know if you remember my name," he started.

"Hunter Diaz," Aurora smiled back.

"That's me. I've known Dalton since we attended BUD/S together. He was an old man and needed a younger friend to help him through."

Dalton snorted.

"I wanted to say how happy I am to finally meet you. Dalton has been a sorry S.O.B. to work with these last five months. So far Dex and I are the only representatives of Black Dawn, but I want you to know that if we need more manpower, you've got more of our teammates chomping at the bit to come up and help sort things out."

Aurora stared at him. He was serious. How could that be? A team of Navy SEAL's coming up to help her for her car being driven off the road?

"But isn't that out of your scope of operation?" she asked.

"Aurora, SEALs never operate in an official capacity on American soil, so we're just here on a little R&R here in Lake Tahoe," Dex said as he ambled over. "Hunter's going to lose money at the penny slots, and I'm going to win money at the craps table." Dex said with a wicked twinkle in his eye.

"If you tell anybody that I play the penny slots we're going to have a serious talk outside the mess hall," Hunter said as he stood up and towered over Dex.

"Yep, penny slots. Sorry man, I call 'em like I see 'em."

Aurora giggled. At that point she realized that everyone had gathered round. They were either in the chairs on either side of the couch where she and Dalton were sitting, or on the loveseat across from her. Well, except for Brody and her cousins. She didn't think she'd ever seen her cousins, Rhys and Luke, actually sitting down unless it was in a saddle. Currently, they were leaning over the back of the loveseat tugging at Lindy's hair, as she sat beside Erwin. Those young men were going to get clocked for sure.

Brody went to the middle of the room and looked up at Hunter and Dex who were still standing in front of the couch. "Please take a seat," he said pompously.

"Absolutely," Dex grinned. "I'm sitting next to Aurora." He plopped next to her and put his arm around her shoulders. Dalton shoved it off. Hunter sat on the other side of Dalton. She looked up at Brody to see what he would do next. It should be interesting.

He pulled out a little notebook.

"I see a few new faces, so I'm going to recap the pertinent details of the case."

She'd never heard Sheriff Brody sound so official.

"Four months ago, Ned Little was wounded with a sharpened piece of plastic in the Washoe County Detention Facility. The corrections' officers were unable to determine who killed him. Also residing in the facility was his cousin Ricky Little. When Ned died, Ricky asked for witness protection. It was determined he had no relevant information to provide to prosecutors to the murder of Hal Dockins or any other schemes that Ned Little might have been involved in. However, Ricky insisted that somebody besides his cousin wanted Aurora harmed."

Dalton sat forward and peered around Aurora, glaring at Dex. "Did you know about this?"

"It was nothing but hearsay that went nowhere," Dex sighed. "But I have feelers out."

Brody frowned. "What do you mean you have feelers out?" he demanded. "It was determined by my office and by the Washoe County DA that there was nothing to Ricky Little's claims."

"Well obviously someone is still after her, so I would say that you and the DA are wrong, wouldn't you Brody?" Dalton said sarcastically. He turned back to glare at his friend. "Now tell me what your feelers saying." he demanded.

"The little shit's trail, pun intended, was tougher to track because he used false names," Dex explained. "Some friends have been sending his picture to all of the ranches throughout the Western United States. Whoever Ned was in league with won't tell us that he worked at their place, but we're narrowing it down to all the places he *has* worked. Then we'll get an idea of the gap and see if we can piece together where he might have been when he met the bad guys."

Aurora kind of kept up with what Dex was saying...kind of. "Sounds convoluted," she said to Dex.

"Dex's theories always are," Hunter said. "But give him a Rubik's cube and he can solve it."

"What I meant was-" Dex started.

"Please don't explain again, I got the gist of it," she said she interrupted him.

Her ears might be bleeding if he started talking again. She was pretty sure she understood she understood him.

Brody cleared his throat, clearly not happy that the focus had shifted from him.

"Both the Sacramento and Placerville authorities are on the lookout for the person responsible for tampering with the horse trailer."

Dalton tapped her on the shoulder and leaned in to whisper in her ear. "Which horse died?" he asked.

"Lucky." She felt the tears coming on, and it wasn't because of pregnancy hormones. The thought that someone could have purposefully killed that beautiful black mare left her feeling bewildered. How could someone do that?

"We're going to get them," Dalton whispered. "I promise you."

"Damn right we will," Dex said beside her.

She saw Hunter, on the other side of Dalton, nod his head in agreement.

It was like she'd just been welcomed into another family.

Brody cleared his throat. He was giving them the evil eye, so she tuned into him again.

"As for the black truck that side-swiped you, we have a little bit more information on that. It was stolen from a Marcus Holt who was in Placerville the same day that the horse trailer was tampered with. The Placerville sheriff's department has had an APB out on the truck since then."

"Was something abandoned in it's place?" Hunter asked.

"What do you mean?" Brody gave him a confused look.

"If he didn't leave something behind when he stole the truck, that means there had to be two people involved, or he took an Uber to the rest stop."

A flush crept up the Sheriff's face. "You have a point," he admitted to the big SEAL. "I don't think a taxi or Uber were probably how he got to the rest station."

"Maybe he used LYFT." Rhys said.

Lindy grabbed the arm of her huge young cousin who had been teasing her hair and yanked him over the back of the couch. "We really don't need color commentary from the peanut gallery, got it?" she growled. "Please continue Sheriff, the rundown you're providing is helping to give us a complete picture." She let go of her cousin who was then punched in the arm by his grinning brother.

"Well, I think you all know that we fished the black truck out of a ditch this side of Squaw Valley. It was wiped clean of prints. We have nothing to go on after that."

The Sheriff looked beaten down. Aurora wanted to make him feel better, but she couldn't think of anything to say.

"All is not lost," Dex said cheerfully. "Jack is going to check in tomorrow with some info on Ned's whereabouts for the last couple of years. Between Jack and his dad, there is no way anybody will not tell everything they know."

"Who's Jack?" Gunnar asked.

"Jack Preston, he and his step-father owns one of the biggest spreads in central Texas. It's mostly cattle, but-"

"But they have a hell of a horse ranch," Gunnar finished for Dex. "Tate, haven't you done business with them?"

"I have," Tate nodded. "Richard Preston is a good man. Fair. Even though he's off in the middle of nowhere and a Texan," he teased. "Preston seems to know everybody West of the Rockies."

Brody brightened at the idea that there might be a lead. "Do you think you really think he might be able to find something out about Ned's whereabouts during those missing two years?"

"I'm betting between Jack's dad's connections and Dex's magic, they'll find out something," Hunter assured the older man.

God, that would be a relief. She wanted this madness to end.

"You're going to call him tomorrow?" Gunnar asked Dex.

"I have a Skype call set-up with the Preston's tomorrow morning," Dex answered.

"I want to be in on it," Brody immediately said.

Aurora looked around the room, almost everybody in

the room nodded or raised their hand to indicate they wanted in on the call. The only hold-outs were her cousins Luke and Rhys, which was good, because she needed them working the ranch since Erwin was going to be in on the call as well.

"I'll make you breakfast tomorrow and we'll do it here," Gunnar announced.

"Breakfast trumps the big screen in my conference room," Brody said as he patted his non-existent stomach. "Apple flapjacks?"

"Whatever Aurora wants," Gunnar said.

Brody gave her a once over pausing on her large stomach, and once again the man flushed. "What was I thinking, of course Aurora gets to decide. What time should I be over here?"

"I'd say seven o'clock." Dex answered.

With that Aurora pushed up off the couch, but Dalton was there to lend her a hand. She could get used to it. Lindy shot her a knowing smile. Dammit, nothing got by her cousin.

"Come on boys," Tate said to his sons. "I've got a hankering for Dickey's Bar-B-Q." She watched as Luke and Rhys grinned ear-to-ear at the thought of food and followed their dad out of the house.

"I need to get going too, if I want to be back here by seven o'clock," Brody said trailing behind her uncle.

"Honey, your Mom probably has something delicious waiting at home. And I know she's baked a chocolate cake for you," Zebadiah said to his daughter. Aurora always liked looking at her Uncle Zeb and Lindy together with their long black hair. They looked regal.

"Chocolate cake? I need to come home more often." Lindy rubbed her hands together.

Zebadiah put his arm around his daughters' shoulders. "Yes, you do."

"I'm going too," Erwin said. "Just call me in from the barn in the morning. Dalton, it's good seeing you again, remember what I said." He gave him a meaningful look and walked out with Lindy and her father. Aurora would have to ask Dalton a little later what that was all about. But if she had to guess Erwin had threatened Dalton. Her ranch foreman had been pretty angry when Dalton hadn't shown up when she was pregnant.

Gunnar was the last one remaining with the SEALs and Aurora. Damn, now came the awkward moment of who was staying where. She sure as hell knew where Dalton was staying, and that was in her bed. There were two other guest rooms she supposed. Before she started to figure out sleeping arrangements, Gunnar faked a big yawn and stretched.

"Well Boys, it was real nice meeting you." He shook hands with Dex and Hunter. "I'm all in. I'll see you in the morning."

Dex and Hunter barely got in their good-byes before Gunnar was down the hallway to his bedroom. As soon as they all heard his bedroom door shut, Dex started to laugh and Aurora started to squirm.

"I think your grandfather didn't want to discuss where Dalton was staying tonight," Dex smiled.

Aurora blushed. How in the hell could she blush when she was five months pregnant with the man's son? She blushed even hotter. Dalton put his arm around her shoulder and she shoved her face in his chest for a moment, then sighed and looked up at the three men.

That's when it hit her. Great, now she had to pee. At most, she had a three-minute window before things got critical and she'd have to make a run for the bathroom. Who knew your bladder would shrink to the size of a peanut?

"You're welcome to stay here, there's two guest rooms," she said as things got worse. Dalton realized something was wrong and gave her a quizzical stare. She gave a small shake of her head.

"While everybody was good-bye'ing, I made reservations for Hunter and me at one of the hotels in-town." Dex said.

"How?" Hunter asked.

"On my phone," he said holding up his I-Phone.

"I figured you had a place to stay," Dex smiled at Dalton.

"Do I?" Dalton asked Aurora.

"If you're up for dealing with morning sickness you do."

He tried to pull her close. Aurora pushed at his chest. "Sorry, along with morning sickness is peanut bladder syndrome." She turned to the other SEALs. "It was good to meet you," she gave them a wave, then rushed down the hall.

"You've got one of the good ones," she heard either Dex or Hunter say as she pushed open the bathroom door.

"Do you really think Jack's dad will come through?" Dalton asked Dex as he stood outside his truck.

"Yeah I do."

"Why has it taken him so long?" Hunter asked.

"Well that is because somebody is dumber than a stump.

That'd be me." Dex sighed in exasperation, letting out a plume of icy air into the night. "I didn't think to call Jack until right before this last mission. I'm a dumbass."

"Shut the hell up," Dalton said sharply. "You've been all over this from the get-go. I'm the fucking dumbass in this scenario." He looked up at the house and saw the light on in Aurora's bedroom. "I've been a dumbass on so many levels."

"I'd say you're doing just fine," Hunter rumbled. Dalton looked at his friend who had a shit-eating grin on his face.

"What?" Dalton demanded.

"Your woman is hot. Not as hot as Aliana, mind you, but pretty damn hot. I saw those pictures in the living room of her on a horse. She is something else." Then Hunter turned serious. Dalton had been expecting it. Hunter, more than anybody else, had stood next to him when he'd lost Reagan.

"So, you're going to be a father again. How's that going to work?" Hunter asked.

Dalton took a moment, trying to find the right way to answer the question.

"I expect it's going to work the normal way, lots of diapers and bottles," Dex interjected with a smile.

"Seriously, Man. How are you coping?" Hunter asked.

He looked from one man to the next. He was lucky to have such good friends in his life. "It's like I've gotten a whole new lease on life. Looking at Aurora today about took me to my knees, but after a few minutes I felt like I needed to be on my knees in another way. I needed to be thanking God for this second chance."

Dex was grinning, but not Hunter. He just gave Dalton a look that spoke volumes, and that's when he realized that his friend had gone through the same thing. Hunter had received a second chance with Aliana, and Dalton knew that he thanked heaven for it every single day.

"Boy or a girl?" Dex asked.

"I'm going to have a son," Dalton answered proudly. "I know why she didn't tell me, what with all the baggage that I've been pulling around behind me I needed a fucking dogsled. I get that, and we're already working through that."

"That's great," Dex said. "And going forward?"

"I'm not going to fuck this up," Dalton said. "You know I want to retire from the Navy, that's always been the plan. First, I was going to stay on the teams for as long as I could, then move into training. But how do I pull her away from her grandfather? This ranch? All the rest of her family?"

"I don't know what to tell you," Hunter said. "I was lucky that Aliana was in Los Angeles, so I wasn't stuck with those kinds of issues."

Dalton looked around, taking in the corral, the tall pine trees, the open fields and the orchard in the distance. "But if I had to give up San Diego and the Navy, this wouldn't be a bad place to end up."

"No, it sure wouldn't," Dex agreed. "And her grandfather cooks, so I think you should totally take this under consideration." Dex looked down at his phone.

"Is that news on Wyatt?" Dalton asked hopefully. They'd been expecting something all day.

Dex nodded. Dalton and Hunter waited impatiently for Dex to read through the incoming information. Then he looked up and grinned.

"He's awake and flirting with all of the nurses down in Costa Rica. They're anticipating a total recovery, not even a limp. He'll be transported to San Diego tomorrow morning."

"Halleluiah!" Dalton exclaimed.

Hunter bumped fists with Dalton, who then slapped Dex on the back.

"And on that note, I'm heading into town," Dalton grinned as he opened the door to his truck.

"What the hell, aren't you going into the house?" Dex asked.

"Just going to make a trip to the all-night grocery store, then I'll come back. There's not a chance in hell that I'm not going to be sleeping with Aurora tonight."

14

————

Aurora felt like she was enveloped in cloud of bliss, her down comforter had never felt so good. It had never smelled so good.

She jerked awake.

"Whoa there. Don't move so quick, or you'll start the nausea going," Dalton whispered into her neck.

She felt her stomach churn and she hated it. She didn't want anything to intrude on this feeling of pleasure.

"Got something that might help," he said. She opened one eye and peered up at him.

"Something besides the saltines?" she asked.

"Yeah, I saw the bag beside your bed," he smiled. "Try this instead," he suggested as he tucked his pillow beneath her head and put a small brown cookie in her hand.

She saw that he also had a glass of water for her too. A cookie? Was he insane? But he looked so hopeful that she fought the urge to throw it across the room. She sniffed it.

"This actually smells good," she said in surprise.

"It's a gingersnap. I texted my friend Zed, it works for his woman. If that doesn't work, there's a bag of lemons for you to sniff too."

Aurora almost choked on her bite of cookie when he said that. "What are you talking about?"

"Didn't you do research on this?"

"Saltines and ginger ale are what Aunt Mary said. When that fails, I go and pray to the porcelain god." She took another nibble of the cookie and waved her fingers for the glass of water. Dalton handed it to her and she took a long swallow of the cold liquid, there was even a slice of lemon in it. She sighed, it tasted good. She wasn't feeling like a cast member of Alien anymore.

She was feeling human.

He'd done good.

"I didn't even hear you come back into the house or get into bed."

"You were out like a light, but that didn't stop you from snuggling right into my arms."

Aurora blushed.

Dalton looked at her with love in his eyes. "You've made me happy," he told her tenderly.

Dammit. She felt the tears coming on and saw Dalton's look of concern. She held up a hand.

"No, don't worry. I tear up if one of the horses eats all their oats. I'm telling you, I'm a regular waterworks factory these days. Maybe if I sniff a lemon I'll stop wanting to cry." She gave him a watery look.

Dalton laughed. "How's your tummy?"

"Let me just rest here for a few more seconds. Maybe I'll have another cookie, then I'll be good to get up. I hope I can catch Crystal in time before she heads over this morning."

"Why is she coming over?" Dalton asked.

"We're wrapping up the research for the Beaumonts on Aladdin."

"Still?" Dalton asked.

"Yep." She gave Dalton a considering look. "You know, when Mark and Taylor find out you're back, they'll want to come over too."

Dalton handed her another cookie. She bit into it and he smiled.

"Pretty proud of yourself, aren't you?"

"Sunshine, I have a hell of a lot of time to make up for. Buying some cookies and lemons is nothing. I want to carry you around on a pillow for the next four months."

He was serious. Aurora set the rest of the cookie down on the nightstand and stroked his cheek. "Dalton, I'm the one who didn't tell you," she whispered softly.

"I'm the one who walked away." His eyes were bright.

"You're here now, that's what matters."

She saw that he was about to protest. Her man who always believed everything was his fault and he wasn't good enough. "Dalton," she said teasingly. "You got here just in time. These next few months I'm going to start needing some extra help moving around. So, your timing is perfect." She kept one hand under the covers and her fingers crossed.

"Little liar," he smiled. "You're probably planning on working with the horses until the day you deliver. So, it is a damn good thing I'm here to stop you from doing too much."

She felt her cheeks heat. "That's not true."

"Are you going to spend the rest of our lives together lying?" he asked.

"No," she lied.

Dalton burst out laughing.

Aurora pushed out of bed and tugged down her sleep shirt over her panties. Thank goodness she'd showered last night so that she'd be ready for the cast of characters to arrive this morning. She looked over her shoulder and saw Dalton staring at her.

"Oh shit. I need to call Crystal. Waking up next to you goes to my head, Mr. Sullivan."

She grabbed her cell phone off the nightstand.

"It'll be good to see her and the boys," he said.

"About that," Aurora started. "I need to give you a heads up."

"Okay," Dalton said. "Hit me."

"Crystal is not your biggest fan at the moment. It was nobody's business why I didn't tell you that I was pregnant. That was between the two of us. I told Crystal that you hadn't abandoned me, but she refused to believe it."

Dalton winced. "You're saying I have some ground to make up with her."

"Something like that."

"I'm just glad you have such loyal friends." Dalton came up behind her and wrapped her up in a hug, his lips at the base of her jaw. "I'll talk to Crystal. It'll be okay, I promise." He nibbled on her earlobe.

Aurora dropped the clothes and turned into his arms. "I think I'll wait to call Crystal."

"Good idea," he said.

"YOU'RE BACK," Crystal said as she walked up the porch steps. It was definitely not a warm welcome.

"Hi Crystal," Dalton said. "It's good to see you. How are the boys?"

"We're not going to talk about the boys, we're going to talk about you being a Baby Daddy, and what all that entails."

God love her, she'd marched right on up those stairs, to the one just below the top of the porch, so that her head almost reached the middle of his chest and she looked like she might take a swing at him. Instead she jammed her finger into his chest. "You know you broke her heart, don't you?"

Dalton winced. He really wished she would have hit him.

"I'm here now," he uttered softly.

"You here for good?" Crystal demanded.

"She won't be able to get rid of me," he promised hoarsely.

Crystal blinked rapidly then swiped at her eyes. "I was counting on you being a good guy. Don't fuck it up again, okay?" Her voice trembled.

Dalton went down two steps and pulled the diminutive woman into his arms and hugged her hard. "I won't. I'm never letting her down again, I promise."

Crystal cleared her throat, "So why are you out here flirting with me?"

"I'm here with some of my teammates," he explained.

They were going to love Crystal. "There's a big Skype conversation going on inside with thousands of Aurora's family members as well as Sheriff Brody."

"I hate him," Crystal said bitterly. "He's been useless."

Dalton chuckled. "You're not alone with that viewpoint.

Anyway, the conversation inside is about where Ned Little might have been working when he left here."

"Okay," she said slowly. "And you're out here with me because...?" she prompted.

"I want Aurora out of the line of fire. Dex talked to Jack this morning before the call. This is call is more for show. We know-"

"We who?"

"My teammates, Aurora's uncles, Gunnar and Lindy."

"Lindy's here," she squealed. "She didn't call me. The Tahoe Trio are back in action!"

"Focus," Dalton said.

"Okay, so who's Jack?"

"Jack's someone I used to work with. He's a SEAL, and his family has a big spread near San Antonio. He found out that Ned had worked for three months at the Windsor Breeding Stables near Sutter Creek. Despite the fact that they had been contacted by Aurora not to hire him, and she sent Freddy Windsor a picture of Ned, the man hired him anyway. It makes no sense."

Dalton could see Crystal's wheels turning. "So, you plan to go pay Freddy a visit?"

"Oh yeah."

"And you want me to make sure that Aurora doesn't go with you."

"I'm morally opposed to laying hands on a pregnant woman, even if it's for her own good," Dalton said.

"Were you here last night?" Crystal asked.

"Yes."

"Then don't bullshit me, because I'm betting there was a whole hell of a lot of laying on of hands going on."

Dalton bellowed out a laugh and looked into Crystal's twinkling eyes.

"I don't kiss and tell," he said.

"Okay, Dalton, thanks for filling me in. I'll keep her ass planted here at Valhalla. Are you expecting trouble down at Sutter Creek?"

"We always prepare for the worst and hope for the best," Dalton answered. That's why we're all going to go pay a little visit."

"Not Lindy though, right? She needs to stay with us. It's been too damn long since she's been in town, so you don't get to have her," Crystal said as she planted her fists on her hips.

"Whatever keeps you happy Crystal. You scare me."

AURORA WATCHED and listened to the two men on the Skype call. She was impressed with their knowledge about the horse industry on the West Coast. She was amazed how they had been able to zero in the Windsor Breeding Stables near Sutter Creek. For God's sake, she knew Freddy Windsor, she'd talked to him six months about breeding one of her mares with one of his stallions. She damn well knew that she'd warned him that Ned Little was bad news. Fine, Ned hadn't given him his real name, but she'd sent Freddy his picture. He should have known better.

The Navy SEAL, Jack Preston, was talking. "Dad had our foreman call around to ranches all around the Western United States. His cover story was that he'd run up against a new form of animal abuse at our ranch and that we'd just had the asshole prosecuted for harming the horses. Our foreman, Enrique, was calling around to other ranches to find out if anybody else had found inhumane practices that were being done to horses by any of their employees that had floated under the radar. When the foreman called Windsor, they were told nothing had happened."

"I'm not surprised," her uncle Tate said. "Windsor has a good reputation."

"Well it won't for long," Jack said. "Two days later, Enrique talked to their former foreman who had moved to a spread in Arizona, the man explained how an employee by the name of Brett Sanders was caught using a wire-snaffle bit on some horse."

"God no." Aurora's hand shot up to cover her mouth.

"What's that?" Dex asked.

She looked around the table and saw that her grandfather and uncles looked as sick as she felt. "Depending on the gauge of the wire, to the horse, it's like using barb wire in their mouth as a bit. They'll stop on a dime, move in any direction at the slightest pull on the reins just so that the bit doesn't go deeper into their mouth. How's the horse?" She asked Jack Preston.

"Not good," Jack answered.

Aurora remembered when she'd found Lily hang-tied in the trailer. She should have just shot Ned and buried him in the woods. Dalton squeezed her hand underneath the table. She looked up at him, had he read her mind?

"Why did the foreman think that was Ned Little?" Gunnar asked.

"He said that Freddy's policy was to hire people under the table, so false names were normal. Enrique texted over a picture of Ned Little to this guy in Arizona and he said Brett and Ned were the same guy."

"I don't get it," Aurora said. "Why would Freddy be covering for him?"

"We're going to have a little talk with him today and find out," Dalton said.

"I can't wait to see what he has to say for himself," Aurora growled.

"Whoa there Sunshine. You're not going anywhere," Dalton said squeezing her hand again.

She shook it off and pushed her chair away from him. "What are you talking about?"

"We know somebody was behind Ricky and Ned, since they're still after you. This is the first real lead we've got. You're the target, and we're sure as hell not having you go into the base of operations."

"Well you don't have much say in the matter," she gave Dalton an angry look.

She heard Dex's muffled laughter.

"You're not going," Gunnar said. "That's the end of the discussion."

"You're not telling me what to do either," she said as she spun around to glare at her grandfather.

"You're not thinking this through," Crystal said.

"Not you too," Aurora turned to her friend. "You can't be on their side."

"Hell no, I'm not on their side. I'm always on your side, Girlfriend. What are you going to accomplish?"

"I want to check out the horses and see if they're all right."

"Like your granddad and uncles aren't going to be doing that. All that you're going to do is slow them down while making them stop every half hour because you need to pee."

Aurora felt herself blush. It was true. She turned to Dalton. "What's your plan?" she demanded.

"It's simple," Gunnar answered. "We're there to look over some stallions to mate with some of our mares. We're bringing some friends from San Diego to look over Windsor to see if they want to use their facilities for their horses."

"I still don't understand why Freddy would be out after me," Aurora complained.

"Neither do we," Dalton answered truthfully. "But this is the only thing that has made sense so far." He raked his fingers through his black hair and gave her a frustrated glare. "I want you off the firing line."

"Amen." Gunnar said.

"Hunter will stay back with you, so that you're protected."

"You're willing to split up the Scooby Gang?" Aurora knew there was a bite to her tone, but she was still pissed about the fact that she was being left out.

"Who are you calling the Scooby Gang?" Dex asked.

"I think that's us," Hunter said easily.

"Please don't ever say that in front of Kenna. I'm begging you," Dex placed his hands together in prayer.

Aurora gave a reluctant giggle, then she sighed.

"We have Rhys, Luke and Erwin here, isn't that enough?" Aurora asked.

"No," Dalton said emphatically. "They're going to be out caring for the animals. I want someone in the house with you."

"Well I'm staying here. I'm pretty sure the LAPD can take care of this, aren't you?" Lindy said.

Aurora saw Dalton squirm in his seat.

"For God's sake, she's a member of the SWAT team," Crystal all but yelled.

Hunter laughed. "I think we're leaving your woman in good hands, Dalton."

"Anyway, I don't want to be part of the Scooby Gang," Lindy said with a grin. "Crystal, Aurora and I haven't been together in years."

"Yeah, we used to do a lot of damage in high school," Crystal said.

Zebadiah groaned, and Gunnar laughed.

"Crystal shut up, we were angels." Lindy said loftily.

"You go get those bastards, and call in the second you know something," Aurora gave Dalton the stare of death.

"I'm telling everyone that Black Dawn's new team name is the Scooby Gang," Jack said from the computer screen.

Dalton groaned. "Are you still out there in Skype land? Turn them off Dex."

"We had to go anyway," Jack said with a smile. Dex turned off the screen.

"Okay, we all have our marching orders, right?" Dalton asked.

Everyone nodded.

15

"Chocolate icing. Graham crackers. Gold medal ribbon ice cream from Baskin and Robbins. I'm going to go into a sugar coma. Did I tell you I love you Lindy Dressler?" Aurora looked at the bounty in front of her. If she threw up after eating this, who cared? At least for once the puking will have been worth it.

"I've missed you little cousin," Lindy said as she pulled Aurora's pony tail.

"Ouch, too hard."

"You big baby," Lindy said as she plunked bowls, spoons and knives down on the table.

"You got it wrong, L, she's big with a baby," Crystal laughed. "Why do we need knives?"

"To spread the icing on the graham crackers, of course," Lindy answered.

Aurora already had her first graham cracker and chocolate icing sandwich made. "You two are slow on the draw. Dish me up some ice cream and fire up the laptop," she said right before taking a big bite of gooey goodness.

"What exactly are you two working on?" Lindy asked after she scooped out the ice cream. Aurora eyed her cousin. She was braiding her long black hair.

"What's with the braid?" she asked.

"Don't want the hair in my ice cream," Lindy grinned.

"You need to cut it," Crystal fluffed her blonde bob. She turned the laptop, so everyone could see it. "Here's the deal. Horse after horse has been coming here to Valhalla for Aurora heal. They've come in physically and mentally abused. Now they've supposedly been purchased from all over Oregon, Nevada and Northern California, but Aurora's seen too many of the same things done to these horses to believe they're coming from different places. They've been abused by the same handlers."

"That's true?" Lindy asked Aurora.

Aurora nodded as she dug in for another scoop of ice cream. She was going to have to stop soon, but Junior was really liking the sweet dairy product. They'd have to get rid of all the evidence before Gunnar came home.

"Aladdin was treated the worst. I'm in love with him, I'm in the process of buying him from the Beaumonts."

"Of course, you are," Lindy smiled.

"So back to me," Crystal said. "Me, myself and I have narrowed down where the abuse is happening."

Aurora's spoon clattered to the table. "Why the hell didn't you tell me this before?" she screeched.

"Well it's not to an actual ranch or anything, it's just an area," Crystal admitted.

"I don't understand. I think I might have a brain freeze," Aurora put the heel of her hand to her temple.

Crystal had a map up on her computer and it had a circle around a small area near Yuba City.

"What are we looking at?" Lindy asked.

"You can't tell anyone, okay?" Crystal asked nervously.

Aurora got excited, and she laughed when she saw her cousin get all cop-ish and frowny. "What did you do Crystal?" Lindy asked.

"Remember Rex from high school?"

"Rex Roberson, the guy who was in the drama club and chess club. The one who followed you around everywhere?" Aurora laughed. She hadn't thought of Rex in forever. Lindy frowned even more.

"Tell us what the hell you did."

"Mindy from the beauty parlor mentioned a couple of years ago that he was a spy or something. I looked up his brother on social media and tracked him down."

"Oh God, so who's the spy?" Aurora asked.

"Anyway, he's really nice, and he's divorced. Believe it or not, he has a daughter who plays soccer. So, I went to one of her games."

"Does he live around here?" Lindy asked.

"No, over in Sacramento."

"You went all the way over to Sacramento to flirt with some guy who's a spy?" Aurora asked incredulously.

"He's not a spy. Well not exactly. He works for DHS. Anyway, I brought orange slices for his daughter's team. Then I asked him for a favor."

"Oh God." Lindy hit her head on the kitchen table. "Orange slices. You traded orange slices for information."

"I told him what it was for. And I wore a push up bra."

"Just tell me exactly what happened," Lindy said.

"This is a Tahoe Trio, pinky swear," Crystal said nervously. "We can't get him in trouble. His little girl is counting on him. What's more, he wants to help horses."

"And he likes boobs," Aurora said helpfully. She needed more ice cream.

"Apparently there's something to do with I.P. addresses and cell towers that he was able to access with things like the conversations that the Beaumont's had with the broker that they did business buying Aladdin. I went and got the same kind of information on the Anderson's buying Lucky, and remember way back when Zeus and Candy came in over two years ago?"

"Oh my God. Just how high up is Rex?" Lindy asked. "Didn't he check you out and find out your married to Danny?"

Crystal opened her mouth. Then Lindy held up her hand. "I don't want to know," Lindy said. "Let me guess, he was able to narrow down where the calls and internet sites originated?"

Crystal nodded guiltily.

"I think I'm going to be sick," Aurora said as she stared at the circle and her heart sank.

"You ate too fast," Crystal said knowingly.

Aurora shook her head and pointed to the circle. "That's why I'm sick."

"What?" Lindy and Crystal asked simultaneously.

"I have to be wrong," Aurora said. "It can't be right."

"For God's sake, tell us," Crystal demanded.

Aurora shook her head, her ponytail flying.

"Aurora Dawn, fess up," Lindy commanded.

"The Lyle's are right there."

"Huh?" Crystal looked confused.

"Elsa and Dennis Lyle. It's the Lyle Olympic Equestrian Center. They've been training horses for twenty years. Their horses are Olympic champions. They can't be abusing horses. They can't be. I know them. I've been to their center. I've seen their horses. It's amazing." It wasn't possible.

"Crystal, how reliable is this information," Lindy asked briskly.

"It was a Frederick's of Hollywood push-up bra. It's gold."

"Aurora is there any place else within this area?"

"I'm sure there is, probably somebody's farm or little ranch," she said shakily.

"Okay. Let's do a google map search." Lindy smiled kindly.

———————

"WHAT ARE YOU DOING?" Lindy asked.

Aurora was once again wrapped in Gunnar's shearling coat in the barn. She was staring at Aladdin.

"I'm an idiot." She looked into Lindy's curious brown eyes, they were so like her own.

"Why do you say that?"

"Come into Aladdin's stall. Stay near the door, I don't want two of us crowding him, but I want you to be able to see what I'm going to show you."

"Okay."

"I never thought about the significance of the scarring on the backs of his legs." Aurora opened the stall door, and they both walked in. Aladdin nickered and ambled over to Aurora, not even caring that Lindy was in the stall with her.

"You are doing so well," Aurora praised the horse. She reached up and stroked the stallion's neck. "You're not afraid at all, anymore, are you? Soon I'll get to ride you and everything."

Lindy snorted. "Maybe in a year."

"Can you turn just a little Big Boy?" Aurora positioned the horse so that Lindy could see the back of Aladdin's legs. "He came to me bloodied because he had fought against the horse trailer. He was out of control. He was tranquilized, and the vet found fresh whip marks on him and focused on those. I was the one who noticed these thin scars on the back of his legs, but I didn't put it together with abusive dressage training."

"What do you mean? You surely saw the marks, I know you," Lindy protested.

"Of course, I did. The vet missed them entirely. Even Doc Barnes did when he examined Aladdin."

"You're kidding," Lindy said.

"Nope. Like I said, he was a mess, so these thin scars were missed by them, they are probably three or four years old." When Aurora touched them, Aladdin pranced back.

"Shhh," she soothed. He calmed immediately.

"So, what made them?" Lindy asked.

"A thin whip that is often used for dressage training. They use them on the back of the legs to get them to do their high step. But never in my life have I ever seen somebody whip a horse to a point to leave scars when training them for dressage. Never. Like I said, I'm an idiot."

Aurora was queasy, and it wasn't the food or anything to do with the pregnancy.

"I guess you're thinking it could be the Lyle's after all, aren't you?" Lindy surmised.

Aurora nodded. "I want to check a couple of more things."

He'd never taken to a bridle or a bit. It was just too much for him. He panicked and fought when she even brought them in the stall. Aurora wasn't even sure she could do anything to check to see if he had been subjected to Rollkur, not without actually pulling on his head, but even that wouldn't tell her anything. Then she did the next best thing.

Aurora stroked the big stallion along his neck, again and again she continued with the soothing petting. She knew that if Rollkur had been used on the horse while training him, it would have forced a deep flexion of the horse's neck through aggressive force to get them to perform well during dressage competitions. She'd seen one video where the pain had brought a horse to its knees.

She looked at Aladdin. "Can you be a Good Boy? Can you?" She kept talking to the horse, petting him and stroking him. Finally, she pushed in a bit along the tendon where the flexion would have occurred. She knew that over the ten months Aladdin had been with her the tendon would have healed, but he might still be sensitive to any kind of pressure in that area. Like it would be a phantom wound.

Aladdin swung his big head in protest and whinnied loudly. His teeth snapped.

Lindy pulled her away. "What the hell?"

"He's fine. Aren't you a big boy?"

"Don't go near him." Lindy commanded.

Aurora shrugged off her cousins' hands. "I just need to check one more thing." It took her another ten minutes of talking and crooning to soothe Aladdin. "I'm sorry Baby, I need you to be patient just a little more. Can you let me do that?"

Aurora could swear she saw him give a look of acquiescence. She went closer to his mouth and muzzle. She carefully looked into his nostrils, and gently touched inside. Aladdin snorted his displeasure.

"Okay, Boy, I'm done with that."

Aurora stepped backwards. "Let's go," she said to Lindy.

When they were out of the stall, Lindy turned to her. "What was that all about?"

"Aladdin has a hell of a lot of scar tissue inside his nose. There is no way that it should be there, somebody was really abusing him with his noseband. Also, he's really sensitive around his neck. As far as I'm concerned it definitely confirms that he was abused while being trained for dressage."

"Help me out here Cuz, it's been awhile since I've worked with horses. Explain the noseband thing," Lindy asked.

Aurora pulled out her hand sanitizer and washed her hands as they walked out of the barn. "I'm thinking the PTSD, the scarring on the legs, and the overuse of the noseband would have all been done if someone was using cruel methods to train Aladdin for either jumping or dressage."

Lindy didn't say anything as they passed the corral.

Aurora was lost in thought. She had to be wrong. Or if she was right, it couldn't be Elsa and Dennis, they couldn't know about it. She came to an abrupt halt.

"What's wrong?" Lindy asked. "Is it the baby?"

"No. We're going to Yuba City."

"Hell no. You're going back in the house, having ice cream, and then we're going to hide it deep in the freezer under the peas and carrots, so you can get to it in the middle of the night."

"Nope, I want to talk to Elsa and Dennis. They have

someone on staff who's hurting horses. They need to be told."

"Fine, we'll call them."

"No this is something I have to do in person. I owe it to them. I know them. I consider them friends. I've actually seen some of their horses compete."

"We'll wait until the men come back," Lindy said stubbornly.

"Oh, for goodness sake, you're an elite member of the SWAT team. Do we really need to wait for them?"

Lindy laughed. "Okay, not really. But if one thing looks the slightest bit suspicious, I'm going to pull in the Yuba City sheriff, got it?"

"Fine by me."

"THAT WAS SURE A WASTE OF TIME," Hunter groused in the front seat of Dalton's truck.

"It was nice to see how just how tenacious and competent my future in-laws are." Dalton had been really impressed by Zebadiah. For a man who had spent his entire life on a ranch, he was almost as hard-core has his brother Tate.

"So, you're getting married, huh? You know Aliana will want to make it a double wedding."

"She can want forever and a day. Aurora and I are getting married before our son is born."

"Congratulations. A son."

Dalton glanced over at his friend and saw the genuine happiness on his face. Then Dalton went back to looking at the freeway. "I'm surprised Dex wasn't the one to tell me. I would have figured he had hacked her medical records, including the sonogram."

"Don't be to sure he didn't," Hunter said sardonically.

Dalton shook his head in wonder.

"A son. The boy is going to be lucky to have you."

Dalton's hands clenched on the wheel of the truck, he could feel sweat forming on the leather. He wished he was as confident as Hunter.

"I worry," Dalton said softly.

"I hope when the time comes, I'm half the father you were with Reagan Elizabeth. There was never a happier little girl."

For the first time, for the very first time, his eyes didn't feel gritty and his jaw didn't clench.

"You're right she was a happy little girl. Remember her second birthday party when she ran around the yard trying to catch her shadow? I thought beer was going to snort through Gray's nose." Dalton smiled at the memory.

"Where in the hell did you find a pink plush seal?" Hunter asked. "I thought she was going to squeeze the stuffing out of that thing."

"That was her favorite toy," Dalton remembered. It had been worth all the trouble tracking the damn thing down.

Hunter's cell phone rang. "Yo Dex." He answered, then put it on speaker for Dalton.

"Gunnar says there's a good place for lunch up ahead, wanna stop?" Dex asked.

"Sounds good," Dalton said.

"Take exit after this one. I'm going to call Tate and Zebadiah," Dex said.

"Okay."

Hunter disconnected the phone.

"A son," Hunter said again. "I can't wait for the day that Aliana and I start a family."

"I AM SO mad that you two get to go and I don't," Crystal hissed as she got into her SUV. "I don't get to do anything fun anymore. I'm such a soccer mom."

"What the hell are you talking about, Miss Fredericks of Hollywood?" Lindy demanded. "Or should we call you Mata Hari? You're lucky we don't tell on you to Danny."

"As long as I wear the bra with Danny, I'm golden."

"I'm going to tell Danny about Rex," Lindy said.

Crystal paled. "Now that's not funny Melinda Sue Dressler. You take that back."

"Go home already, we've got to get to Yuba City, you know Lindy is just yanking your chain. I expect to see you, Taylor and Mark the day after tomorrow for their riding lessons. Got it?" Aurora said.

"Got it," Crystal saluted. "I'm saluting so you can get used to your new life as a Navy wife," Crystal smirked.

"Get the hell out of here. Go. You've worn out your welcome." Aurora was still laughing as Crystal's SUV was halfway down the drive.

"You ready?" Lindy asked Aurora.

"Yep, I've already gone to the bathroom. I'm raring to go."

"We're taking my car," Lindy said pointing to her Dodge charger.

Aurora rubbed her hands together. "Can I drive?" she asked as they walked toward the electric blue car.

"Not on your life. You flunked driver's ed."

"Just the written," Aurora pouted. "I passed the second time. It wasn't my fault that Tony Lawler sat in front of me. How was I supposed to pay attention?"

"You have a point, but still, you don't get to drive." Lindy opened the passenger door for her.

"Again, only pregnant, not an invalid."

"Just be happy I'm not going to make sure your head doesn't hit the roof of the car," Lindy grinned.

It sure was good to spend time with her cousin again. They ended up giggling almost the entire trip, just like they had when they were in high school together.

"Are you and Dalton going to make it permanent?" Lindy asked as they were closing in on the Lyle's place.

"He hasn't asked me to marry him, but if he doesn't ask me, I'm asking him."

"Thatta girl. So where will you live?"

Leave it to Lindy to get to the heart of the matter. "Valhalla's in my blood."

"Is it? Or is it Granddad and the horses?"

"Valhalla's beautiful." Aurora insisted.

"Look around, it's awfully pretty around here. You told me that the ranch you go to at Torrey Pines is gorgeous. And as I remember, it's not that far away from the Naval Base in San Diego."

"And how do you know about Torrey Pines?" Aurora asked suspiciously.

"I might have talked to Granddad."

"Lindy, you need to stay out of this," Aurora cried. "I'm serious. This is not your business."

"It is too. This is family business. Granddad knows that you would not follow your heart because you're worried about him. You need to know he's all right. Hell, there's

Uncle Tate, and my mom and dad are on the ranch right next to his."

"Yeah, but they're not living with him, that's a big difference. He'd get lonely." Aurora couldn't stand the idea of Gunnar roaming around in his house all alone.

"You know my mom would pop in for a visit every day. She loves Gunnar. They'd play scrabble."

"He hates scrabble." Aurora crossed her arms over her stomach. She felt her baby flutter. "Grandpa does like gin rummy," she admitted.

"Mom could learn," Lindy said sparing a glance over at Aurora.

"You're talking like it's a done deal that I'm moving. Hell, he hasn't even asked me to move in, let alone get married."

"You already said you were planning on asking him. The man's besotted, he's not going to say no. Should we pick up some flowers and a man's ring after we're done talking to the Lyle's? What size does he where?"

Aurora laughed. "Hmmm. What kind of flowers do you think he would like?"

"You can never go wrong with roses," Lindy answered.

———

"It looks like something out of 'Gone with the Wind'," Lindy said.

"Nah," Aurora laughed. "Think J.R. Ewing and Dallas."

They drove past the long line of low white fencing and the field of cut green grass.

"Well I can't miss the sign," Lindy said as she turned under the towering crest above the drive that proclaimed the Lyle Olympic Equestrian Center. "How big is this operation anyway?" Lindy asked.

"They've had sold plenty of gold medal horses. I'd say they have probably close to one hundred horses on-site at any given time." Aurora answered as the drove up the long-paved drive.

"How much do they go for?"

"The best of the lot won't go as high as a racing thoroughbred." Aurora sat forward in her seat to look at the big house and office.

"Yeah, but how much?" Lindy asked.

"I've heard as much as a half a million, maybe more."

Lindy whistled, as they parked the car near a bunch of others. Aurora took note of a Bentley amongst a bunch of BMWs' and a Mercedes. "Your Dodge is kind of out-of-place."

"Yeah, but a notice a lot of good old-fashioned work trucks," Lindy smiled. "Let's go mingle with the rich and famous."

The woman at the front desk didn't seem all that impressed to begin with when she saw the two of them, but things soon changed when she got Dennis Lyle on the phone.

"Mrs. Chance, I didn't realize you were such a long-time friend of the Mr. Lyle. Please take a seat in the drawing room while I get Chuck Zimmerman to give you a tour while Mr. Lyle finishes up with his meeting."

It wasn't long before Lindy and Aurora were checking out the expensive indoor training arena.

"You could eat off the floors in the stables," Aurora teased Chuck.

"We set very high standards here at L.O.E.C.," he said stiffly.

He'd been like that the entire tour. Aurora was intent on getting him to loosen up.

"There you are!" Aurora and Lindy turned at the same time to face Dennis Lyle. Aurora lit up. She really liked this man. She held out her hand.

"Ah come on, none of that," he almost leaned in for a hug, but then took her two hands. "I didn't know you were expecting. When did you get married?"

"I didn't," Aurora answered.

"Are you and the stallion on speaking terms? Are you thinking of getting hitched?" Dennis asked jovially. Aurora had forgotten his penchant for speaking in horsing terms. God love the man, he meant that in the nicest way possible, so Aurora smiled. "Yes, we're going to get married."

Aurora saw Lindy roll her eyes. "Who's this pretty filly?" Dennis asked as he turned to Lindy.

"I'm Officer Melinda Dressler of the LAPD," she said gruffly. Aurora could read her cousin's mind. She was asking if Dennis Lyle was for real.

"You must be either Tate or Zeb's little girl," Dennis said.

"What, no handshake?" he asked.

Lindy gave him a reluctant handshake. "This is quite the operation you have here, but I noticed that Chuck was reluctant to give us a tour of some of the out buildings," Lindy noted.

Dennis waved his arm expansively. "Those are Elsa's projects. She thinks that she can eventually get even more horses trained with a new method she's working on perfecting. For now, I'm leaving that to her and Chuck. She's very protective of her system." He turned to whisper conspiratorially with Aurora. "You know she's an Olympic champion. She won gold at Atlanta and Sydney."

It was a familiar story. Aurora nodded and smiled.

"Perhaps Elsa will show us." Lindy said doggedly.

"No, that's not possible. I already told you this," Chuck said emphatically.

"Well, there you go," Dennis smiled. He looked up and his smile got brighter. "And here's my beautiful wife. Elsa, look who's come to visit; Aurora Chance and her cousin Melinda Dressler. Melinda works for the LAPD."

Elsa tripped on the cement but quickly righted herself. She gave a quick smile to Aurora and then held out her hand to Lindy. "What brings you here?"

"My dad buys horses along with my uncle Tate," Lindy smiled as she let go of Elsa's hand. "Aurora told me about the great training facility you have here."

"You compete?" Elsa asked.

Aurora watched the two women together. It was an odd conversation, Lindy was definitely suspicious of something.

Dennis put his arm around Aurora and walked her over to the entrance of the arena. "Those two seem to be hitting it off," he said. "Look, I'm late meeting a new client, so I'll leave you in Elsa and Chuck's capable hands." He bent over and kissed Aurora's cheek. "Tell your grandfather I expect to see him at the next horseshow in Reno."

"Will do, Dennis," Aurora smiled.

She turned to see Chuck, Lindy and Elsa all talking. She went back to them.

"Just in time," Elsa said with a sunny smile. "Chuck told me that you're interested in seeing my new training facilities. I would love to show you. You just have to promise not to tell anyone about it," she said coyly.

Ick. Elsa being coy was not attractive. Judging by the look on Lindy's face she was thinking the same thing. Aurora stole a glance at Chuck and saw the man looking happy for the first time. Apparently, he liked coy.

Ick again.

"Let's take one of the SUV's," Elsa said as they exited the training arena. "I hurt my hip doing a jump a couple of days ago. What with you being pregnant, and me needing to take it easy, it makes sense," Elsa said. "Mort!" she called out to a ranch hand that was walking from the office to the arena. "We need a driver."

"Coming, Mizz Lyle." The man looked like a linebacker.

"Come sit in the back with me Aurora. I want to hear what's been going on at Valhalla." Aurora kept Elsa entertained the half mile to the outlying buildings. It was the friendliest Elsa had ever been. Maybe flirting with Chuck was giving her a new lease on life.

"What's the new training program you're doing with the horses?" Aurora asked.

"It's when the horses fail using regular methods. We just use a little more attention and tender loving care. I know you would approve of that Aurora."

"What do you do specifically?" Aurora asked.

"Some of the horses have done marvelously well. You know Sutter? He took Gold at Rio," Elsa said proudly.

Aurora remembered Sutter. He had done really well. "What's he doing now? I haven't heard of him competing in any other events since Rio." Mort opened the door for Aurora to get out of the vehicle and Chuck got Elsa's door. Aurora noted that Lindy was on her own.

"We put him out to stud."

They walked toward the corrugated building with

Chuck in front, then Lindy and Mort behind her. Chuck unlocked the door.

Aurora turned to Elsa, "Why did you put Sutter out to stud? He was at the top of his game, I would have thought that he would do more events and compete in the next Olympics."

"What the fuck?" Lindy yelled.

Aurora whirled around in time to see Mort shoving her cousin through the doorway of the darkened building. Then she heard a sickening thump.

"What happened? Lindy!"

"Shut up and get in there." Elsa pushed Aurora. She didn't need to, she had to get to Lindy. When she got through the door she saw that the far back corner of the building was illuminated. She heard the sound of horses whinnying, but for once she didn't care. Instead she was focused on Lindy. Oh God, please say she wasn't dead.

Aurora slammed down to her knees and felt for a pulse and sobbed with relief when she felt one in Lindy's neck.

"We need to get rid of them," Elsa said. "And this time don't fuck it up. I need you to make it look like an accident."

Aurora stared up at a woman she'd known for years. Things became pathetically clear. "You've been abusing these horses to get the results you wanted."

"Not all of them," Elsa said. "A lot of them didn't need extra incentives. But some of them, like Sutter, needed a firmer hand."

"You whipped him."

Elsa nodded in agreement. "Used sharper nosebands and Rollkur too. But in the end Sutter was a champion. Of course, I also ended up with some rejects," she said dismissively.

Chuck snorted. "Yeah, and somehow they kept ending up at your place." He glared at Aurora as if it was her fault.

"That's because you hired stupid people to sell the horses. The brokers needed to sell the damn horses to Arizona and New Mexico, not to our own backyard," Elsa practically yelled. "Look at this mess. I told you she was going to find us out. Now she's here. Dennis saw her!"

Aurora clutched her stomach. This crazy woman wanted her dead. She was going to try and kill her.

Kill her son.

No.

No!

That was *not* going to happen. Not on her watch.

"Grandpa knows we're here, Elsa. Do Uncle Tate and Zeb."

Lindy groaned.

"Why is the cop really here?" Elsa demanded.

"Why do you think? She wanted to look around. She was suspicious. I told her she was imagining things, you and Dennis couldn't possibly have anything to do with the things that had been happening to me. But she said I was too trusting," Aurora spat.

"She's a smart girl." Elsa nudged Lindy with the toe of her riding boot. Her cousin didn't move. Elsa looked up at the two men who were waiting for her orders. "I need them disposed of. Far away from the property, and I need it to look like an accident. Do you understand? Do better than that worthless Ned Little did."

"We need to wait until it's dark," Chuck said.

Aurora considered screaming, but knew it wouldn't be any use, since horses had probably screamed in here and nobody had come to their rescue.

"Fine, wait until dark. Do whatever you need to. Just get rid of them." Elsa spun around on her boots, slammed open the door, then yanked it shut behind her. Aurora stared up at her two executioners.

"We can't tie them up, people will notice the rope burn around their wrists," Mort said as he looked down at her.

"We can tie her up around her ankles, over her boots," Chuck said. "Go find some rope. Also get a blanket, we can wrap that around them, then tie the rope around that."

Mort shrugged. "That'll work." He headed to the corner with the horses.

This was her chance. Aurora gathered herself to pounce.

"You make one fucking move, and I'll kick you in the stomach." Chuck said it with no emotion whatsoever.

Aurora shivered. She believed every word.

Mort came back with a rope. "Have you checked the cop for a gun?"

Chuck looked at Mort with a blank expression, and Aurora felt just as stupid. Mort shoved Aurora away and yanked up Lindy's shirt. There at her waist was a gun in a holster. He pulled it out. "You're useless," he glared at Chuck. He checked Lindy's pocket and grabbed the car keys from her too.

Aurora wanted to cry. Why hadn't she known that Lindy was carrying a gun? It's time to start thinking. She had a phone, didn't she?

"Wrap 'em up." Mort threw a blanket at Chuck. "I'll take the live one, since you can't seem to handle the simplest of tasks."

After what Chuck had said about kicking her son, Aurora was happy that Mort was tying her up. That was until he yanked her hands behind her back.

"Please, that hurts too much, can't I put them around my stomach? It's too awkward that way when I'm pregnant."

Mort gave her a considering look. "Fine," he said.

Aurora placed her hands around her stomach and he swaddled the blanket around her, then he wound the rope on top of that. Aurora kept her arms away from her body as best she could so that she had a little bit of play, it was difficult because Mort was intent on tying the rope tight, but in the end, the rope was a little loose around her arms, but it wasn't around her legs.

"We'll be back."

"Please come back in an hour. Pregnant women have to pee often."

"You should have thought of that before you went all Nancy Drew," Chuck said dismissively. He turned to Mort. "Are you going to move their car?"

"Of course. Why else would I have taken their keys?"

Aurora watched the door close behind the two men.

So much for the pity vote.

She looked over at Lindy then down at herself. Great there they were mummy and the mummy mommy.

She wanted to cry.

16

"THAT'S THE THIRD TIME SHE HASN'T ANSWERED. AND SHE hasn't replied to my text. Are you satisfied now?" he asked Dex.

"Okay, you gave it fifteen minutes," his friend said slowly.

"You would have only given it ten minutes if it was Kenna," Hunter said to Dex.

"What are you boys talking about?" Gunnar asked as he pushed back from the restaurant table.

"Aurora isn't answering her phone and hasn't been for fifteen minutes."

Zebadiah frowned and pulled out his cell phone and made a call. He looked at everyone. "Lindy's went straight to voicemail."

"Anybody know Crystal's number?" Dalton asked, looking mainly at Gunnar. The old man fumbled for his phone and took a hell of a long time to go through his contacts, at least in Dalton's opinion.

"Got it," Dex said. "Dialing now. It's ringing." He pushed his phone over at Dalton.

"Crystal?" he asked as soon as he heard her voice. "This is Dalton."

"Why are you calling me? Why isn't Aurora? Is something wrong?"

"I can't get ahold of Aurora or Lindy, are you all still together? Can you put Aurora on the phone?"

"They left hours ago," Crystal answered.

Dalton's blood turned to ice water.

"What do you mean they left hours ago? Where did they go?" He got up from the table, Hunter and Dex on his heels.

"Lindy and Aurora were going to go check out a stable near Yuba City to see if they might be responsible for all the abused horses." They were just outside the restaurant. Dalton put the phone on speaker. Dex and Hunter leaned in close. Gunnar and the two Dressler's crowded in the best they could. "Aurora was convinced it couldn't be the owners at someplace called the Lyle Olympic something-or-other."

"Lyle Olympic Equestrian Center," Gunnar whispered.

"She and Lindy were going to go check it out."

"They shouldn't have gone anywhere," Dalton all but yelled.

"Calm your ass down, Baby Daddy." There was a pause. "Oh shit, now you've done it. Now I'm scared. You couldn't get ahold of either one of them?"

"They're not answering," Gunnar called over Dalton's shoulder.

"Do you know when they left Crystal?"

"Three and a half hours ago," she said worriedly. "You don't think something bad has happened to them, do you?"

"Yes," Gunnar growled. "Where's your common sense?"

Dalton put his hand on the older man's arm. "Crystal, when exactly did they leave? What car did they take? I'm handing you over to Dex to talk to him while I drive, okay?"

Dalton pushed the phone to Dexter who had already handed his keys to Hunter. The SEALs moved like a well-oiled machine. Hunter pulled Gunnar with him to Dexter's truck and the Dressler's were already running to their vehicle. Dalton got into his truck with Dex and skidded out of the parking lot. Hunter had Gunnar with him and was driving right on his ass. He listened as Dexter finished up the call with Crystal.

"How fast can we get to Yuba City?" Dalton asked Dexter.

"Let me just pull up a map," he said as he plugged his phone into the charger. "You know that Lindy will keep her safe, right?"

"Really? Then why isn't she answering her phone?" Dalton asked sarcastically. Thank God for the super charger in his truck, but he couldn't press the pedal to the metal until Dex told him exactly what fucking highway to take.

"Hurry up with the directions."

"We're going to take Latrobe Road, that way we can avoid Sacramento. It's a two-lane road." Dex explained.

"Sounds good to me, just point me in the right direction. What does your phone say the ETA is?"

"An hour and forty-six minutes," Dex answered grimly.

"Okay, call Hunter. The plan is to be there in less than an hour."

"DON'T CRY," Lindy mumbled.

"I'm not crying," Aurora cried. She wiped her snot filled nose against the blanket and wiggled and squirmed.

"Honey, we're going to get out of this," Lindy assured her.

Aurora watched as her cousin who wiggled and squirmed too.

"Do you have to pee too?" Aurora asked.

"No. Trying to get to knife. It's in my boot." Aurora heard Lindy's deep intake of breath. "Fuckers tied my hands behind my back."

Lindy sounded angry and determined. But her breathing didn't sound good, and her voice was slurred.

"Can you move over toward me?" Aurora asked. "My right hand is almost free. Maybe I can get your knife." Aurora had been trying to get to the cell phone stuck in the front pocket of her maternity pants.

Lindy's eyes glittered with excitement. "Holy fuck, you're amazing." For just a moment she was SWAT Team Lindy, then her eyes dulled. "Give me a minute or two, then I'll come to you, all right?"

Aurora heard Lindy take another deep breath, then she bucked up and down on the floor like a seal or walrus. It seemed like an eternity before Lindy was able to plop her leg on top of Aurora's. "It's my left boot."

"Lindy, cell phone or knife? Which first?"

"What? I don't understand." Lindy was slurring her words again.

"Should I try to get the cell phone out of my jeans, or the knife out of your boot?" Aurora clarified.

"Knife. I want us out of this, and me with a weapon."

"Got it." She pushed past the blanket and got her hand and forearm free. She looked dubiously at the rope around Lindy's jeans. "Fudgenugget! Getting this undone is going to be impossible."

"It's okay, Aurora. There's just one loop, you can do it," Lindy said calmly. "You're going to be fine."

Aurora prayed her cousin was right. Aurora grunted as she yanked at the stubborn rope. Her fingers burned but she put the pain out of her head and took a tighter grip. Again, and again and again she pulled. As she was doing that she continued to wiggle her other hand loose. Finally, it was free.

"Turn over," she told Lindy fiercely.

"What? Why?"

"Both my hands are free. I want to just work on the knot," Aurora said as she helped her cousin turn to her side. She could see the knot. It'd been tied by Chuck, he didn't know what he was doing. Mort would have tied a much better one. She went at it.

Aurora let out a yelp.

"What's wrong?" Lindy asked. God, she didn't sound good.

"Nothing, my nail ripped out. Just let me concentrate."

Aurora gasped with relief when the knot finally gave.

"You did it!" Lindy laughed and gasped. Okay, that sounded like her cop cousin. Aurora smiled.

Caught between tears and laughter, Aurora carefully pulled out the knife and worked at the knot around Lindy's arms. The second it was sawed through, Lindy sprang out of the blanket like a super heroine.

"Come on Honey, now you." Lindy grabbed the knife

and had her uncut in seconds that felt like hours. Maybe Aurora had been wrong, maybe her cousin was fine.

Aurora was so relieved she started to cry. She didn't mean to, but the tears wouldn't stop. She ignored them. She needed a bathroom, but she ignored that too.

Lindy was checking the door, and Aurora saw she was swaying as she crouched in front of the door knob. "Goddammit, we're locked in."

"Sit down, before you fall down," Aurora said.

"Oh shit, I think I hear Mort's SUV pulling up," Lindy said.

"How do you know it's Mort's?" Aurora asked.

Lindy shot her a weary look, "I'm a realist."

The door knob rattled.

Lindy pulled Aurora so that they were both plastered against the wall. Lindy held the knife as they waited for the door to open. The knife was trembling in her hand. This was not good. Not good at all.

"WHAT ARE our weak points in the plan?" Dalton asked. They were all on one big conference call amongst the three vehicles as they drove up the drive to the Lyle Olympic Equestrian Center.

"The new staff they have at the ranch," Zeb said. "The old timers will be fine with Tate and I nosing around. They'll know us. But there are literally millions of dollars of horseflesh in those stables, so they are going to be suspicious if we aren't with a Lyle employee," Zeb finished. Dalton could hear the worry for his daughter in his voice.

"You're not thinking this through brother," Tate said

easily. "Once we run into somebody we know, we get them to show us around. That way we can start nosing into every nook and cranny."

"If I know your daughter Zeb," Gunnar spoke up, "she's probably kicking ass and taking names."

God, Dalton hoped to hell that was true. But he had a bad feeling about this.

"Okay, now for my part. I get to go to the reception area with my soon to be grandson-in-law. We're just going to ask for Dennis and Elsa and ask where the hell Aurora and Lindy are. I like the direct approach. See if we can scent if there's a problem."

"Meanwhile Hunter and I will just do some reconnaissance everyplace but at the stables. See what we can see," Dex said.

Dalton was the lead vehicle in the convoy, he circled the parking area. "I don't see Lindy's car, do any of you?"

"Nope," Zeb said.

Dalton headed to the furthest area away from the ranch house near a copse of shade trees. He parked beneath them. Everyone got out of the trucks. Hunter and Dex disappeared into the trees. Soon Zeb, Tate, Dalton and Gunnar were moving toward the big white building. As they got closer, Zeb and Tate veered to the left to circle around to the back.

Dalton took a vague note of the nice white paint job as they walked up the steps into the foyer.

"May I help you," the receptionist asked.

"Becky?" Gunnar said with a smile. "Is Dennis or Elsa around?"

"And you are?" she asked questioningly. "Oh wait," she smiled. "You're Gunnar Olsen. Your granddaughters were here earlier today."

"Did they leave?" Dalton asked abruptly.

The young woman's smile faltered. "What's your name?"

"Just answer the question."

"I'll get Mr. Lyle," she said as she picked up the telephone.

Dalton stepped forward, leaned in, and placed his fists on her desk. "You call Mr. Lyle, but in the interim, you answer my question. Did you see Aurora and Lindy leave?"

She shook her head, her green eyes wide with fear. "Mr. Lyle, Gunnar Olsen is here to see you. Please come quick."

In less than a minute the closed door to the reception area was flung open and a balding man burst in. "What's going on?" he demanded to know. "Becky are you okay?"

She pointed a shaky finger at Dalton. "He threatened me."

"Where are Aurora and Lindy?" Dalton asked Dennis. The man blanched at Dalton's aggressive behavior.

"What are you talking about?" He saw Gunnar and turned to him. "What's going on Gunnar? Aurora and Lindy came for a tour, but that was hours ago. They've left."

"Not according to your girl here," Dalton pointed his thumb at the redhead.

Dennis ignored Dalton. "Gunnar, seriously, your granddaughters are gone. Elsa took them for a tour, but they left. You have to believe me. Who is this man, and why is he acting like this?"

Should have had Aurora's phone synched with his already so he could track her whereabouts. Dammit, his head hadn't been in the game!

"I'm your worst nightmare," Dalton answered Dennis's question. "You're going to take me on the same damn tour that your wife did, you got me? Better yet, get your wife in here, and you both will take me on this tour."

"Becky, call security," Dennis said.

Gunnar ripped the phone out of the wall. Dalton smiled.

"Guess you can't call your wife, or security, but you can still take me on that tour. Gunnar, stay here and keep Becky occupied so that she doesn't raise the alarm, won't you? As for you Dennis," Dalton pulled out his military issued pistol and shoved it into Dennis's side. "Keep in mind that I have this on me. Aurora's going to be my wife. I will do anything for her. Don't do anything that will get you killed."

Dennis gulped.

"Are you ready to give me a tour?"

Dennis continued to stare down at the gun.

"Answer me," Dalton said grimly.

"Yes. But do you need to see the places where I saw her?" Dennis stuttered. "I mean I know Lindy and Aurora were safe and okay then."

"What do you mean?"

"I know Elsa and Chuck were going her special facility. That's where Elsa's doing some experimental training."

Gunnar pushed close to Dennis's face. "What kind of experimental training?"

Dennis gave Gunnar a helpless look. "It's her project. I don't know."

"So you're saying you saw them in good health until they went on an expedition with your wife and some guy named Chuck?"

Dennis nodded.

"Tell me exactly where they went, and when."

"The out buildings are about two acres back behind the training arena. They're two big corrugated buildings that are secure. They're locked tight. There are some horses out there, so Aurora would be interested."

"When was this?"

"I'm not sure. A couple of hours ago?" Dennis said helplessly.

"That's where we start. Gunnar can you sit on both of them?" Dalton eyed the big Norwegian who was a head taller than Dennis.

"You give me that gun, and I'll keep them from sounding the alarm," Gunnar said. "Becky, move to the couch over there," Gunnar ordered.

Dalton agreed with the old man's plan. Better to have the two of them sitting together. He shoved Dennis down on the couch beside Becky, then handed his pistol over to Gunnar. He went over and turned the sign in the window to closed, shut the drapes, and locked the front door.

"You okay?" Dalton asked Gunnar one last time before he left.

"I'm fine. I'm going to call the others and tell them about the out buildings, just go get my granddaughters."

"DON'T THINK I'm doing this for you," Mort said as he the door opened. "I can't stand the thought of piss stinking up my car for hours on end, so you're getting your bathroom break." The big man took two steps into the gloom of the cavernous building. "What-?"

Lindy jabbed her knife into his neck. Blood sprayed so far and wide that Aurora felt splashes hit her face and hair.

With the knife lodged in his throat, one of his hands went to the knife and his other hand reached forward like

Frankenstein, attempting to grab Lindy, but she ducked and then shoved him.

"Come on," she grabbed Aurora's hand. "He's not dead yet."

Aurora tried to block the gurgling sound coming from Mort who was now slumped against the wall. When they got out into the early evening air, Aurora got a good look at Lindy. She looked ready to fall down. Her face was covered with blood, not just Mort's.

"We need to get back to the ranch house," Lindy said determinedly. "Are you okay to walk?"

Her cousin was damn near staggering, and she was asking about her? Aurora was incredulous.

"Do you think Frankenstein is dead yet?" Aurora asked.

"Huh?"

"I want his car keys."

Lindy was bent over with her hands on her knees. "We should check the driver's side visor. Dumbass probably put them there." Her voice was so slurred it took a moment for Aurora to comprehend what she'd said.

Aurora guided Lindy to the SUV and Lindy crossed her arms on top of the hood of the vehicle then laid her head on them. Aurora hit pay dirt when she found the keys exactly where Lindy had said.

Sh-Shoot. Lindy hadn't moved. Aurora lumbered out of the driver's seat. "Come on Honey, let's get you into the car." Aurora looked around. It was getting darker. What if Chuck was coming?

"I'm fine," Lindy waved her off. Then she turned and doubled over, throwing up. Aurora saw bits of graham cracker. She swallowed convulsively, sweat sheeting her body. No way, they weren't going to have two of them puking.

"Lindy, you have a concussion. We need to get you to a hospital."

Apparently, her cousin had only been able to keep it together long enough to stab Mort, now it was up to Aurora. She pulled a trembling Lindy into the passenger seat and ran around the front of the car to the driver's side.

"What an idiot!" she said as she pounded the wheel of the car.

"What?" Lindy asked. Blood from Mort and vomit covered the front of Lindy's blouse. Aurora rolled down the window to let in fresh air, then she fished out her phone from the front of her jeans. She almost screamed when she saw it was dead.

"Lindy give me your phone," she begged.

Lindy lifted up off the seat and pulled it out of her back pocket. It was cracked. "Must have happened when they hit me," she said weakly.

Aurora started the SUV. She needed to get Lindy to a hospital. She needed to avoid Chuck, Elsa and whoever else was willing to kill them. They didn't have cell phones. Think!

She started to drive. Fuck it, she was going to head toward the front driveway where all the Mercedes were. Other clients weren't out after them, and one of them would have a cell phone. She aimed for the wide-open field that would eventually lead to the front of the property. She couldn't have gotten more than one-hundred yards when she felt a tire blow. She skidded in the wet grass.

Another tire blew, this time she'd heard the gun shot before the impact of the back tire made the SUV career sideways. Her eyes shot to Lindy and she gasped in relief. Her cousin had put on her seatbelt.

"Give me the knife Lindy," she yelled. She saw two men running toward the car. In her rearview mirror she thought she saw another man tackling one with a gun. What was going on?

She rolled up the window and made sure the doors were locked. Why hadn't she checked to see if Mort had had a gun?

"Got 'em!" A man's voice roared.

They were surrounded, one on each side of the car. She couldn't tell which one was Chuck.

She heard the passenger door crash open.

"Ooomph." A man grunted. Lindy shoved against the door and jumped out. Aurora spared a quick glance to see her cousin crouched on the ground beside the car arms up, ready to fight.

Aurora had the knife in her sweaty hand. She was going to fight this bastard to the death. But she sure as hell wasn't going to open the door like Lindy had.

"Aurora, open the door." A big hand slapped on the window. Aurora cringed.

"Sunshine, it's me."

Aurora couldn't comprehend what she was seeing.

"Honey, open the door, it's me, Dalton."

Her hand wouldn't let go of the knife. She couldn't press the button to unlock the doors. She continued to stare at Dalton's beautiful face through the smeared driver's side window.

She jumped when the door unlocked. She looked over to the passenger side and saw that Hunter had pressed the button to unlock the door. Dalton had her door open in a heartbeat.

"We need to get Lindy to the hospital," she said. She couldn't take her eyes off Dalton. He was prying her fingers off the knife.

"Dex is on it," Hunter said.

"How badly are you hurt?" Dalton asked as he wiped at the blood on her face.

"I'm not," Aurora assured him.

"You're bleeding."

"Not my blood."

He looked scared to death. Aurora held up a finger. "I broke a nail."

"Goddammit Sunshine," he pulled her into a rough and tender hug.

"Elsa Lyle is the one behind everything. She's been abusing the horses. She's evil. Don't let her escape."

"We won't."

She pushed at his shoulders and looked at his face. "No seriously. She's the mastermind. Go get her."

"Hunter!" Dalton called.

Over his shoulder she saw her uncles, Zeb and Tate, running up towards her, Zeb veered off to the other side of the vehicle where Lindy was.

Hunter came over to Dalton, he looked pissed. "What?" Dalton asked.

"Lindy just told me everything. We need to get her to a hospital. It's a bad concussion."

"Elsa Lyle is behind everything, she needs to be secured," Dalton said harshly. But no matter how angry he sounded, the hands that were stroking Aurora were gentle and loving.

"Dex has it taken care of. The piece of shit he took down. The one who was shooting at this car. He gave her up," Hunter explained.

So much for that love affair, Aurora thought. She snuggled deeper into Dalton's hold.

Siren sounded in the distance.

17

IT WAS ONLY THREE WEEKS SINCE THE RESCUE. SHE AND
Gunnar were in the orchard. In some ways it was more
special to her than the stables, because it was where she had
had picnics with Grandma Mae and Gunnar.

"It's kind of cold for a picnic," Gunnar smiled. "But I
think it works out well."

"I'd say so. You kind of made it winter proof." Aurora
spread her arms wide to take in the tarp, covered by the five
horse blankets and the propane heater.

"Just remember what your soon-to-be husband has to
live up to." His eyes twinkled.

Aurora blushed. She was glad that her grandfather
hadn't questioned Erwin too closely as to why they had the
tarp and propane heater, otherwise he'd realize Dalton had
already purchased them for a more intimate outing not so
long ago. He'd also brought along flowers and a ring.

"Drink your cocoa Darlin." She sipped the hot chocolate
he'd poured from the thermos.

"What did you want to talk about?" she asked.

"Everything. Anything," he answered.

"That's quite the list." Aurora settled down in the little camp chair. Seriously, she had everything to make a pregnant woman feel comfortable. She smoothed her hand over her round stomach.

"Have you decided where you're going to live? Have you decided if you can really and truly deal with marrying a Navy SEAL?"

"Grandpa, he said he would quit and move up here with me. Can you believe that?"

Gunnar snorted. "Are you seriously going to ask him to do that?"

"Good God no."

"How do you feel with Dalton being away on a mission right now?" Gunnar asked seriously.

Now that was a hard one. "You know the other Navy wives tried to reassure me at the baby shower they threw for me."

"Didn't you say there were like ten of them or something?"

"There was Kenna, Aliana, Miranda, Sophia, Lydia-"

"Stop already," Gunnar laughed. "Obviously you're surrounded by estrogen down in San Diego. So they tried to reassure you about the SEALs going on missions, huh?" he prompted.

"Yeah, but it was when Lindy and I went to dinner that everything came into focus. One, she couldn't be anything else but a police officer. Two, she's trained down to the 'nth degree. Grandpa, you should have seen her at the Olympic Center. The doctors said she should never have been conscious, let alone up and killing Mort. This is in her blood. Having seen it up close and personal, I know it has to be the same for Dalton. I trust him. I trust him to come home to me and our son."

"I worried how you might handle that."

"Well if you think you're worried about me, I'm worried about you. Yeah, it looks promising moving down to San Diego, I could definitely make some friends, and Lindy's close by in L.A. But I won't have my Grandpa."

"I worried about you having a support system when he was gone. It's good to know that won't be a problem."

She leaned over awkwardly and grabbed his hand. "I want you to move down with us. Dalton and I have talked about it. He's looking for a house that'll be comfortable for all three of us, and the baby."

Gunnar cupped her cheek. "God love you. There is no way I'm going to move in with newlyweds and a new baby. But I've been thinking, you're not going to be happy just being a wife and mother, you're going to need horses too."

Aurora sighed. She was going to miss Valhalla. "I'll be up for lots of visits, especially when Dalton is on a mission."

"I've already talked to Myrna Englewood at Torrey Pines. You're hired whenever you want to be."

Aurora sipped her cocoa until it was gone. "That's a bit presumptuous, even for you."

"She's okay with you taking five of the horses, including Aladdin."

"Not interested. I want to come up here whenever I can instead. I want Aladdin to stay here, and I want to be involved with rehabilitating the horses from the Lyle's place."

"Stop," Gunnar held up his hand. "That's been taken care of and you know it. Elsa is well on her way to wearing an orange jumpsuit, and for the next six months Tate is going to oversee the place."

"But-"

He looked at her. "Honey, your place is with your husband and your son. Your horses will be at Torrey Pines. Now tell me the real problem.

She felt the tears start. Damn hormones.

"I told you the problem. I can't leave you Grandpa. I can't stand the idea of you being alone in this house," she whispered hoarsely.

Gunnar grabbed her hand in his and ran his thumb over the sapphire and diamond ring on her ring finger. "It matches your eyes," he said.

"It matches his eyes," she disagreed.

"Believe what you need to believe. You need to be with your husband. On a full-time basis. Anyway I have something to tell you. That's why we're having this picnic. I'm not going to be alone. I've met someone."

Aurora couldn't believe her ears.

"What? What did you say?"

Gunnar laughed loudly. "You heard me, Darlin."

"Who is she? Who have you met?" she demanded to know.

"Kim Sokolov." At Aurora's confused look, Gunnar laughed again. "You know her Aurora. She works at Safeway. I've known for over a year that you've been feeding me turkey bacon."

"Oh, Kim. I just didn't know her last name. Is this real?" she asked softly.

"I think I'm old enough to know real. I want to explore this. You're not leaving me alone, I promise."

Her hot chocolate spilled as she threw her arms around her grandfather's neck. "Oh my God, I'm so happy for you."

"Really? She's not Barb," he teased.

"Kim's so nice. I think the world of her. I was just worried she'd tell you about the food."

Gunnar grinned. "You thought right."

He kissed her forehead.

Both of them looked around the orchard. "Grandma is so happy for you, I just know it."

"So do I, Aurora. So do I."

EPILOGUE

THE MINUTE, THE SECOND, THE MOMENT THAT DALTON HAD seen her pregnant, Aurora had known that there would never be a better father in the world for their child. She stood in the shadows outside the nursery and soaked in this moment.

"Your name is James. Not Jim. James. But right now, you can be Jamie. At least until you start school."

Aurora smiled. Her husband was a huge softie.

She watched as Dalton's big hand covered the whole of Jamie's back. Her son knew he had it good because he snuggled in against his father's bare chest. He wasn't hungry, she'd fed him an hour ago. Nope, Dalton had heard the same snuffle she'd heard on the baby monitor and couldn't help himself. Their boy had them both wrapped tightly around his little finger.

Jamie let out another little sound. Nothing of importance, just a sound to let his father know that he was there, that he liked the attention he was getting. Aurora saw Dalton's thumb move up, so he could touch the back of

Jamie's head and play with a silky black curl. She'd been right, he looked like his big sister Reagan. All big blue eyes and black curls. Jamie was going to be a heartbreaker.

"So why are you up in the middle of the night my boy?" Dalton asked their son.

Jamie moved his little fist upwards and touched it against Dalton's whiskered jaw.

"Nope, none of that. That's too rough for you." Dalton brought the little baby's hand to his lips and kissed it.

Jamie let out a little cry. He never liked being told no. He was seven weeks old, and already knew that word and hated it. Dalton went over to the rocking chair and turned on the small lamp. He had to move the blue plush seal off the seat, so he could sit down.

Aurora gulped a watery breath as her husband and son settled down in recliner. Dalton took the little soft toy and put it next to Jamie, who grabbed it's little tail. It always hit her hard when she saw him sit in that spot with their son.

She remembered when she'd had Dalton sit on that same rocking chair in their San Diego home, she'd been almost nine months pregnant.

"Don't kneel down," he'd admonished. "Get up."

He'd pulled her onto his lap.

"The chair's going to collapse," she protested.

"It's a rocking recliner," he smiled. He brushed back her hair. "Why is there a package on the table?"

She fought back tears. "It's for you. I hope I did good. I don't want you to be sad."

He frowned.

"Or mad," she said. Did she do the right thing?

"What's in the package?" he asked.

"It's something for both you and Jamie."

276

"Our son's name is James," he smiled. "What's in the package?"

She handed him the present. "Just open it, okay?"

Because she'd made such a production about it, he took his time opening it. She could tell he was freaked out, but then again, so was she. Please God, say he'd like it.

He froze when he pulled out the picture frame. Reagan's little face was smiling up at him.

Dalton's eyes turned indigo bright and filled with tears. Reverently, he held the picture up over Aurora's swollen belly. He spoke to their son. "I know you can't see this right now James, but this is your sister Reagan. She's watching over you."

Dalton's tears fell as he smiled and put the picture on the table. He cupped Aurora's face between his hands.

"It's perfect. You're perfect," he whispered against her lips.

It took a moment for Aurora to come back to the present and realize Dalton was whispering to her.

"I see you," he was saying.

"You can't see me," she protested.

"Okay, then I can feel you," he laughed softly. "Come help put James to bed."

"Jamie," she corrected.

"James," he smiled as she walked into the nursery.

She watched him put their son gently into the crib. She stood next to the table with the lamp and she kissed her fingers and placed them gently against the photo of Reagan.

"I love you," they said simultaneously to the two adored children.

ABOUT THE AUTHOR

USA Today Bestselling Author, Caitlyn O'Leary, adores writing Military Romantic Suspense and Paranormal Romance. She started publishing books in 2014. Storytelling has been a tradition in her family for years, and she still holds on to the letters she has received from family members since her childhood.

Caitlyn lives in California with her husband John of sixteen years who often makes guest appearances in her reader group, Caitlyn's Crew. Getting to know so many people within the reader community is almost as much fun as writing each new novel. So join her reader group so she can get to know you, and see if she and John can make it to year seventeen!

You never know what kind of book she'll write next, it all depends on what strikes her fancy. Be sure to keep in touch.

Keep up with Caitlyn O'Leary:

Website: www.caitlynoleary.com
Email: caitlyn@caitlynoleary.com
Newsletter: http://bit.ly/1WIhRup

facebook.com/Caitlyn-OLeary-Author-638771522866740

twitter.com/CaitlynOLearyNA

instagram.com/caitlynoleary_author

amazon.com/author/caitlynoleary

bookbub.com/authors/caitlyn-o-leary

goodreads.com/CaitlynOLeary

pinterest.com/caitlynoleary35

ALSO BY CAITLYN O'LEARY

THE MIDNIGHT DELTA SERIES

Her Vigilant Seal (Book #1)

Her Loyal Seal (Book #2)

Her Adoring Seal (Book #3)

Seal with a Kiss (Book #4)

Her Daring Seal (Book #5)

Her Fierce Seal (Book #6)

A Seals Vigilant Heart (Book #7)

Her Dominant Seal (Book #8)

Her Relentless Seal (Book #9)

Her Treasured Seal (Book #10)

BLACK DAWN SERIES

Her Steadfast Hero (Book #1)

Her Devoted Hero (Book #2)

Her Passionate Hero (Book #3)

Her Wicked Hero (Book #4)

Her Guarded Hero (Book #5)

THE FOUND SERIES

Revealed (Book #1)

Forsaken (Book #2)

Healed (Book #3)

Made in the USA
Coppell, TX
21 December 2019

13644351R00164